THE MADNESS OF THE FAITHFUL

THE MADNESS OF THE FAITHFUL

RH Williams

Copyright © 2022 RH Williams

The moral right of the author has been asserted.

Apart from any fair dealing for the purposes of research or private study, or criticism or review, as permitted under the Copyright, Designs and Patents Act 1988, this publication may only be reproduced, stored or transmitted, in any form or by any means, with the prior permission in writing of the publishers, or in the case of reprographic reproduction in accordance with the terms of licences issued by the Copyright Licensing Agency. Enquiries concerning reproduction outside those terms should be sent to the publishers.

This is a work of fiction. Names, characters, businesses, places, events and incidents are either the products of the author's imagination or used in a fictitious manner. Any resemblance to actual persons, living or dead, or actual events is purely coincidental.

Matador
Unit E2 Airfield Business Park,
Harrison Road, Market Harborough,
Leicestershire. LE16 7UL
Tel: 0116 2792299
Email: books@troubador.co.uk
Web: www.troubador.co.uk/matador
Twitter: @matadorbooks

ISBN 978 1803132 112

British Library Cataloguing in Publication Data.
A catalogue record for this book is available from the British Library.

Printed and bound in the UK by TJ Books LTD, Padstow, Cornwall
Typeset in 12pt Bembo by Troubador Publishing Ltd, Leicester, UK

Matador is an imprint of Troubador Publishing Ltd

For Rachel, Kitty and Idris, and
the glorious chaos of each day.

ONE

February tenth would mark the beginning of a new age for humanity but for Paul Harris of Salford, England, it started like any other rotten Monday. Since he quit drinking, waking up each day was a stark rebirth. He would emerge from the peaceful depths of slumber and burst to the surface gasping for air. It was a pattern he was familiar with – the shock, breathlessness, and racing heart, he was used to – but the subsequent long shadows of guilt that followed, always filled him with dread.

His routine was the usual. He used coping techniques that his friend, Father Michaels, had taught him. He sat up, closed his eyes, and took ten deep breaths. He tried to focus on the memory that brought him most comfort. It started with the sea – a thick blue layer flickering and sparkling in the bright daylight. The sun warmed his face. On his lap, he could feel the weight of her head resting as she dozed. His fingertips tingled as he stroked her arm. Her skin was soft but peppered with sand granules. The sound of waves filled his ears. He scanned the horizon. To his left, he saw a quiet harbour where bobbing boats sheltered next to a stone pier. To his right, a green headland rose out of the water. Where it plateaued at the top, there sat an ancient grey building with a crooked crucifix protruding from the roof like it was reaching out into the sky. He wanted to stay, but as always, the real world pulled him back.

He opened his eyes and glanced at his father's Bible lying next to him on the bed. Falling asleep when sober was still something he struggled with. Skimming through the pages of the old book seemed to help. As he reached over to pick it up, he noticed the time and realised he was late.

"Sorry, Mr Harris, they've gone now. They were expecting you at nine."

"But it wasn't my fault," Paul said, "I was caught up in an emergency."

"There's nothing I can do, I'm afraid."

"I need that job."

"I'm sorry. They picked another candidate."

Paul smashed the handset down and collapsed onto the sofa. He punched the arm before looking over at the armchair where she used to sit with a cigarette in her mouth watching the television. "You'd be laughing at me now, wouldn't you?" He huffed. "It's not fair. The alarm was set. Getting up is impossible after these long nights."

He rubbed his jawline and felt a slight stubble on his chin where the cheap razor had missed a patch when he shaved the night before. He looked around the room and back at the chair. "Why does it always have to be so hard?"

He pursed his lips, got up and headed to the kitchen to put the kettle on. The fridge was empty – he needed to go to the shop so went back upstairs to get dressed. He saw the Bible on the bed, picked it up and flattened the creased pages before carefully placing it on his bedside table. He stroked the aged black leather cover and patted the book like he was comforting an old friend.

He left the house and headed down the street. Near the corner shop, a familiar voice spoke up from the alleyway.

"Alright, dickhead."

Paul sighed and turned towards the side street. Sheltering from the wind was a short, skinny figure dressed head to toe in denim. Hunched by the bins, he was trying to light a crooked cigarette with a failing lighter. His normally styled bowl cut was a mess and there were dark circles around his eyes.

"You've been out all night," Paul said.

"Jesus speaks." Karl's voice was husky and slurred. He was still drunk. After a few attempts, he managed to light the cigarette and his wheezy lungs inhaled with all their might.

"About to start again, are you?" Paul asked.

"I never stopped, mate."

Karl sneered and advanced towards Paul. "Don't you be judging me – you're no better. You run with those church freaks now but it's all the same. Just another way to numb the pain of all this shite."

Paul edged away. "I'm not in the mood, Karl."

"Mood, Paul? What's your mood, moody Paul? That's what I say."

He stuck his finger in Paul's face. "You're a moody bastard, Paul. Moody, judgemental bastard. You used to be different. Man, I loved you. Remember those nights we had? Now, you're just like the rest of the sheep."

Classic Karl. Able to go from nought to crazy in seconds. Karl would never forgive Paul for abandoning him – particularly the way he did. Losing Paul to the church was a betrayal of the worst kind. Paul shook his head and stepped away in the direction of the shop.

"Get on your way then, Bible-basher. Get back to your empty house to fucking cry yourself to sleep."

Paul shut the door of the shop and leant against it. He peered through the glass and watched as Karl staggered away. "Nutter," he muttered under his breath, fully aware that the complexities of their relationship couldn't be dismissed away with a simple one-word insult.

He turned and nodded to Mo, who was stood behind the counter reading a newspaper. The shelf behind him was lined with spirits. Paul gazed at the bottles for a moment before shaking his head and heading over to the fridge to grab a carton of milk.

As he examined the tinned foods, he heard ringing. Not like church bells, but more like the chiming of a distant grandfather clock. He looked around the shop but could see no source, so he ignored it.

He examined the soups and jars of sauces and stroked the back of his head. He wasn't picky. So long as it was hot and tasty, it would suffice. On a lower shelf, there were tinned pies all marked with handwritten discount stickers. He picked one up and tried to read the price. The numbers looked blurry. It wasn't just his ears that were failing.

An odd sensation – like a presence – came to him and he felt the hairs on the back of his neck stand on end. He turned his head expecting to see someone there. As he did, a wave of nausea hit him, and he covered his mouth with the back of his hand. After a couple of breaths, it passed, and he tilted his head and looked down the aisle to the counter.

"Mo, what price are these pies meant to be?" Yelling left him breathless.

"What's that, Paul?"

He took a large gulp of air and readied himself to shout again. The sound returned, and the chiming was louder this time. Paul's eyes darted around the shop. Where the hell was it coming from? It grew in strength like the clock was coming closer. He started to feel faint. He tried to focus and looked to the shopkeeper, who himself appeared distracted.

"These pies – how much?"

Something pushed against his back and his face hit the shelves. Then it pushed against his front and his back landed against the wall. Spooked, he twisted his head one way and the other as he searched for his tormentor. It happened again but this time faster. The force batted Paul to and fro like an invisible bully. He was unable to escape. It grew in strength and size until it surrounded him. Inside, he shook from side to side until the vice closed and he was no longer able to move. He cried out as he fought against it, but he was trapped inside like an insect in amber. His sight was fixed on Mo who himself appeared stuck inside his own energy field. The shopkeeper howled. His gaze was fixed upwards towards the heavens and his jaw hung open as if he were waiting for something to be poured into it.

Bright speckles of white light floated down and surrounded Mo's head. There, they flickered and began to change colour like ignited flames. Paul watched, terrified, but also in awe of the sight. Never had he seen anything so glorious. *Was this it?* he thought. Was this God coming to take the worthy ones away? Oh, the joy of that prospect. Was this the moment of judgement? Would he be worthy enough?

"Please," he mumbled, "I've tried so hard to change."

The lights now came to him and something was happening in his head. Images shuffled through his mind's eye like playing cards. He felt drunk, elated, and aroused. His spirits lifted and his whole body tingled. He could not see the coloured flames, but he knew they were with him. It was his time to be taken. He would ascend and be with her – be with his love – sheltered by the gracious arms of Christ. *Oh Lord, take me*, he thought. He tried to speak but the words were a mess of noise. It was sublime and it was perfection. He felt a release. Fear was forgotten and he was in the care of the lights. But as he gave himself to their mercy, he came to realise that the experience was not what he hoped. This was a phase of transition; a temporary state before he fell back to earth. Abruptly, the chiming stopped, and three separate notes rang out as though the clock had struck the hour of three.

The fire left the shopkeeper's body, dropping him to the floor. Then it was Paul's turn and the world went dark. But the dark was followed by light. He was sat on the beach from his memory, and he saw the usual – the blue water, the boats in the harbour and the church on the headland. Yet one thing was missing – her head was not resting on his lap. He scanned the horizon looking where she might have gone and then he saw her. She appeared out of nowhere, naked and waist-deep in the sea directly in front of him. She faced away – towards the horizon and he examined the pale skin of her back and the curvature of her body. Her long brown hair covered her shoulders and upper back. In her hand she held his father's Bible. He called out to her, but his voice was muted and she started walking further into the sea. He tried to scream but she didn't respond. He knew he was losing her and when she was gone, she would not return. He tried to get to his feet, but he could not. He remained seated and still; tied up and gagged by the cosmic forces that brought him to this place. Her arms went under – and with them the Bible. As the water reached her neck, she turned her head slightly and glanced back at Paul before disappearing beneath the sparkling blue water.

At that moment he was back in the shop. He opened his eyes slowly as though expecting to see something horrendous waiting for him. But there was nothing there. Beside him on the floor was a pile of tinned foods. The place was quiet apart from the gentle sound of someone sobbing. His head pounded and the spinning world pinned him to the floor. This was the atomic bomb of hangovers, but he hadn't had a drink in a long time. Something else had knocked him down.

He needed to get out of there. He tried reaching for the shelf to pull himself up, but he felt too weak. He tried again and slipped on one of the tins.

"Bastard," he called out before crawling towards the door. He pushed it open with his hand and shoulder and made his way outside. He squinted as the daylight hurt his eyes. He rubbed his temple and tried to remember the last few moments.

Outside, a rubbish truck had driven into a house on the other side of the street. The front of the building had partially collapsed, and masonry and broken glass carpeted the ground. Paul could not see the driver's side from his position, but he heard the howls and banging of someone struggling to get free. As he stared, he felt himself drift away until a surge of energy hit him, and he was able to sit upright with his back against the shop door. He thought about trying to help but he could barely get to his own feet. He shook his head in disbelief. "Home," he said, licking his dry lips.

He began to crawl down the street. When he came to a drainpipe at the corner of the building, he stopped and reached up to try and lift himself. His strength was growing but he had to hold on tight. His balance had not yet returned. He looked around at the houses and his chest became tight and his heart raced. He tried breathing through it and regaining some calm.

Something caught his eye – on the other side of the road, an elderly woman was sat on a doorstep. She held her head in her hands and was completely motionless. Her shopping covered the ground around her. Paul tried to call out, but his voice was too faint. He shook his head and gave a muted roar.

He pulled himself along the walls of the terraced houses, grabbing protruding features and leaning on windowsills when he could. After three or four buildings, the walking became easier. He heard a shriek of laughter behind him and turned. Next to the lady on the doorstep was a younger woman in a green summer dress howling with laughter.

"What the…?"

She looked familiar to Paul but he couldn't see her face. He struggled to focus his thoughts or gain enough clarity to recall where he might know her from. Faces flashed in front of his eyes, but he couldn't discern those important to him from strangers, or reality from fiction. The tightness in his chest hit him again and he wanted to cry. *Get home now*, he thought, and he pushed on without seeing another soul.

He reached his house and pulled the keys from his coat. His hand trembled and he struggled to get the key in the lock. He pushed hard and the door slammed against the wall. He fell into his living room and collapsed on the sofa, face down. There, he rested. His breathing calmed and his mind fell silent. Seconds before he drifted off, he heard Father Michaels' voice.

"He will wipe away every tear from their eyes, and death shall be no more, neither shall there be mourning, nor crying, nor pain anymore, for the former things have passed away."

The voice hung there, and he welcomed the quiet hand of sleep.

*

Paul's eyes opened wide, and he sat up straight on the sofa. He still wore his coat, and the front door was open. He couldn't tell how long he'd slept for but sunlight now filled his living room and the shadows had eased.

He rubbed his face. *What happened at the shop?* he wondered. Was he sick? Had he had a stroke or burst a blood vessel in his brain? Aside from a sore head, he felt okay physically, but he struggled to focus his thoughts and think clearly. A dull aching sorrow emerged, and as he sat there, it grew stronger and more crippling. Something was gone, but what? Tears formed in his eyes and streamed down his face. He searched his coat pocket and took out his phone. He dialled 999 for the emergency services. Whatever happened scared him and he couldn't ignore it.

Paul listened to the ringing tone for over a minute, at least. No answer came. He held the phone away from his ear and looked at it. *This shouldn't happen*, he thought. Then an image came to him and he dropped the phone on the floor.

He saw her at the hospice. Eve. Her laboured breathing as she slowly suffocated from her failing lungs. She was fading away and leaving him for good. His hands became numb, and he felt chills down his spine. He tried to think of something else. Anything. He focused on the light from the window as it made the hanging dust dance.

His thoughts turned to the church and he remembered the comfort and support he'd received after her death. He remembered how reassured he'd felt by the pastor's words about the afterlife and God's love. It felt strange and Paul felt sick to his stomach. Something was not right. His jaw dropped as he realised that it wasn't just Eve who'd left him for good. His faith had departed as well. He shook his head in disbelief. He saw through it all – God, Christ, the Bible. Somehow, he knew it now. The whole lot was made up – just myths and fairy tales. None of it was real and he was unable to accept any of it. He had no doubt – it was clear as day and he felt cold and empty. He felt cheated. Betrayed. Everything the pastor had told him was fiction; lies to make Paul feel better. False reassurances and whatever else he needed to hear to calm him down like a scared child.

His breathing became faster, and he started clenching and unclenching his hands repeatedly. The sorrow was turning into fury. He leant his chin onto his chest and growled and hissed and bashed his fists on the sofa cushions. He was overwhelmed by the anger and needed to do something. He got up, ran upstairs, and grabbed his father's bible. He examined the book with his quivering fingertips; an object that had once filled his heart with hope and joy. Now, it was nothing more than a book of lies. His hands began to shake more vigorously. He dropped it onto the bed, opened it in the middle and started to tear out the pages. The thin paper was stronger than he expected.

Frustrated with his progress, he took it outside to the garden and threw it into a rusty metal bucket before drenching it in lighter fluid and setting it alight. The fire erupted and yellow and blue flames danced over the aged leather covers. He popped the matches in his pocket and continued to pour the fuel into the bucket until the container was empty. The fumes from the fire were strong and made his eyes sting. He turned away, kicked the fence and screamed.

The rage subsided and Paul sat down and stared into the flames. He couldn't make any sense of what happened, and his mind was a maelstrom of sad memories and odd feelings. He took a moment to compose himself, nodded to the fire and got up. He needed a drink.

He checked the back of the cupboards in the kitchen and the sideboard in the living room. He didn't hold up much hope since he'd cleared out all the bottles earlier in the year. He checked he still had his wallet in his pocket and headed out of the house.

Mo's shop door was locked. Paul looked up and down the street. The rubbish truck was still there but the sounds of struggling had ceased. The place was deserted and there was no sign of anyone. Brief flashbacks of the event returned to him.

"Jesus," he said. He rubbed his eyes and his forehead – he still had a dull throbbing headache. How many more people could this thing have affected?

He decided to check whether the Sailor's Return was open. He turned the corner and arrived at St Luke's Square, home to his old local and – more recently – the church he attended each week. Upon seeing the church, his nostrils flared and he grinded his teeth. A woman laughed behind him but when he turned his head there was no one there.

Paul was desperate as he pulled on the nearest of the two doors of the Sailor's Return. To his surprise, it opened. He walked in and looked around – the place was silent and empty. The television on the wall was on and it showed a message on the screen, *IBC News: Normal services will resume shortly*. Beneath those words, rolling text repeated the sentence, *Unknown event affects billions across the world*.

"Paul, are you alright there?" Geoff – the landlord of the pub – leant on the bar.

"I don't know," Paul said. "What happened?"

Geoff shook his head. "I was asleep upstairs. Lizzy woke me up, telling me she'd collapsed. I told her to lie down, and I tried to call for an ambulance. I was on the phone when I noticed the television."

Paul shook his head and looked at the screen again.

"Were you affected?" Geoff asked.

"Something happened. I thought it was just me."

"Paul, it was… everyone."

"Do they know what it was?"

"Not yet. The only news we're receiving are these short alerts. There was one before from the government telling people to keep calm and not panic. Seems the emergency services have been overwhelmed so we're on our own. Keep calm and carry on, Paul. That's the best advice they can give us right now. Keep bloody calm."

"Right. Jesus." Paul turned back to face Geoff. "Can I get a drink at least?"

"Too right. Something strong?"

"Whiskey, large. Keep the bottle handy."

TWO

Paul stared at his reflection in the dirty mirror behind the optics. He still wore the same clothes from the morning. His hair was unkempt and his eyes were red. He exhaled slowly and looked to the clock on the wall. It took him a moment to focus on the timepiece – was it ten something? Shit, where had the day gone? He'd been there since the afternoon, drinking and watching coverage of the *unknown event* – as they kept calling it – on the news. Inside the pub, things seemed normal enough. There was a brief power cut in the afternoon and Geoff had stacked up candles behind the bar in case of a similar recurrence, but it didn't happen again.

Over the course of the day others had joined them and as he looked around the room, he saw that the dusty, dated bar with faded wallpaper was full of regulars. All of them had been affected by the event in one way or another and being around familiar faces with a drink in hand seemed like the best option given everything going on. Paul remained in his seat by the bar throughout – listening to incomers regaling

Geoff with their war stories. Most of them spoke of blacking out after seeing and hearing things that weren't there. They described waking up feeling violated, dazed, and sorrowful. This event – whatever it was – had evidently messed with people's heads. Lingering mental problems were widespread according to the TV. Loss of faith was frequently brought up as one of a number of aftereffects. Paul's experience was not unique although this provided him little comfort. Experts had no answers, and the public, well, all they could do was work themselves up into a frenzy.

He heard some commotion and turned to see Kevin the Postie limping in. He held a blood-stained rag to his nose and had bruises on his face.

"Kev mate, are you alright?" Geoff yelled from behind the bar.

Kevin sighed and wiped his forehead. "Yeah. Better now I'm inside. It's mad out there."

Geoff crossed his arms and leant on the bar. "What happened to you?"

"I was jumped near town. I was coming back from my sister's and these lads came out of nowhere."

"Did they take anything?"

Kevin shook his head. "No, they just attacked me and legged it."

"Did you report it?"

"Not much point with everything going on."

"Yeah, it's crazy. Do you want a pint of the usual?"

"Give me a shot of something first, will you?"

Geoff reached for the bottle of whiskey next to Paul and poured Kevin a drink. Kevin lifted the glass and Paul could see his hand shaking.

"I hear it's all kicking off outside," Geoff said.

Kevin took a sip and made a face. He wasn't a whiskey drinker, Paul thought.

"Parts of the city are like war zones," Kevin said. "Fighting and looting everywhere."

"News is saying the emergency services can't handle it," Geoff nodded to the television. "Don't worry though – you're safe here."

Geoff stepped away to serve another customer, but Paul kept watching Kevin. Kevin was the only other person in the bar who also attended the church. Paul cleared his throat and moved closer. Kevin looked up and their eyes connected in the mirror.

"Paul. I didn't see you there."

"I heard what you said. You alright?"

Kevin closed his eyes briefly and nodded.

Paul rubbed his hands together. "I need to ask you something."

The bleeding from Kevin's nose had stopped but his eyes were bloodshot, and he had open cuts and bruises all over his face.

"This thing," Paul said, "it knocked you out?"

"Yeah."

"Right. Got us all, it seems." Paul took a deep breath and licked his lips. "Afterwards though, how did you feel? Anything different?"

Kevin looked down at his glass and tilted it from side to side. "You want to know about my faith, right?"

"Well, it's crazy but…"

"It's okay. I've heard the same thing. People are saying their belief is gone." He turned his head towards Paul and had a vacant expression on his face. "Yeah, it's gone. All of it – disappeared. God means nothing to me. You?" Kevin's words were huge and affecting but his voice was unemotional and empty.

"Same." Paul reached over to his glass and took another sip.

"What do you think it means?"

"I've no idea."

Kevin raised his glass to Paul and left him. He went and sat alone in the farthest corner of the room where he stared into the middle distance. The look of shock was fading from his battered face, leaving behind an expression of loss and grief.

Paul made eye contact with Mary – another old drinking companion who he'd not seen in a while. She came over and sat next to him, placing a large white wine next to his whiskey glass.

"Been meaning to come say hello," she said in her gentle Glaswegian accent, "but you looked like you didn't want company."

"Odd kind of day, I guess," Paul said.

"It's madness alright."

Paul glanced at her and nodded.

She took a sip of her drink and sniffed. "We haven't seen you here for a while."

Paul cleared his throat. "No, I suppose you haven't."

"How long's it been?"

He sighed. "Nineteen months."

"That was for Eric's birthday, wasn't it? We all wondered what happened to you after that night."

He rubbed his hands together. "Had to call time on things. I was spiralling."

Mary blinked and leant towards Paul. "Spiralling?"

He stroked his chin. "I woke up the next morning in the alleyway next to the church. Father Michaels found me soaked in piss and half frozen."

"Call the pigs, did he?"

"No, he took me into the vestry and cleaned me up. Sat me down with a hot tea in front of the heater. We ended up talking."

"Ah. So, you found God?"

"I found something." Paul looked at his reflection again in the mirror and started to cackle.

"At the time, I believed I'd been saved. Michaels and the church helped me, and I bought into the whole thing. Hook, line and sinker."

"You believed?"

"So much so, it hurt, Mary."

"And now? Is what they're saying true?"

Paul shrugged his shoulders. "All I know is everything he told me was bullshit." He turned to face Mary. "Switching booze for faith was like swapping one pair of out-of-focus specs for another. You want to see a reality you're comfortable with, but it isn't the truth. I didn't have the guts to see the truth of it all."

He raised his glass and sipped on his drink. "And look at me now. Back where I started and still blind as a bat."

Mary stroked her hair and bit her lip. "If it's any consolation, I don't think much has changed here."

"These bastards certainly haven't."

"I bet they're a livelier congregation than you had at the church."

"That's true."

"Also, we have Father Karl…"

Karl stood among a group of men near the television.

They gazed at the screen like they were watching a football game. He'd arrived earlier in the day and had made a beeline for Paul when he saw him at the bar.

He'd greeted Paul with the usual charm. "Well, well, dickhead. Must be the end of days if holy Paul has fallen off the wagon."

"Yeah." Paul didn't know how to respond. He knew Karl would run with whatever he said.

Karl leant on the bar next to Paul and turned to face the television. "So maybe you could help me with something. Social media's crawling with people saying this thing's fucked with their belief in the almighty. *Fucked* meaning wiped out. Not just your god either – we're talking all faiths and religions. As a fully paid-up Bible-basher, what's your view on this, mate?"

"Not now, Karl." Paul got up and went to the toilet. He didn't need to go – he just had to get away. Things were weird enough without having Karl mess with his head. Karl despised religion and everything that went along with it; whatever this thing was, he was likely relishing it.

When Paul returned, Karl had gone off to revel with the other regulars. Paul tried to keep a low profile, but he frequently heard Karl's voice. Initially, he appeared at ease and was entertained by all the drama. But as the day progressed, he became agitated and louder as the drinks flowed. This was a pattern that rarely ended well.

"…And it seems Father Karl is hitting his stride," Mary said.

From afar, Karl looked the same as he ever did. He could have been wearing the same tight jeans and Joy Division T-shirt that he wore thirty years ago, but his face could not hide his years of drink and drugs. Beneath the bowl haircut, he had the tired, gaunt face of a middle-aged man twisted from a life searching for escape. His voice was loud and clear across the room. "You don't see it, do you? You're all fucking idiots."

He got up on a chair and addressed the room. "Like it or not, your god is gone. Something out there has done us a service today and I say good fucking riddance. Good riddance to organised religion that's done nothing but rape, murder, and abuse since... forever. Good riddance to the insecure old bastards trying to control us with their bullshit contradiction and manipulation. Good fucking riddance to all that shite. And fuck any of you who think otherwise."

Paul and Mary looked at each other.

He got down, and sat on the stool, taking out his tobacco and papers to roll a cigarette. Paul could see that his hands were trembling. There were raised voices. Old Charlie from the bookies who'd been stood nearby was mocking Karl. Karl got up and lunged forwards, headbutting Old Charlie and breaking his nose. Some of his friends stepped forwards and Karl smashed a bottle against a table and held it out ready to stick it in the nearest face that came his way.

Geoff approached with his hands raised. "Come on, Karl. We can't have that here."

"I'll fucking show you." Karl bared his teeth, smashed the bottle, and strode out of the pub.

"He hasn't lost his charm," Mary said.

Paul shook his head. Mary gently sipped on her wine.

"What do you make of all this shite, Paul? What do you think happened?"

Paul rubbed his brow. He looked down at his glass and started laughing.

Mary appeared confused. "What?"

"I thought it was the rapture, Mary. I thought it was God coming for us true believers." He rubbed his eyes. "I thought I would be up there with Eve, but instead it was the opposite – a hard slap in the face and a plunge into icy cold water."

Mary placed her hand on his and squeezed. Paul looked into her eyes. "Do you feel different, Mary?"

"Well, I'm a wee bit pissed now."

"You know what I mean."

"I don't know, Paul. In some ways yes – but Jesus was never a close acquaintance. Do you?"

"I'm not sure. I started falling but I don't think I've hit the ground yet."

"But you know, love. A few drinks won't help the situation. Especially after so long on the wagon."

"You're right, Mary. A few won't help." Paul glanced over to see that Geoff was still sweeping up broken glass – albeit with his eyes trained on the television. He dashed around the bar, stepped up onto a small ladder, and searched the upper shelves. He needed something with more of a kick and he knew Geoff usually had a bottle of high-proof vodka hidden that he used on special occasions for flaming cocktails. Geoff's cousin in Poland sent him crates of the stuff so he always had a supply. Paul saw a bottle with the word *Diabeł* and a picture of a smiling devil on the label and grabbed it. He returned to his seat, unscrewed the cap, and took a large gulp. His face twisted as the liquid burned his insides. He offered the open bottle to Mary.

"No thanks, love. You should probably take it easy on that stuff as well."

"Everyone shut up." Geoff scrambled to the bar to grab the remote. He turned the volume up on the television. Paul and Mary both turned to see what was happening. A very sober-looking young man in an expensive suit stood outside 10 Downing Street. He stood behind a podium and nervously shuffled a handful of papers.

"Where's the prime minister?" someone yelled and Geoff hushed at them.

"As press officer, in Her Majesty's government, I am here tonight to make the following statement on behalf of the government of the United Kingdom. More information will follow, but at this moment in time I will not be taking questions." He cleared his throat.

"At eleven thirteen this morning, Greenwich Mean Time, an unknown event took hold of the people of the world resulting in temporary loss of consciousness."

Paul took a mouthful of vodka and grimaced as it hit the back of his throat.

"At present, the cause of the event is unknown. But the temporary loss of consciousness resulted in countless incidents across the world and we're sad to say this has led to widespread loss of life and injury. We are currently working with governments and agencies around the globe to understand what happened."

Paul took another drink.

"We have the best minds helping us to understand the event, whether there were any warning signs, and if there are any learnings we can apply to detection of potential future threats."

"This could happen again?" someone yelled and murmurs followed. Paul filled his mouth with as much vodka as it would take.

"Regarding the various rumours circulating about the aftereffects of the event, we currently cannot confirm or disprove any hypotheses. What we do advise is that citizens try and be rational in their interpretation. Our assessment right now is that the physical effects were temporary, but any extended impact on the mental health and well-being of individuals beyond that is unknown."

What the hell does that mean? Paul thought, and he lifted the bottle to his mouth again.

"To conclude, the government wishes our nation to know that we have the best scientists, researchers and medical personnel working around the clock to find out what happened. We're also coordinating with other nations to answer questions at a global level. However, at this stage, we advise citizens to remain calm, stay at home and keep news channels open for further updates from the government. Thank you."

There were no answers. The greatest minds may be on it, but they knew nothing. Paul belched and tasted sick in his throat. He needed some fresh air, or at least somewhere more private to throw up. He lifted himself from the bar stool, almost dropping to the floor as he descended.

"You alright?" Mary appeared concerned.

Paul stood up straight. He nodded, coughed and put his hand up against his mouth. He leaned on the bar and turned to face her.

"I have fought the good fight, I doubt I'll finish the race, and the faith, well that's… whatever." He took the bottle of vodka and left Mary at the bar.

Outside the pub, the street was empty apart from the silhouette of a lone, thin figure surrounded in smoke. Paul walked over to him. Sirens from all directions filled the air and a smoggy mist hung in the sky like it was bonfire night.

Karl saw him approaching. "Happy to talk to me now, are you?" Karl's voice was flat, and his gaze didn't shift from the end of his cigarette.

"Seems you're more certain of what happened than those idiots in charge."

Karl sucked hard on his cigarette and the burning end lit up his face. "They're too scared to call it what it really is."

"And what is it?" Paul asked.

"An opportunity."

"What do you mean?"

"It's a chance to be free of all that bullshit." Karl signalled his cigarette in the direction of the church.

"That can't be why this thing really happened though, can it?"

Karl cleared his throat and spat on the floor. "Everyone's knocked out and something comes and takes all their stupid beliefs away. Makes perfect fucking sense to me."

"You make it sound like an operation. What kind of surgeon could do that?"

"Why don't you ask your Bible-bashing buddies? They gave you answers, didn't they?" Karl made no attempt to hide the derision in his voice.

Paul swayed and turned to face the church. He pressed his fist against his mouth and puffed out his cheeks. "I believed so much in that place. I thought it saved me, but the reality was…"

"They played you like a fiddle."

"I had no choice, Karl. It was either that or let the darkness take me."

"You had people in here behind you." Karl nodded his head towards the pub.

"These people did nothing more than grease my wheels."

"Always the victim. You made your own choices, dickhead. No one twisted your arm."

"Yeah, right. I'm going for a walk."

He left Karl by the pub and crossed the square to the church. The lights were still on but there was no sign of anyone about. He reached the wall and touched it. The stone felt cold. He staggered around the building, dragging his fingers against the walls.

Played you like a fiddle. He scoffed and jerked his hand away from the stone surface.

Paul shut his eyes and shook his head. That night after the pub, when he'd hit rock bottom, he believed the pastor had saved him; that he was the lost sheep the pastor always spoke of – the single sinner who repents and inspires more joy in heaven than the ninety-nine righteous people who did not go astray. But the truth was he was easy pickings, a vulnerable soul desperate for help. They fed him lies and got their claws into him.

He felt used and disgusted. He gritted his teeth and felt his toes curl in his shoes. He felt the fury rise inside again and took a sip of the vodka. This time, the face of the smiling devil on the bottle caught his attention and he thought about his time in Belfast during the Troubles. He patted his trouser pocket – the matchbox was still in there. He opened his coat and pulled on a piece of open lining. After a few attempts, he managed to rip off a piece of the material and he stuffed the end into the bottle. He shook the bottle repeatedly and inverted it until the edge of the cloth on the outside was soaked and dripping. The stench of alcohol was strong. He walked further around the building to the window next to the altar. The glass here was old and it wouldn't take much to penetrate it. He stood motionless looking up as the light shone down and the window frame cast a shadow of a cross on the ground. Paul acknowledged the shape by marking it out with his finger in the air. A peculiar feeling of being watched came to him and he turned around but there was no one there.

His hands shuddered as he took out the matches. He took a deep breath and lit one before holding the flame under the wick. It started to burn – a tiny blue flame at first, but this soon grew, became darker and then a bright yellow. He felt the heat from the burning cloth against his skin.

"For the fiddler," he said. He pulled his arm back and readied himself to launch the projectile. He felt the anger circulate in his veins and tried to focus and draw strength from it. He threw the bottle at the centre of the lower windowpane, and it broke through like fingers through a tear-soaked tissue. Inside, it hit something, and an eruption of light emerged.

Before long, he could smell burning. The odour had a distinct character – a mixture of old timber and burning lacquer. As he watched the window, his legs buckled beneath him and he fell to the ground, all the while watching the lights as they flickered though the glass. Everything was spinning and he was dizzy – even as he sat with his back against the alleyway wall. He watched as the illumination from the fire grew – his gaze pulled towards the bright spectacle. As he stared, colourful lights began to dance around his field of vision, and they were glorious. When their time came to an end and they faded into the night, Paul felt disappointment. But he could still hear the flames. For as long as he could, he sat and listened to the wholesome sounds of the crackling and snapping of burning timber.

THREE

Paul woke up in a state of blind panic on his living room floor. His cheek was stuck to the carpet and he struggled to raise his head. The stench of sick and smoke filled his nostrils. His face was caked in dry vomit and it smeared between his skin and the carpet. He felt uncomfortable and desperate to move but his body was paralysed by horrifying thoughts. He remembered flames, fumes, and the dancing lights of the fire through the glass. But nothing after that.

Paul growled as he pulled his head away from the ground and turned on his side. He looked down at his body and examined his clothes. His knees were covered in dirt and his trousers were ripped open to expose red, sore skin. Most of his front was covered in gravel and stained with filth. His hands ached from scratches and cuts. His head pounded like it was under attack from heavy artillery shells.

He turned onto his back and looked at the ceiling. His lower lip quivered and tears started streaming from his eyes. Unable to hold back, he cried like a hurt child. He saw flashes of the church during the funeral. A small attendance, kind words from Father Michaels, and then that stupid song she liked playing throughout the building at the end of the ceremony.

The tears slowed and he was left panting. He tried to sit up, but the world around him was spinning, and he fell back down. He tried again – this time with more determination – and managed to get to his feet by holding on to the sofa. The television was on. Still more of the same rolling news. *Unexplained global event...*

"Yes, I know," he said.

He stretched upwards and staggered into the kitchen. He turned the tap on and stuck his head under – lapping up what he could like a dog. He splashed water on his face and rubbed his cheeks hard.

He sat down at the kitchen table and placed his clasped hands on the surface. First things first, he needed to know what happened and the only way he could be certain would be to go back there and see. He looked down at himself and sniffed his sleeves. He needed to get cleaned up before he went anywhere.

Upstairs, he took off his clothes and placed them in a bin bag. In the shower he scoured his hands and face like he was trying to erase what happened. His mind could not recall how the night ended, but his skin appeared to have kept track of everything.

After getting dressed, he returned downstairs. He felt sick and sat down on the sofa. He looked up at the television. Still, no one had anything new to report.

"Global deaths now estimated to be somewhere between one to two million," a young woman said. Healthcare systems were overwhelmed and emergency services in many parts of the world were still in chaos. The army had been mobilised in the UK and some cities were under martial law. All flights were grounded. Stock markets remained shut and people were advised to stay at home and only leave the house in case of medical emergency.

The never-ending stream of information made his headache feel a thousand times worse. He got up and went over to the sideboard to search for some painkillers.

"Now let's go to news teams in your local area," the news anchor announced before the theme music played.

"As the world this morning tries to understand what happened yesterday, here in the north-west, inhabitants were themselves attempting to make sense of the chaos."

Hearing a local accent, Paul glanced at the television before continuing to dig through the drawer.

"Hospitals in the area remain full of those injured during the event yesterday… Liverpool and Manchester city centres are in lockdown and under the control of riot police and the army following widespread rioting and looting… Fire services across the region spent most of the night clearing wreckage from roads… Greater Manchester Police, the Cheshire Constabulary and Merseyside Police reported that numerous violent crimes were committed over the course of the night – including a spate of attacks on religious leaders and buildings…" Paul pricked up his ears.

"…In one particularly horrifying scene at St Luke's in Salford, a local pastor, Father Phillip Michaels…" Paul looked up. "…And his wife and son appear to have died when the church was burnt down late last night. Police are investigating and trying to understand what happened…"

The man carried on speaking, but all Paul heard was white noise. His chest became tight. He couldn't breathe and he put his hands to his ribcage. This was the end, he thought. Something pulled him downwards. It wanted him in the ground. He dropped to his knees. He gasped for air and shook his head from side to side.

"No, no," he said. "Can't be true."

His mouth and throat were trying hard to keep the air coming in and out of his body. He swallowed big gulps of air. The pain in his chest kept growing and the voice in his head was screaming. He opened his mouth again, but no sound came out. He could see himself being pulled into a dark tunnel. But as he entered, a switch was flicked, and a strange calmness fell upon him. He released the tight hold on his chest, and he could breathe again. His eyes moved from side to side as he struggled to accept that the panic had passed. But really, it did seem okay. Then a familiar voice spoke, and he realised he was no longer alone.

"You've made a complete pig's ear of things here, haven't you?"

It couldn't be, but it was. He felt like the shock should've hit him hard – it should have hurt. Yet he felt fine – like he was waking up from a bad dream. He sat up and looked at the armchair. There, sat Eve. They both stared at each other. This wasn't her like he remembered her. This was a younger Eve – the one from his memory of the beach. He got up from the floor, and without losing eye contact with her, went and sat on the sofa. She was wearing that summer dress. The green one covered in small red tulips. The same one she wore that day at the seaside. Her skin was fair and her cheeks glowed. Her beautiful eyes shimmered and were not puffy and yellow like they were in her later years. Her long brown hair draped over her exposed shoulders. Yes, that is how he remembered her. A single tear rolled down his face.

"Burning down a church and killing that man who did so much for you?" The tone of her voice was also different. "And his poor young family as well. That won't do. No, that won't do at all."

Paul looked on, without shifting his gaze.

"A loyal, loving wife and a happy four-year-old boy. You burnt the whole family to a crisp."

"I didn't know."

"Doesn't matter. It was careless. After all these years, you still can't take responsibility for your actions."

"It was an accident."

"No one firebombs a church by accident. You've put us both at risk."

"It wasn't—"

"We're in danger and we have to leave."

"Where… to?"

"I know where we need to go."

Paul nodded. "Well, maybe it is time for a break. There's been a lot going on here recently."

"Good." She sat back in the chair. "Now go pack a bag."

"Right." He got up slowly and headed towards the door, but he was unable to stop staring at her.

"Go."

Upstairs, Paul opened the wardrobe and reached for a small canvas holdall that had been there since he recovered it from the hospice. He filled it with a selection of clothes and toiletries from the bathroom. The wardrobe was empty apart from a dark green British army jacket. Paul stroked the left sleeve. He rubbed the gold buttons to clear some dust and let them shine again. He slammed the door and returned downstairs.

Eve now stood looking out of the window.

"Ready?" she asked without turning around.

"Just a minute."

Paul went out into the garden and examined the metal bucket filled with rainwater and ash. He dug his fingers into the sludge and felt the remains of the old Bible between his fingertips. He found himself biting his lip. He emptied the bucket onto the grass, wiped his hands and went back inside. In the living room he grabbed his coat and put it on.

"Right," he said. "Where are we going?"

"Follow me."

Without even glancing at Paul, Eve headed out into the street. He followed, closing the front door behind him. They walked in the opposite direction to St Luke's Square, and briefly, he thought he could smell burning. He imagined what the corpses looked like and had to stop as he was overcome by nausea. Eve turned around and gave him a cold, hard stare until he carried on.

The streets were empty. Deserted. They were walking south. The city skyline was black from smoke and pervasive sirens still hung in the air like they hadn't stopped. From the terraced avenues of Salford, they passed through the modern developments of the quays and the shadows of Old Trafford stadium – its own place of ritual and worship for many.

Eve carried on unless Paul stopped. She walked with clear determination of where she was going. He followed her as best he could, but his movements were sluggish and – despite the blackened overcast skies – the daylight still made his eyes hurt. He couldn't shake the feeling that he could vomit at any second. Many things about the situation were unnatural.

Their route took them across a park. In his peripheral vision Paul saw a group of children stood by a grove. They were looking at something. One of the larger boys in the group – no older than eleven – had hold of a smaller boy. He was pushing him to do something, and the younger boy fought back as best he could. Paul's curiosity got the better of him and he walked away from the path to see what the children were looking at. Eve called after him.

Nearer to the group, he saw the underside of the black shoes of someone on the ground. He cocked his head to try and see between the children, but it wasn't until he was right behind them that he could see the body. Sat upright against a tree, with his eyes and mouth wide open, was a motionless and pale-faced young man. The larger boy pushed the younger one to interact with the body.

"Go on, touch your dead boyfriend."

"What the hell are you doing?" Paul pushed his way through.

"It's alright. He's dead, mate," another of the boys said.

The man was dressed in a black suit and white shirt and his body leant against the tree. His head hung to one side and partially rested on his shoulder. On his lap was a black book with a golden star of David on the front. He had a skullcap on his head. Next to the body was an open plastic pill bottle and a few pills were littered on the grass.

Paul looked around at the boys and shook his head. "Jesus Christ. Show some respect."

The larger boy let go of the smaller one and the rest put their heads down.

Paul was uncertain of what to do. He felt despair at what he saw. How helpless the young man must have felt to do this. He reached for his phone but the battery was dead. From behind, he could hear Eve's voice. She was getting louder.

"Have you called the police?"

"Chris has gone to get his dad," the older one said.

"We need to keep going," Eve said. "You don't want the police finding you here."

Paul glanced at Eve. He felt tears in his eyes. There wasn't much he could do now. He gazed at the dead man.

"Let's go," she repeated. "Now."

Paul nodded, turned on his heels and made his way back to the path. The children stared at him as he walked away.

*

Suburbia passed around them and there were few souls to be seen. At an intersection, they came upon the aftermath of a car crash; two car wrecks had been moved to the side of the road after colliding. Further along they reached a row of shops where windows had been smashed, and a cash register had been plunged through the glass door of a phone box.

In Stretford they crossed a football field and went through a gate that opened out on to the River Mersey. Paul recalled coming down to the spot in the summer with Eve and swimming in the cold, fast-running water. The river snaked past him into an area hidden by bare trees. The sun was high in the sky and it was late morning. Despite the mad events of the last twenty-four hours, nature appeared unaffected. Paul stared at the scenery and tried to clear his mind of the image of the pale, young corpse. He became aware of Eve's stare.

"Don't you remember coming here?" he asked.

Eve shook her head. "We need to keep moving."

"Why do we need to keep moving? Why can't I stop for a minute?"

"Why can't you take anything seriously for once?"

"I remember this place. We used to come here."

"Have you forgotten what you've done? The past doesn't matter now."

"What do you mean the past doesn't matter? You were here with me."

Eve stepped forwards and gazed into his eyes.

"It doesn't matter now. Everything has changed. Nothing will ever be the same again."

"Look, just over there. By that tree – that's where we sat and drank your dad's cider. You must remember?"

Eve glanced at the tree and then swung at Paul with her fist. She struck him on the side of his face and knocked him to the ground.

He held the side of his head – his mouth hung open and his jaw trembled as he searched for the words. "Why did you do that?"

She bent over and brought her face close to his. "You thought I couldn't hurt you because I only exist in your stupid little head."

Her eyes moved over his body and Paul lifted his arm, ready to defend himself.

"Well, I can hurt you, so you need to listen to me. We can't stay here cowering. We need to act. We need to get moving."

Paul rubbed his cheek and spoke hesitantly. "And… what if I don't?"

"Then I will keep reminding you in whatever way I need to."

Eve got up, walked away a few paces, and then turned to look at Paul. He got to his feet, dusted himself off and followed her along the riverside path beyond the trees.

FOUR

Paul was dead on his feet having walked for hours without rest. He had no sense of the time, but the daylight had faded a while ago. Ten paces ahead, Eve's pale figure marched in the darkness like some storybook phantom. They were now well clear of the city having walked in a south-westerly direction, through the green suburbs of Cheshire and then out into a more rural space. Lining the country lanes were huge fields – each surrounded by dark hedges and thick stone walls. He'd seen farms and a few cottages, but aside from the odd twitching curtain and a tractor driven by a glum-looking farmer, he'd encountered no other persons.

The only thing he'd eaten the whole day was a handful of overripe apples from a tree next to an old barn. He quenched his thirst by lapping up water from a rusty farm tap.

Marching on an empty stomach for hours reminded him of basic training. Had the circumstances been different, he might have enjoyed the experience.

Without any stimulation in the darkness, his mind took him away. He thought about his last conversation with Michaels. That Sunday – like every other Sunday – he helped the pastor clear up after the service. He picked up hymn books and placed them in an empty wooden crate on the floor next to the organ. The pastor packed away his notes.

"Nineteen today. The cold weather must be keeping them away."

Paul nodded.

"Still, at least the youngsters made it." Michaels turned to Paul and smiled. Paul tried to mirror the man's expression.

"Paul, you look ever so tired. Are you still not sleeping?"

Paul sighed. "Some nights are longer than others."

The pastor's eyes narrowed, and he looked fixedly at Paul. Paul felt uncomfortable.

"It was the anniversary of her death, wasn't it?"

"On Wednesday."

"Oh Paul." The pastor put his hand on Paul's shoulder and looked down at the floor.

"I have fought the good fight, I have finished the race, I have kept the faith. Do you know who said that?"

Paul shook his head.

"It was your namesake – Paul the apostle. Two, Timothy four, seven." Michaels grinned. "Those words are a reminder that faith and belief in Christ really are part of the lifelong struggle against evil – both within us and externally in the wider world. Satan takes many forms and presents us with challenges almost every day. Suffering is all around – whether it's on the news or staring us in the face at home.

"And you, Paul, really are one of Christ's soldiers. Here you are, still facing your own challenges, yet you faithfully attend here each Sunday helping with his work. You're an inspiration."

The pastor's words felt good. But for Paul, attending church service wasn't a chore or a job, he needed to be there.

"I do what I can. It's good to have a routine. Be around familiar faces."

The pastor nodded and signalled to the nearest pew. "Why don't we sit down and have a chat?"

"Thanks, but I better be getting off. I have stuff I need to do at home. Got that interview tomorrow."

"Ah, of course." The pastor smiled. "I spoke very highly of you. I think you're in with a very good chance. I just hope you don't mind maintenance work. That community centre needs a lot of it."

"No, it's perfect – really appreciate it."

Paul picked up a worn blue anorak that was hanging on the nearest pew and put it on. "I better be off."

"Okay, well thanks again, Paul. And remember, I'm always here if you need to chat, or even if it's just a theology lesson you're after."

Paul sensed a little attempt at humour but raised his hand and walked away. Before he got very far, Michaels called after him.

"Hang on, Paul, you left your phone."

Paul returned and the pastor handed him the device.

"That's quite a vintage piece you have."

"Does the job for me." He nodded to the pastor and then retreated again. Behind him, Michaels was preaching to an empty church.

"Go therefore and make disciples of all nations, baptising them in the name of the Father and the Son and the Holy

Spirit, teaching them to observe all that I have commanded you."

As Paul pulled on the faded brass handle of the heavy church door, the pastor yelled his words. "And behold, I am with you always, to the end of the age."

But he wasn't. He was now cinder and ash, a charred shadow of non-existence – he, and his family. Paul could taste smoke on the air and his stomach dropped.

He stopped walking and saw Eve's still outline in the dark facing him. He shuddered.

"I'm coming," he said, his voice cracking.

*

The darkness had now swallowed Paul and a storm had moved in, bringing strong winds and heavy rain. He was soaked and shivering, and his body felt heavier with each step. He wiped away the rainwater from his brow so he could view the road ahead more clearly. The route took them through a wooded area and there were trees on each side of the road that gave him some shelter. He had not seen a house for a while but ahead was a cottage. As he got nearer, he noticed that all the lights were on and the front door was wide open. He slowed his steps and approached the building. He looked through the windows with his hands cupped against the glass. No sign of anyone. No car in the driveway either.

He popped his head into the open doorway.

"Hello?" He listened but heard no response. He called out again and knocked on the door. He stepped into the hallway and looked around. All the lights in the rooms that he could see were on. The cottage was small, and the door opened into a living and dining area. He walked further into the house and surveyed the space. He entered the kitchen at the back and then called out again.

"What the hell are you doing?" Eve asked from the doorway. "We need to keep going."

Paul did not reply. He glanced over at her before treading carefully up the stairs, calling out again a few more times but to no response. All the lights were on in the upper floor and, despite this and the open door, there were no other signs of anything out of the ordinary having taken place. He walked back down the stairs before stopping at the bottom step and sitting down.

"Look, I can't keep going like this all night. I'm cold and about ready to collapse."

"You're weak," Eve replied. "You know we have to keep going. Trouble will catch up with us if we stop here. We can't stay."

"I have to rest. I'll die of exposure out there."

"Stupid behaviour like this is why bad things happen to you." Eve sat down on the sofa near the window. Paul looked at her expecting more pushback, but she seemed compliant, for the moment at least. In the kitchen he opened cupboards and examined the food situation. There wasn't much, but he found a tin of beans with a ring-pull top. Spoon and open tin in hand, he sat in the dining area and devoured the cold beans in seconds. Eve shook her head.

On the near wall was a picture of a man, a woman and young girl. A happy family. On another wall, he could see a shape where the paint was less faded, indicating that an object had been hanging there until recently. It was the shape of a crucifix.

There were many questions, but Paul was exhausted and not thinking straight. He emptied the remaining beans into his mouth, before closing the front door and going upstairs. There were two bedrooms and a bathroom. One had a small bed, boxes of toys and unicorn posters on the walls. He walked into the parents' room and looked around. The bed was made, and the room was immaculate. He dropped his bag on the floor and collapsed onto the bed face first and closed his eyes. The wind outside howled like an angry banshee, and the storm hit the trees hard. One of the branches scraped the roof of the house like it was clawing to get in. Paul opened his eyes and ran back downstairs. Eve was no longer sat on the sofa. He looked around the living area but saw no sign of her. *Screw her,* he thought, she could take care of herself. He went into the kitchen and picked up a butcher's knife from the sink. He dashed back upstairs and lay down again – this time on his back – with the knife in his hands. He left the lights on, but still managed to close his eyes and drift off.

*

Paul was back in St Luke's and sat in his usual pew surrounded by the faces he saw every Sunday. He looked up into the pulpit and saw Karl dressed in Michaels' choir dress turning the pages of his Bible. He looked around at the congregation expecting to see confusion on their faces, but he saw only content expressions and smiles. Karl raised his head and spoke.

"Jesus, console those who are grieving. Let them be comforted by your love. Share it with those who mourn and surround them with peace." Paul wanted to leave but an invisible force held him stationary.

"Give us your strength to know that when a loved one passes, you our lord will gain more than we have lost. We know that you are the resurrection and the light. And you will guide us to eternal life. Though our bodies will one day die, we take comfort in the knowledge that our souls will continue on. We know and believe this to be true with all our hearts."

Karl closed the book and smiled – exposing crooked, blackened teeth.

"Now we shall sing one of my favourite hymns, 'Light Shining Out of Darkness', by William Cowper."

The force holding him pushed Paul to his feet. The organ started playing and he leafed through the hymn book searching for the right page. He couldn't find it and he struggled to remember the words despite having sung the song a hundred times. The congregants around him started singing and he began to panic.

"*God moves in a mysterious way, his wonders to perform; he plants his footsteps in the sea, and rides upon the storm.*"

Beyond the organ, in the background, he could hear bells chiming along in time with the music. When he looked again at the congregants, he saw they were all burnt corpses. Red and smoking cindered flesh surrounded him. He could smell burning meat and at the tip of his tongue he could taste bacon.

Up in the pulpit, Karl had been replaced by Father Michaels. He had the same burnt appearance as the congregants. His eye sockets were empty and what was left of his eyes streamed down his exposed muscle and sinew like runny egg. Paul wanted to run, but he could not. Small flickering lights came down from above and danced around him. They changed colour the way flames evolve as a fire burns through different fuel. He desperately tried to move and get away, but he could not. He tried to scream but his voice was lost in the hymn. A jolt of energy hit him, and he emerged from the horror and out of sleep to a more shocking scene. Eve leant over him with the knife in her hand. Her knees pushed on his arms and pinned him down. The blade hung over his neck and he saw fury in her eyes.

FIVE

Paul twisted his body and pulled his hands from under her so he could grab her wrists. He pushed to move the blade away and she toppled to his side of the bed and as she did the knife caught him on his left arm. He screamed and she released the knife, before dropping off the bed onto the floor. The long diagonal slash across the underside of Paul's forearm began to gush blood. He pushed his palm against it and ran into the bathroom where he grabbed a towel and twisted it around his arm. Paul's heart raced and he sat down on the toilet to catch his breath. A red patch appeared and grew on the towel where it pressed against the wound. He got up and returned to the bedroom.

"What the hell were you doing?"

Eve lay on the floor quietly with her eyes closed. "Don't be so dramatic," she said. "Don't tell me you haven't thought about doing that before."

Paul paced around the room shaking his head. Then he stopped and looked at her.

"Why do you keep trying to hurt me?"

She smiled and got to her feet, straightening her dress. "You know it's not me – it's the universe. It's always had it in for you. I'm just doing its bidding – helping things along."

"I…" he started before a banging sound came from elsewhere upstairs. Paul grabbed the knife and stepped out into the landing. He tiptoed into the child's bedroom and looked around. Everything appeared as it did before. Nothing was out of the ordinary. Behind him, Eve shuffled in. Then another bang, followed by muffled whining. There was someone in the wardrobe. Treading as lightly as he could, he stepped nearer and slowly opened it with one hand while the other lifted the knife up, ready to strike. There, sat on the floor, and covered in the content of a box that had fallen from the shelf above, was a young girl with blonde curly hair. Her eyes were red, and her two small hands held up a piece of clothing to her mouth. It was soaked and covered in teeth marks. She was wide-eyed and full of fear. Paul stared at her before throwing the knife to one side. He turned his head slightly and looked to see if Eve was still there.

"What do I do?"

"We need to leave," she said.

The girl stared at him.

"I can't just leave her here."

"You can. She's not your responsibility. Come on, let's go now before her parents return."

Paul looked at his arm. "I don't want to go anywhere with you."

"You're not free of me yet."

Paul looked around at the child's room. There was a soft green dinosaur in the corner on the floor. He reached over and picked it up. He then forced a smile and tried to offer the toy to the child. The girl was reluctant at first, but he persisted, and she grabbed it with both hands.

"Where are your mum and dad?" Paul tried to soften the tone of his voice.

The girl shook her head.

"How long have you been in there?"

The girl bit her lip.

"You've no idea what you're doing so let's just get out of here now." Eve spoke but the girl kept her eyes on Paul.

"Just shut up. You're not helping. I need to think." Paul got up.

"I bet you've been in there a while, haven't you? Would you like me to get you some milk and biscuits?"

Reluctant, the girl gave a gentle nod.

Paul walked out of the room, signalling to Eve to follow him.

"Come on, I'm not leaving you here with her."

In the kitchen, he searched the cupboards until he found a small pink plastic cup with a large smiley face printed on the side. He filled it with milk from the fridge and then took two chocolate biscuits from a tin on the side. On the fridge was a photo of the girl with her parents at the beach. They were all smiling. The father had the same curly hair, albeit darker. She had her mother's eyes.

"Something bad happened here," Paul said. "These people wouldn't have left the girl alone like this."

"Maybe one of them snapped," Eve said. "It happens." She smiled and Paul shivered.

"I should phone the police," Paul said.

"After what you did? That's a stupid idea."

"But I can't leave the girl here like this. What if it's dangerous? If one of her parents has lost it, what if they come back here?"

"What if they do? The fate of their own is theirs to deal with."

"No, that's not right."

In the living room he found the base of the phone but no handset.

"It must be here somewhere." He picked up cushions on the sofa and searched underneath the furniture but there was no sign of it. Eve watched with her arms crossed.

"You have to leave her here," she said. "It's too risky to take her with you. Arson, murder and now child abduction."

"I'm not the one to blame." Paul stopped what he was doing and gave Eve a stern look. "And I can't leave her here alone."

"You said yourself, her parents won't have gone far. They'll be back soon for her."

"Shut up and stay here." Paul took the milk and biscuits upstairs. The girl raised her eyebrows when she saw him. Was she pleased or scared? He couldn't tell. He knelt in front of her and walked a couple of steps nearer on his knees.

"There you go."

After a few prompts, she took a biscuit and then the beaker of milk.

"Is that good?"

She gave a single silent nod.

Paul watched her eating. She finished the first biscuit and took a sip of milk. She placed the beaker on the floor and reached for the second one. This time, her bites were bigger, and she finished it off in quicker time.

She was looking at his arm and he realised the towel was now drenched in blood. He went back into the bathroom and stuffed the old, red-stained hand towel into the bin. He examined the wound – it was still moist, but the blood flow had slowed. He ran it under the tap and wrapped it in a thin bandage he found in the cupboard beneath the sink.

From outside, he heard a scream, and he turned his head in the direction of the frosted glass. He couldn't tell if it was a man or a woman, but it was a person.

"We need to leave," he said.

Eve was in the doorway.

"She's coming with us."

Eve dropped her head.

*

Paul had built up a little trust with the girl. She was willing to leave her hiding spot in her bedroom and follow him downstairs where he got her to don her small puffer jacket. She wore leggings and a pink jumper with a picture of a bear on it. He found shoes for her to wear and asked her if she needed to go to the toilet before they left. He put his own coat on and placed the holdall strap over his shoulders. He took a few deep breaths and looked around the room to check that he had everything he needed.

The girl yawned and Paul looked at the clock on the mantlepiece. It was just after five in the morning. Still dark and windy but at least the rain had stopped. As he readied to leave, all the lights went out and they were plunged into darkness. The girl started crying. Paul reached out for her and grabbed her shoulder.

"It's okay. Just the wind knocking trees onto power lines."

"Or our executor is here," Eve said.

Paul looked out of the window but could see nothing in the darkness. He heard noises from the back door and dashed into the kitchen. The handle turned. It remained locked but someone was trying to get in. On each of the windows on either side of the door, dark red crosses had been smeared on the glass. They could wait no longer. He lifted the girl and whispered to her. "Now remember what I said. We need to be very quiet as we play this game. When we get to where we're going, you'll get lots of nice treats. Your mum and dad will be waiting there for you. But until then it's very important that we are very quiet."

He wasn't certain whether he needed to say this – she hadn't spoken a word since he found her. But he had to be sure.

Sounds from the back of the house were getting louder. Someone was banging against the door. They were trying to kick it open. Paul opened the front door as softly as he could. Then he picked up the girl and stepped out into the night. Eve followed behind. As soon as they were outside, he picked up the pace and treaded lightly but swiftly. He looked back in the dark but could barely make out the road let alone see whether anyone might be following them. He thought he could hear footsteps, but he couldn't be sure. He stopped and there they were – heavy, slow feet plodding along behind them.

"Death is stalking us," Eve said.

Paul ignored her and picked up the pace. He tried to run but his lungs said no. He wheezed and felt sweat dripping down his back. He kept to a steady, fast walking pace, but it was tiring. He didn't want to slow down but the weight of the child was proving more considerable by the step. Throughout, he could hear Eve whispering in the dark.

"Terrible mistake. Firestarter. Killer. Child abductor."

Her voice repeated like a tape player in his head. He wanted to scream at her and tell her to shut up, but he was trying to make as little noise as possible.

Despite what he heard and the distress it caused him, the girl fell asleep in his arms. She looked at peace and he tried to listen to the sound of her breathing. It provided a soothing counterbalance to the hateful running narrative he was receiving from Eve.

His left arm ached where the knife had cut it open, but he didn't want to think about that now. His priority was to get them away from the cottage and the person who was following them. He didn't know what he would do with the girl yet.

*

They were out of the wooded area as slivers of daylight slipped out from the darkness. The trees were replaced by green pastures surrounded by farm fencing and stone walls. The wind died down, and, like the panic and the terror of the night, the storm had passed. Ahead, Paul saw smoke rising from a building. Finally, a house. He stopped and listened. He heard sheep bleating, birds singing to signal the start of a new day and the gentle snores of a young child – but he heard no footsteps.

"Here's your chance," Eve said.

This time he nodded. The farmhouse was positioned next to the road and surrounded by stone buildings covered in corrugated iron roofing. There was a light on upstairs. He crouched down near the hedge as he approached the building and examined the layout of the property.

At the back of the house, he saw an enclosed porch. Watching the windows, he dashed around the building. He peered into the porch and saw coats hanging on a series of hooks. He tried the door and felt relief as it opened. He pulled the coats from the wall and dropped them in a pile on the floor. Then – carefully as he could – he placed the small sleeping girl down on the small nest. He expected her to wake up and was ready to run but she did not. He remained crouched next to her and gently brushed a long blonde curly strand away from her face. He grabbed a fleece that was next to her on the floor and pulled it over her. Then he stepped back out of the porch and gently pulled the door closed. He took one last look at her through the glass before running from the driveway and down the lane in the opposite direction to where he had come from. He stopped by the hedge and crouched down to look back. This was the best place to leave her. His arm ached like it was reminding him of something else and he looked to Eve who stood ahead of him on the road. She signalled to him to come and he complied with her wishes and followed.

SIX

A few hours after the farmhouse, Paul looked up at the sky. He was thinking about the girl. He felt a twinge of pain in his arm and stopped. Eve came over.

"We can't keep doing this. We need to get away before the police catch up."

Paul rubbed his arm. "I don't regret what I did. She – we – were in danger there."

"You keep telling yourself that but what if there was no one there?"

"You heard what I heard. That child was left because something bad happened."

"When the police catch up, we'll find out."

"We'll see."

"For now, we keep going." Eve walked away but Paul stood still. She turned her head before marching back.

"Have I not demonstrated to you yet what I am capable of?"

Paul grabbed his arm.

"Do you ever wonder?"

"What?"

"Do you ever wonder whether we would've been good parents?"

"Thankfully that was never meant to be."

"But if we had?"

"Do you think you would have been more present than your own father?"

Paul didn't have an answer for her.

"Stop dawdling and get yourself together."

*

They came to a road sign that said *Croeso i Gymru. Welcome to Wales*. Paul stopped and called out to Eve.

"You're taking us back there, aren't you?"

Without responding, Eve turned on her heels and walked on.

They reached an area full of factories and warehouses. Paul saw a line of lorries parked up and ready for transit. He listened and heard only the breeze and birds above him. The industrial estate was devoid of any activity. He walked along a tall boundary wall surrounding a depot and saw a sentence painted on the cinder blocks that stretched far along the wall, despite it comprising only three words, *GOD IS DEAD*.

Away from the warehouses, the road widened. A car went past and slowed down as it drove through debris from a road accident. At the side was a burnt-out transit van. Paul peered inside and saw blood stains on the seats.

They crossed the Flintshire bridge over the River Dee. As he reached the middle – and what appeared to be the highest point of the bridge – he turned to see the English countryside behind him. The rising winter sun drew out long shadows across the bleak landscape.

On the other side of the river, they followed a road along the banks of the Dee and went past a strange-looking building with four chimneys; a power station perhaps given the thick cables and pylons that connected to it. The river widened as it opened out into Liverpool Bay and the road became nondescript with thick hedgerows on either side. There were more cars on the road and nearer the sea, Paul saw a man and a woman on foot. They paid him little attention.

His arm was hurting, and the exhaustion was catching up with him. He'd barely eaten anything since he'd left the city. Next to a bus stop he went into a public toilet. There, he supped water from a leaky tap. He tried to see his face in the remaining pieces of smashed mirror that hung on the wall but all he could see were his bloodshot eyes. He pulled up his coat sleeve and removed the bandage around his arm. He dripped water onto it and tensed his jaw as he felt the sting. The wound looked red and tender. It did not bleed but it was still moist, so he wrapped the bandage tightly around his arm again before gently easing down the sleeve.

The road turned inland, away from the estuary, where the route became flat and green. They passed a golf course, then a farm machinery shop and a garage that was open for fuel only. As his pace slowed, he came upon a sign for Prestatyn. This place he remembered. It was a decent-sized town. Bigger at least than the villages he'd seen that day. Somewhere would surely be open. The sun now hung low in the sky. He would need to rest soon.

On the outskirts of town, he walked past a large field full of caravans. He could see the odd person moving around in the campsite. Further along, the town itself was quiet. All the pubs on the main street were closed, as was the shopping centre and supermarket. Jesus, he thought, what was the plan here? Life had to go on at some point.

Eve became impatient as he peered through shop windows and tried to open doors. In the glass of the post office window, something caught his eye in the reflection. Behind him on the other side of the road, a train was pulling into the station. Somehow, he had failed to hear its engine. Unable to believe his eyes, he turned around. No one appeared to be boarding nor alighting the train but there it stood. Much to Eve's annoyance he crossed the road and ran up the steps to the platform. As it moved away, a boy in the last carriage caught his eye and smiled. He held out his still hand as if to wave. The boy did the same and Paul watched as the train faded into the distance.

He gasped. On the other platform was the station shop and it was open. He ran over the bridge to the central reservation. An older woman wearing a faded tabard stood behind the counter.

"You're open?" he said with disbelief.

"Yes, love."

"But there's no one here?"

"You'd be surprised. End of the world for some – for others it's time to visit their caravan."

If he hadn't been so tired, he would have laughed.

"What about you?" he asked.

"Why am I here? I needed to get out of the house. I know everyone is scared to do anything, but I'd rather be out here keeping busy." She extended her neck and looked up and down the platform.

"Saying that, I haven't had as many customers as I would like. Can I get you anything?"

Paul was overwhelmed by the choice. He ordered sandwiches, two pies, a large bottle of lemonade, three chocolate bars, and a selection of miniature spirits.

"How frequent are the trains?" Paul asked after paying for his feast.

"Not often. Mostly essential services to and from the cities. Are you travelling far?"

"I won't be taking a train. My journey is by foot."

"You do look tired, love." She glanced down towards the ticket office.

"You know the station manager's not around today, and he left the waiting room down there open. It has some very comfortable seats for somebody in need of a rest."

Paul looked down the platform then up at the darkening skies. "Right. Thank you."

He gathered his provisions and turned to see where Eve had gone, but she was nowhere in sight. He walked down the platform to the waiting room. The seats were comfortable and there were no armrests so he could stretch out, perhaps for the whole night if undisturbed. The surroundings looked familiar. Was this where they had stopped on their journey home all those years ago? Yes, he thought, it could well have been. He closed his eyes and tried to remember.

*

He and Eve were returning from their honeymoon in Wales. They had travelled along the coast from Anglesey – taking buses and hitchhiking where they needed. From the station they planned to take the train back to Manchester. It was late in the day and both were tired. They slouched in the waiting room chairs – Eve's head rested on Paul's shoulder. She wore his jacket, and the sleeves reached the tips of her fingers – her covered hands rested on his. Between Paul and the rucksacks, a small battery-powered radio hummed sounds from a local radio station.

"I wish we didn't have to go back," Eve said.

"I know, but at least we'll have a few weeks before I leave for Catterick."

Eve pulled up her sleeves and grabbed Paul's hand.

"Are you still sure about the army?"

"It's the only option – there's nothing for me in Salford."

"I'll be in Salford."

Paul turned to face Eve. "You know what I mean. There's no jobs, no future. This way I can take control of my own fate. If I don't, I'll remain trapped and I don't know what I'll do. I don't want to end up like Karl."

"You could never be like Karl."

Paul stroked her hands.

"Couldn't you get a job with a building company? Do an apprenticeship? That's the type of thing you want to do, right?"

"We've been through this, Eve. No one's building anything in the north-west. There's no money in the city and since they closed the dockyards, any available labour work is being snapped up by those with experience. I've got no hope."

She turned away from Paul and sighed. "Can I ask you one thing, though?"

"I know what you're going to say."

"Well, are you?"

"Am I trying to escape my mother?"

"You know that shouldn't be the main reason that you're leaving."

"Mum's a complicated woman, but this isn't about her. It's about you and me. About us building our lives together. I do a couple of years in the army – I get to learn some trades and skills, and when I come back I'll have lots of options."

"Only if you're sure it's the right move."

"It's the only move."

Paul reached over and kissed Eve on her lips, before reaching his arms around her and pulling her close.

"I don't know what the future holds for us," he whispered in her ear. "But what I do know is that it's our future. You're my destiny, my life, my everything and we'll always be together."

Eve looked into his eyes – tears were forming in the corners of hers. "I know." Then something caught her attention and her expression switched.

"Turn up the radio, it's that song again."

He turned the volume dial as high as it would go. Eve stood and pulled him up and they both danced along to the song that had become their holiday anthem. Together, they sang along to the chorus and cheered each other on with smiles and winks.

"*Stick with me baby, I'll show you the way. We'll keep each other shining, we'll never fade away.*"

*

Paul looked around at the waiting room. The colour was different, but it was the place where they talked and kissed and danced. He wanted to tell Eve, but she probably knew already and at that moment was elsewhere, which suited him.

He managed his way through an egg mayonnaise sandwich before opening one of the vodka miniatures, raising it in the air and pouring the spirit down his throat. He did the same again five or six times before laying down on the bench with his head on his bag. He closed his eyes and in a matter of minutes was sound asleep.

SEVEN

Paul opened his eyes and scanned his surroundings to see if she was near. He sat up and squinted as the morning sunshine fell on his face. His head was sore and he felt sick. He looked at the empty vodka miniatures in the bin next to him and shook his head. He drank a few sips from the bottle of lemonade and – as if out of nowhere – Eve appeared in front of him on the other side of the glass. Her stern look was a stark contrast to the face he remembered in that very same spot so many years ago. He knew it was time to leave and packed up what was left of his supplies.

As he stood, a chill went down his spine and he zipped up his coat. He touched his left arm and recoiled in pain. A bump had formed around the healing wound. He should be seeing a doctor but there was no time to think about that now. Eve glared at him through the glass. There was something about her appearance that caught Paul's attention. Perhaps it was the morning light. Perhaps it was her cheekbones or the way the dress cradled her body. She signalled her head towards the exit, telling him it was time to go.

Neither of the two exchanged any words and Paul followed her down the platform, past the closed shop and over the bridge and out of the station. To Paul's surprise, there were people out and about on the street that morning – a postman, a baker delivering bread to a shop, and a lady walking her Labrador. There were empty glasses, bottles and cigarette ends outside of the pub on the main street. Seems the place had come to life later in the evening.

The air didn't feel as cold as previous mornings, but Paul still shivered. The shadows were stark as the sunlight peered in between the buildings. He looked through the window of a newsagent. A handwritten sign on the door said, *Opening from 12 until 4 today*. But what caught his eye was the headline on a stack of newspapers inside the shop, *DAY OF REVELATION HAS ARRIVED*. He couldn't really make out any of the text underneath, but these words were striking. In his head he heard Father Michaels' voice.

"Well, Paul, I'm glad you asked. The Book of Revelation describes John's warnings to the seven churches who had gone astray and what would happen to them if they didn't correct their paths. The word apocalypse means to uncover or reveal and actually it's about revealing God's real intentions as opposed to the dark end-of-world images that most people connect it with."

Eve stood close to Paul and he turned to see her gaze.

"He was right, you know," Paul said. "What greater divine reveal could there be than it was all bullshit?"

They left the town centre and followed a route through a residential area. Despite being close to the sea, it was mostly bungalows and gardens that lined the road. In the distance, Paul heard crashing waves. It was a reassuring and calming sound. But he now felt a great deal worse than he did before. The shiver was constant. He felt light-headed and weak. His arm appeared to be the epicentre of the malady taking over his body. He thought about Eve and the dirty knife that she wielded in the cottage.

The road they followed was straight and felt never-ending. Walking was becoming an increasing chore and he felt his whole body was getting heavier with each step. He stopped and sat on a wall. He took out the lemonade from his bag and battled the nausea to bring the bottle to his lips. His dry mouth and pounding head told him he needed to drink something. As he lifted the bottle with both hands, he felt a sharp pain in his left arm. He put the bottle down, pulled up his sleeve and felt the bump. The wound had darkened in colour and blood vessels contrasted starkly against the increasingly pale-looking skin. It throbbed and wept and – oh lord – it was beginning to smell. Paul retched. He vomited a little over the side of the wall, before wiping his mouth and standing up straight.

Out of nowhere, Eve stepped into his field of vision. She grabbed his left arm and squeezed it. Her blunt fingernails dug into his tender flesh and his face contorted as he gasped from the pain.

"Feel that?" she said. "That pain is your punishment for all the bad things you've done. You own that pain so get used to it."

She walked off and Paul tried to calm his breathing. He looked up and saw her further down the road watching him. He pulled the sleeve back down over his wrist and stroked his arm. He raised a hand telling her to give him a moment. She began walking away. He picked up his bag and threw the long strap over his shoulder. Nursing his arm against his chest like a baby, he followed her.

Distractions became necessary. He looked up at the sky and across at a field of caravans. He breathed in the sea air and tried to listen to the waves and the wind blowing past his ears. He focused on anything that would keep him awake and away from the hole that the dark forces were pulling him into.

They reached the seafront on the outskirts of a seaside town. The sun burned in the sky and Paul felt the heat of the flames as they billowed down towards the earth. The wind picked up and played with the scenery like an invisible spirit. It collided with the water making huge waves. It picked up handfuls of sand and scattered it across the beach.

He closed his eyes and tried to focus on positive memories – Eve on that summer's day, laughing with Karl in the pub, sitting in church with Father Michaels. He tried to recite his friend's favourite hymn as he walked.

"*God moves in a mysterious way... His wonders to perform... He plants his footsteps in the sea... And rides upon the storm...*" He stopped and coughed.

"*Blind unbelief is sure to err... And scan his work in vain...*" He struggled to remember the next line.

"*God is his own interpreter... And he will make it plain.*"

Paul pushed on for what may have been minutes or hours – he couldn't say. His strength was failing him. The corners of his vision began to shimmer. He looked around to see where it came from, but it followed his view no matter where he looked. The shimmer grew. It came from heat –

from flames. He walked in fire and the blaze expanded until it was all around. He was inside the burning church and he felt the heat and smelt the fumes. Stood somewhere near the water, he saw three charred humans – a man, woman, and child – watching him with their arms wide open.

"I'm sorry. I don't know why I did it," he said. "I don't know."

Then his attention was drawn to the other side; stood in the road were two young soldiers – each with a gunshot wound to their head.

"I wish I'd been there with you. I should have been there."

Other faces appeared across the landscape, but as the flames filled his vision, it all became too bright, and he closed his eyes shut and listened to the seagulls above.

When he opened them, he was sat in the Sailor's Return like he had done two years earlier. It was a Tuesday afternoon, and the bar was empty. He sat alone with his pint – not his first or his second, or third. Next to the drink, his mobile phone was on silent, but the screen illuminated to show that someone was trying to call him. He pressed the button to see call history; thirteen missed calls from the hospice. *It must be time*, he thought. He picked up his glass, finished his drink and walked over to the bar to order another. As he waited to be served, Eve came over.

"This is where you were? The only company I had was a young care worker who stared out of the window. She wanted my life to end sooner because the whole experience was an inconvenience. My lungs were failing, and I was drowning in my own rotting flesh. Each desperate gasp I made sprayed bloody spit onto my chin. Over and over, I tried to wipe it off because I felt shame. But there was no end to it. There was only one way it ended. I was scared and in terrible pain and worried the process of my death was an unbearable and horrifying experience for anyone who visited me. But thankfully, no one came. Those were my last conscious seconds before I suffocated, and my thoughts faded away. I was afraid, alone and suffering, and this is where you were."

Paul turned away from her and closed his eyes – trying to direct his attention elsewhere. In the outer world he felt himself begin to fall and as he did the vision that surrounded him in the inner world became fixed within a framed square box. He looked around and was sat next to his mother in her house watching television. He saw people and places he knew on the old box.

"Be quiet, will you?" she said as his breathing became loud and laboured. "I'm trying to watch my programme."

He choked, struggled for air, and shivered – feeling colder than he ever had before. At the same time he was drenched in sweat.

His mother turned to him.

"The Lord preserves all who love him but the wicked he will destroy."

"Mum, I think I'm dying."

"You, my boy, sow discontent and then surprise yourself when you reap suffering. Now please be quiet – I'm trying to watch my soaps."

His heart beat harder and faster like it was out of control. He tried lifting his left arm, but it felt like an anchor pulling him down into the ground. He felt his head hit the bottom of a hole, and as the light left his vision and he entered a darkness that now felt familiar, he heard a voice behind him calling out like an echo from another world.

"Are you alright, mate?"

EIGHT

The first thing Paul noticed was the children's cartoon on the small television hanging on the wall. A cat and a dog argued about their right to sleep on a chair. There was also a mouse but his or her role was less clearly defined.

He was in a hospital ward with five other beds around him. The television was loud, and the cartoon sounds filled the room. He wore a patient gown and had a tube running from the back of his right hand up to a bag that was hanging on a metal pole. On the index finger of the same hand, a small plastic clip connected him to a machine to his side. He couldn't see the display, but he heard the regular beeps it made.

The air held a particular fragrance – not an entirely unpleasant one – but a unique smell nonetheless, a mixture of bitter disinfectant and sweet antiseptic.

His left arm was tightly wrapped in a bandage. When he tried to lift it to look, it felt mildly sore. The extreme pain from the day before – or whenever it had been – had subsided. He was in the bed nearest the door. On the left side was a large window. Through it, he could see the peaks of mountains and a cloudy blue sky. The countryside below was beneath his field of vision.

Most of the beds appeared occupied. In the nearest to his, was a young man in striped pyjamas who was captivated by the television and the ongoing conflict between the cartoon animals. The curtains were closed around the bed on the opposite side of the room. Sat in the chair next to that one was a gentle-looking man with glasses and a permanent smile on his face. From his position, he was unable to see the television above him, but he seemed happy enough watching the room. He nodded to Paul.

"Oh, you're awake." A petite nurse with dark brown hair stood at the bottom of his bed. In her hand was a jug full of water. She placed the jug on a table at the other end of the room, near the window, and then returned. She checked the tubes and the sensor on his finger before placing a blood pressure pump around his arm. Squeezing on the little bulb, the cuff inflated and tightened. She looked at the gauge and then wrote something down in the file at the end of his bed.

"How are you feeling, *cariad*?" She had a similar accent to the lady at the train station.

"Fine, I think," he said. "What happened? How did I end up here?"

"The doctor will be with you shortly and she can fill you in with a bit more detail. But it seems you collapsed on the beachfront in Rhyl and when you were brought in you were suffering from sepsis."

"Sepsis? Like blood poisoning?"

"Yes. To be honest, it was pretty touch-and-go from what

I understand. You were just going into shock when they found you. Do you know what day it is?"

Paul thought for a second. "Must be Friday?"

"No, it's Monday. You were in the intensive care unit for over three days."

"You're kidding."

"Don't worry – that happens. After ICU, people often feel like they've been through a time warp. Just be glad that you're through the worst of it now. We'll have you back on your feet in no time."

The nurse's tone was reassuring but Paul felt bewildered.

"So, I'm here because of this?" He lifted his left arm slightly.

The nurse's eyes narrowed. "Yes, that seems to be the case. But why don't I see if the consultant can come here and have a chat with you about everything."

"Okay, thanks."

"She'll be with you within the hour. If you need anything, call me using that button there. My name is Anwen."

Paul forced a smile and nodded.

Monday, Paul thought. One week since the event. What was the state of things now? Did they know much more about what happened? Some news might be good. He pressed the call button and around the corner Anwen came at pace.

"What is it, Paul?"

"Is there any chance we can change the channel and see if the news is on?"

Anwen turned her head and glanced at the screen.

"I'm afraid we can't right now. I don't think the news is on and maybe it's best we wait for the doctor and she can explain everything to you."

"There must be news on some channel."

"Please hang on for a moment." She turned and walked away.

That was peculiar, he thought.

As he waited, he thought about his last waking moments before losing consciousness at the beach. He shuddered. Where was Eve now? Did she come with him in the ambulance or was she still out there?

A head popped in from the corridor. A girl – in her late teens perhaps. She glanced at Paul and then looked to the floor.

"Sleeping beauty awake now, is he?"

Paul looked around as though she were speaking to someone else.

"Yes, I do mean you." Her voice was impassive.

"Do I know you?"

"I was here last night when you were brought into the ward. You looked dreadful."

"What?" Paul didn't know how to respond.

"My name is Kat."

Kat ambled in from the corridor in her denim jacket and spotty trousers; trousers that could have passed for pyjama bottoms. Her blonde hair was tied back exposing the full features of her young, fair face. She didn't smile. The expression on her face didn't say much, in fact.

"Are you a resident here as well?" Paul asked.

"Oh God no, just visiting. Funny isn't it how people still say that? – *Oh God* I mean. And *oh Lord* and *Jesus Christ* as well. They don't really have the same impact now, do they? Maybe we should switch them for other prominent historical characters? I always thought Genghis Khan was a good name. Oh, my Genghis – I can't believe you just said that."

Paul half smiled, still a little unsure of what to make of her.

"But I guess the whole idea was to make an impact by taking the Lord's name in vain. So maybe we should use the names of people we respect. Abraham Lincoln, for example, or Marie Curie or – and this one is perfect – Anne Frank. Yes, Anne Frank." Her eyes darted around the room. They went everywhere apart from Paul's direction.

"You're a strange one," Paul said.

"Oh P-Paul, Paul, you would say that." She stuttered and repeated his name.

"How do you know my name?"

She pointed to the file.

"You read my charts?"

"What can I say? I'm a sucker for graphs."

"Right. So, who are you visiting here?"

"My d-dad. Yes, my dad. He was in a car accident and had to have an operation on his legs. The bones were badly broken. Very bad. He's recovering but needs observation for a few days in case more work is needed. You know how these things go."

"I don't really."

"What about you? I heard the nurses say they found you collapsed and talking to yourself on the beach in Rhyl."

"I was quite unwell I think."

He signalled to the television. "What's the deal with the cartoons? This isn't a children's ward… is it?"

"Ha, no. That's just to keep the animals happy."

"What do you mean?"

"Well, you know which ward you're in, right?"

"No, which ward am I in?"

Anwen came in with a South Asian woman who wore thick-rimmed glasses and had a stethoscope hanging around her neck. Kat turned to see what Paul was looking at and Anwen greeted her with a scowl. She gasped like she'd been up to some mischief, got up and dashed out of the room.

"Paul, this is Dr Khan. Our current on-duty consultant. She can explain everything to you and answer your questions." Anwen pulled the curtains around the bed, giving Paul and the consultant some privacy. The doctor picked up his file and looked through.

"So, Paul, how are you feeling today?"

"A bit sore. More confused than anything."

"That's quite normal. You've been through quite a trauma."

"I don't really remember what happened."

"Some memory loss is not uncommon for patients who've had your experience."

"Right."

She closed the file and rested her clasped hands on it.

"I'm not sure what the nurses have told you so far?"

"Not much."

"When you were brought in, the infection in your arm had spread to other parts of your body causing sepsis. Your blood pressure was very low, and your body was starting to go into shock. I'm sure I don't need to tell you that you were very lucky. An hour longer and the outcome could have been much worse."

Paul listened and nodded.

"When you were brought in, you were just about breathing by yourself, so intubation and mechanical ventilation weren't needed. You were, however, admitted into the ICU for monitoring."

Paul became very aware of the background noises from the cartoon as the consultant spoke.

"They gave you oxygen, pain relief, and a broad-spectrum antibiotic through the IV line in your arm, which seemingly dealt with the infection over the next couple of days. You were in ICU until last night and then when it seemed like you were through the worst of it, they brought you down here."

Beyond the curtain, he heard the younger man to his side laughing.

"Your current vitals are looking good from what I can see, but an infectious disease consultant will come and check on you later this morning to ensure that the antibiotic is still doing its job."

"How long do you think I'll need to stay here?"

"Well, in terms of physical recovery, I think we're making great progress," she said. "However, it's important you're aware that sepsis can really take its toll on the whole body and full recovery may take some time. You may find yourself feeling very tired and weak, suffering bouts of insomnia, or losing your appetite."

Something in her words stood out to Paul. "You said *physical recovery…*"

"I'm a psychiatrist and this is the psychiatric unit of Gwynedd Hospital."

Paul tried to sit up as though he'd just been insulted.

"What, why? I'm absolutely fine."

"Please remain calm, Paul, and let me explain. One week ago, something happened to people across the world and everyone was affected in one way or another. Since that event, the hospital has been bursting at the seams with patients. Initially, admissions were because of injuries related to the loss of consciousness. But after the first two to three days, we saw a shift to patients coming in with psychiatric and neurological conditions – everything from anxiety and depression to mania and hallucinations."

He turned his head and thought about the other men in the wardroom.

"There's been a considerable increase in the number of suicide attempts and cases of self-harm. So many – in fact – that we've had to expand our normal psych unit. This room was actually a general ward until last Thursday."

Paul's eyes widened.

"Don't feel any unease though. This is a low-security unit. The patients here are mostly harmless. In fact, we have a few outpatients that come and go each day."

She took her glasses off and gave them a quick wipe with the edge of her sweater.

"Anyway, bringing it back to you; the concern was that the cut on your arm that led to the infection was self-inflicted, and given last week's event, it's not the only injury of this type we've seen."

Paul glanced at his tightly bandaged arm.

The doctor leant closer to Paul and frowned. "Let me ask you, how did the injury happen, Paul?"

Paul thought about the question for a second.

"I – er – put my arm through a glass window."

"Accidentally?"

"Yes."

She pushed her glasses up the ridge of her nose and narrowed her eyes. "You accidentally put your arm through a glass window. So, you didn't do this to yourself?"

"Absolutely not. To be honest, it's a bit embarrassing. I'd

had a couple of beers beforehand, so my fall was not elegant."

"Okay." She paused, opened the file, and looked at the notes again before looking up.

"Tell me about your Revelation, Paul. What was your experience like?"

"My Revelation?"

"Yes, sorry, the event that took place on February tenth. For lack of a better name, it seems like *Revelation* is the word that's sticking."

"Right. I was at work and felt a bit dizzy so sat down, got myself a fizzy drink and had a breather. I felt fine after a few minutes and carried on as normal."

"Okay. That does sound more on the asymptomatic end of the spectrum."

"Sorry, what?"

"No one knows for certain what happened last week. But what we do know is that the Revelation resulted in a spectrum of symptoms for people. At the one end, people like yourself describe their Revelation as asymptomatic. On the other end of the spectrum, people experienced a variety of different symptoms like loss of consciousness, seizures, disorientation, and aura-like visions. Many of them have been left with long-term mental health conditions that require further management and need extended recovery times."

Paul was taken aback. His real experience was without a doubt on the symptomatic end of this spectrum.

"Why so different for everyone?"

"That's the strangest thing about the whole event. The one unifying factor appears to be pre-Revelation faith or supernatural belief in a religion or god. The stronger the belief, the greater the symptoms."

"And afterwards?"

"Afterwards..." She sighed. "Afterwards, it seems that all religious belief was gone. Faith has been eliminated. Everyone is an atheist."

Paul's head dropped as the implications hit him. "It did really happen..."

He looked up at the psychiatrist again. "And the stronger their faith was, the more painful it was to have it taken away?"

"I suppose you could say that."

"Like tearing off a plaster?"

"Yes, like tearing off a plaster. Based on your experience, I guess you weren't a regular at church?"

Paul faked a smile. "No, not much of a feature in my house growing up, I guess."

He looked down at his lap again. "But how did it happen?"

The doctor started shaking her head before he had even finished asking the question. "No one has any idea, Paul. It's completely mind-boggling. A person's faith is – *was* – an intrinsic part of their being. It's not something that could be shut off or cut out. Their belief would be deeply intertwined with other parts of their mind and personality."

There was an equal mixture of horror and fascination in her voice.

"And the cause?"

She shrugged. "There's certainly no technology, drug or infectious agent that we are aware of that can have this kind of effect."

She crossed her arms and her gaze drifted up like she was pondering a question. "What I do know is that it adversely affected many, many people. Quite frankly, if it was an External Force that decided humans would be better off without religion, there must have been some anticipation of the negative effects of doing something like this."

"External Force?" He wrinkled his forehead.

She blinked and made eye contact with him again.

"Doesn't matter – it's all speculation."

She turned to her notes again and Paul looked around – he could see through a gap between the curtains. The young man in the bed next to his still gazed at the television. Paul couldn't see the screen, but the noises suggested the animals were still fighting.

"Paul, since the Revelation, have you experienced any other physical symptoms?"

"Aside from the cut and the infection, no."

"And regarding the wound, why didn't you go to the doctor sooner? Surely it must've been hurting – and perhaps even looking and smelling like something wasn't right?"

"It did cross my mind. But with everything else going on, I didn't want to be a burden."

"Right," she said, narrowing her eyes. "And mentally, any strange feelings or moods?"

"No more than usual." He feigned a smile. "What do you mean by strange?"

"Well, perhaps seeing or hearing something or someone who wasn't there."

"Certainly not."

"And no feelings or compulsions to hurt yourself or anyone else?"

"No."

Dr Khan wrote more notes in the file and Paul heard a familiar voice.

"She knows you're lying."

Eve.

It caught him by surprise. He looked around but couldn't see her or identify where the voice was coming from.

"No, she doesn't," he said.

The doctor looked up. "Sorry, Paul, did you say something?"

"No, nothing. I was just adding that there's nothing out of the ordinary."

Eve spoke again. "She's on to you. Bet she knows about the church and the kidnapping."

Paul scanned his surroundings, trying to see where she was hiding.

"Paul, I'm going to leave you now," the doctor said. "Dr Jarvis, our infectious disease specialist, will be with you shortly to talk you through your physical recovery."

"When can I leave?"

"Assuming Dr Jarvis is happy the infection has cleared, perhaps in a few days. You may not be feeling ready yet, so please don't feel the need to rush out of here. Your body has been through a lot and recovery after sepsis may take some time."

Paul nodded.

"Also, do please remember what I said to you about feeling anything out of the ordinary. If there is anything, it's easier for me to help you while you're in here with us."

Dr Khan stepped out through the curtains and he heard her shoes tapping on the hospital floor as she walked out of the room.

"Don't worry. I'm still here with you," Eve said. "We both know how you struggle alone. Alone and sober – that's the worst for you, isn't it?"

"Where are you? I can't see you." Paul was getting frustrated.

"I'm right here."

He reached for the call button and pressed it. Anwen's head appeared between the curtains.

"What is it, Paul?"

"Can I please get some water? Also, could you open these curtains? I'm feeling a little closed-in."

"Of course, let me do that now." Anwen pulled the curtains around the back of his bed. "I'll just go and fill your jug up. I'll be right back."

As the nurse left, Paul listened to the noises around him – the buzzing of the machines and the sounds of a cartoon cat trying to outwit a wily mouse.

"Why did you lie to her, Paul?"

His eyes darted around the room like he was watching a fly.

"Just leave me alone, will you?"

"If I leave you, you really will be alone."

"Get away from me." Paul closed his eyes and started humming *God Moves in a Mysterious Way*.

"I'm still here. I should get away from you. You really are trouble, but you need me."

He flinched as someone touched his arm.

"Paul, are you okay?" The reassuring face of the nurse appeared close to his.

"I sometimes calm myself by humming hymns."

"My father did the same." Anwen smiled. "Here's your water."

Anwen placed a full jug of water on the cabinet next to his bed and filled his glass. Paul took a sip of water, then closed his eyes and lay his head back on the pillow. Calm, he rested a moment as he waited for Eve to return. But it was another voice that spoke to him.

"Had a chat with the big chief then?"

Paul opened his eyes to see Kat. She stood facing him with her arms crossed and they briefly made eye contact. She started blinking and then looked away.

"Apparently so." Paul had one eye open.

"What's the diagnosis? Self-mutilator? Suicidal? Compulsive masturbator?" Her words implied humour, but her voice was flat and expressionless.

"All of the above." Paul smiled and it felt good.

They spoke for an hour until Dr Jarvis turned up to give Paul a physical examination. Kat disappeared once again but Paul knew she would return.

NINE

Getting some shut-eye in the ward was hard. Outside, there was constant coming and going near the nurses' station. Inside the room, there was the humming and beeping of machines interrupted by the odd outburst in the dark from the other occupants.

Not long after the lights went out, a female figure strode into the room. At first, Paul paid little attention – expecting it to be the nurse on night duty. But her movements were erratic, and she paced around the room like a caged tiger. He caught a glance of her ghostly face in the dark. Eve had returned.

He'd heard her voice earlier in the day, but this was the first time he'd seen her in the hospital. She glanced over at him. She looked angry and ready to lash out at anyone who caught her attention, but the other occupants – by now – were dead to the world. She said nothing to Paul. She sneered at him occasionally. He watched and saw her edge towards the door – looking like she was about to leave but then she turned and lunged over at him.

"Look at you – helpless like a child."

"You did this to me," Paul said.

"You deserved more."

"You might have managed it, had I not woken up."

She stepped closer to Paul and gazed into his eyes. He pulled his head back against the pillow.

"Get ready to leave. I'm going to get us both out of here."

"I can't leave yet," he replied. "You almost killed me. I need time."

"You're the only killer here." She turned away and circled the room a further few times before leaving. Paul rubbed his forehead. He closed his eyes and tried to see the beach, but his mind's eye saw only flames.

*

In the daylight, the mood in the room was different. The residents weren't a chatty bunch, but they were awake. The ward was livelier – meals were served, and daily routines were underway. The only person who was less visible was Eve. Paul felt she was still around – somewhere – but she didn't make her presence known.

He hadn't slept much after his interaction with Eve in the dark and he wasn't in the best of spirits. Physically, he felt a little stronger and he was able to sit up in the bed, but he felt far from ready to leave the hospital. That became clear earlier in the morning when he tried to use the toilet. Anwen – who had just started her shift – saw him struggle and suggested he would be better off with a bedpan. Paul grudgingly conceded.

He had come to know the names of all the men in the room as Anwen went about tending to their morning needs.

In the bed next to Paul, was a younger man they called George who never said a thing – he just stared all day long at the cartoons, which played on the wall-mounted television. He had red hair, wore pyjamas, and looked like a large child. An older man in glasses, called Mal – short for Maldwyn – sat in a chair next to the bed opposite to George. He rarely stopped smiling. He was pleasant and polite and spoke very little. The curtains around the bed next to his – the one facing Paul – were always closed. An angry and unpleasant man who everyone referred to as Mr Phillips hid in there. Paul rarely saw him, but he heard the man on several occasions tell the poor nurses where to go when they disturbed him. The two sleeping areas by the window were currently empty – although the one in the furthest corner was usually occupied by a thin and very nervous man by the name of Tommy.

Paul was still awake at dawn when he noticed Tommy was up by the window staring out. He looked like he was watching and waiting for something. When he appeared to have had enough, he mumbled aloud and then went back to his bed. Before long, he was back at the window. He repeated this action a dozen times at least before rushing out of the room yelling something about someone's imminent arrival.

Paul had stopped waiting for Tommy to return and after eating a few spoonfuls of cereal and drinking a mug of tea, he felt his eyelids become heavy and he lay back. That is when he heard commotion out in the corridor. At first, Paul tried to ignore it, but the yelling grew louder. Everyone in the room turned their heads towards the door. Even George briefly glanced away from the television. A bedpan came flying into the room and clattered on the floor. After that, Tommy goosestepped in with his fist up in the air. In his other hand, he held onto scrunched-up pieces of a newspaper. Pages fell behind him leaving a trail.

"Brothers, it's true," he said. "The External Force lives and we are all witnesses to its power."

Paul looked around at the other men. George sneered as Tommy became an obstacle between him and the television. Mal smiled at Paul with wide eyes.

Two male orderlies walked into the room after Tommy. Behind them was the on-duty nurse, who held a blood-stained tissue to her mouth. Tommy turned around and wagged his index finger at them.

"Don't you come near me, you dirty deniers. The Force has made itself known, loud and clear." He threw the remaining pages at the nearer of the two orderlies – who flinched. Tommy stepped back and stared at them both with a piercing gaze. "The Force killed your God and showed us its true strength."

Tommy leapt back and then climbed onto his bed. "The Force has freed us from the tyranny of Christ and Mohammed and the rest of them."

He started to move his hips like he was dancing. He pulled on the drawstring of his dressing gown and held it around his head like it was a feather boa – moving his body to music that no one else could hear. The two orderlies looked at each other before stepping closer to the bed. Mal started to clap along in time to Tommy's dancing. Dr Khan appeared at the entrance of the room. She whispered something to the nurse and showed her a small syringe in her hand. As the two orderlies stepped even closer to the bed, the nurse pulled on the curtain so that it fully separated Tommy's bed from Mal's. From behind, Tommy continued to chant or sing or whatever it was he was doing.

"God is dead and the Force lives on. We are all witnesses now."

The curtains were pulled further, and Tommy was almost fully enclosed. Dr Khan stood at the entrance watching.

"Get your filthy denier hands off me."

There was a loud thud that sounded like Tommy being pulled down onto the bed. Dr Khan immediately rushed in, and within seconds, Tommy's protests were silenced and the only noises in the room came from the cat and dog on the television.

Paul looked over at the door of the room and saw Kat watching, deadpan. She turned to Paul.

"Matey over there have too much coffee?" Kat spoke in her usual matter-of-fact tone.

Paul shrugged.

*

Tommy was taken away from the ward on a trolley and Paul did not see him again. The young nurse with the cut lip finished her shift and Anwen took over for the day. Paul explained to Kat what he'd seen. Before the nurses cleared up, Kat had picked up the scrunched-up newspaper page that Tommy had thrown at the orderly.

"What does it say?" Paul asked.

Kat turned it around to show him. The headline said *EXPERTS SAY, 'EXTERNAL FORCE LIKELY'.*

"External Force?" Paul said.

"Have you not heard about the Ex-External Force?" Kat said, tripping over the words.

Paul raised his hand to the television. "The news coverage in here hasn't been great to be honest."

Kat turned to look.

"Right." She nodded. "Well, it's something some expert said. The Revelation couldn't have just happened randomly like that. There must have been some External Force behind it."

"What, like aliens?"

"Who knows." Kat closed her eyes and took a deep breath. Paul felt uncomfortable and scratched his head.

She opened her eyes and looked towards the window. "Thing is, though, all the crazies have grabbed on to the whole External Force idea. Like it's this all-powerful thing that has done humanity a huge service with the Revelation."

"And they worship it like it's a…"

"Yeah."

Kat looked down at the newspaper.

"The Witnesses," she said.

"What?"

"The Witnesses of the External Force is what they call themselves. Like your matey boy over there."

"I never spoke to him." Paul glanced over at the empty bed.

"To be honest, a lot of their ideas are not that crazy given the current level of crazy in the world," Kat said, continuing to look down at the newspaper page.

"You sound like you have a soft spot for them."

"Some of their messaging is catchy." She put her finger on the page. "*God is dead, and we have awakened. With eyes wide open, we are all witnesses now*."

She lifted her head and her eyes moved past Paul. "Quoting Nietzsche is definitely something I approve of."

"They sound like a cult." Paul crossed his arms.

She shrugged. "It's mostly people meeting up online and sharing ideas in forums right now. But they're getting more popular."

"What's a forum?" Paul asked.

"You really are old, aren't you?" She bit her lip. "A forum is like a virtual noticeboard where people write messages to each other and share stuff."

Paul shook his head.

"Wow. Do you even have a smartphone?"

"I have a phone, but I don't think it's very smart."

Kat pulled on a strand of her hair and twisted it. Her eyes looked past Paul up at the wall behind him and she whispered something like she was talking to someone. "…He doesn't know."

"What?" Paul traced her gaze and looked to where her eyes focused.

He bit his lip and sighed. "Who's this *Neechah* person?"

"Nietzsche. A German philosopher from the nineteenth century."

"Right. You like to read about stuff like that?"

Her head dropped again as she examined the newspaper page.

"It's not the liveliest place to grow up. A Smiths' album and a bit of *The Gay Science* is not a bad option for a Saturday night."

"Gay Science?" Paul grimaced. "Is that something kids have to learn about at school?"

Kat cocked her head. "It's a book, Paul."

"Right," he said, rubbing his chin. "I may have a bit to learn."

She nodded. "Gay science," she repeated. "It's my favourite lesson after gay maths."

Despite her tone, he knew she was joking, and he smiled. "Could be for all I know."

TEN

That evening Paul felt anxious about falling asleep, but exhaustion meant that slumber would not wait. As soon as the ward lights were off, his breathing slowed, and his eyelids became heavy. He slipped away to another place. He saw the blue of the sea flickering in the sparkling sunshine. He felt the warmth of the sun on his face and the weight of her head as it rested on his lap. Her skin was velvet. He heard the crashing waves. To his left, bobbing boats were sheltering – as they always did – next to the stone pier. To his right, the green headland rose out of the water, and at the top, he saw the shape of the ancient church.

"Why do you keep torturing yourself with this image?" Eve said, her eyes open and looking up at Paul.

"I like coming back here," he said. "This was the calm before the storm."

"But the storm still came. It changes nothing."

"The storm always comes. That has been the way of my life."

"Because of the choices you make."

"No, it doesn't matter what I want. I always end up cold and alone in the dark."

Eve sat up and she sneered. "Poor little Paul. Life has always been so hard for you."

"Stop it."

"Curse this horrible nasty universe for having it in for little Paul."

"Please, leave it."

"All he wants is a happy day at the beach in the sunshine with his dead wife."

"No."

"Do you want to touch my skin, Paul? Or can I feel yours?"

Eve grabbed his arm and pulled it towards her. He tried to resist, but she was too strong. Narrowing her eyes, she then dragged her nails down the underside of his forearm and Paul screeched. The pain pulled him from the scene and he awoke on his bed. Confused, he looked around from side to side in the dark but there was no sign of her. He felt a stinging sensation on his right arm and lifted the pyjama sleeve to see four long scratch marks running from near his elbow to his wrist. For the rest of the night, he skimmed between waking and sleeping states, ever-wary that another attack may be imminent.

*

"I'm ready for a change of scenery." Paul lay on his bed with his arms crossed. It was late morning and the only time he'd got up was to visit the toilet.

"This cartoon has some strange messages," Kat said.

"What do you mean?" Paul asked.

"Well, the cat is naïve – a fool. Loyal to the owner, yes. But a complete idiot who gets trodden on by the other animals. The dog is a sadomasochist and the mouse, the mouse is a complete dick. Why would parents let their kids watch this stuff?"

"This one's old. I remember seeing it on television when I was a child."

"They had televisions back then?"

"They did but they were steam-powered."

"Right." She turned back to face Paul and seemed to scan his face before looking over at the wall. "You look rough. Did you sleep at all last night?"

"It's noisy at night."

"What did you say about the scenery?"

"I said I need a change of scenery."

"When can you get out?"

"Don't know yet. Soon, hopefully."

Kat twisted a curl that hung over her ear. "I know where we can go. Is that dressing gown warm?"

"Warm? Where do you want to take me?"

"You'll see."

Paul shuffled along the corridor after Kat. He wore pyjamas, a dressing gown and slippers that were provided for him. They recycled clothing left at the hospital. Paul preferred to imagine that these had been forgotten by previous patients after they had left the hospital as opposed to the alternative reason for their departure. Anything was better than the gown he'd worn for the first few days after he had awoken in the makeshift psych unit. He still had his holdall with him but had not prepared for a hospital stay on his journey.

"This way." Kat signalled, and he followed her down another corridor and then into a lift. She pressed the button for the top floor.

"Can we go that high?" Paul asked. Kat shrugged her shoulders.

When they reached the twelfth floor, Kat stepped out of the lift and pointed to a service door. On the other side was a poorly lit stairwell. Kat bounded up the stairs. For Paul, each step was a chore and he ascended at a snail's pace.

"You okay?" Kat asked.

Paul took a few deep breaths through his mouth and nodded.

"How many more steps?"

"Only seven hundred or so."

"What?"

Kat came back down to Paul's step and signalled to him to follow her. "Come on, you're almost there."

She counted out loud as they walked up the final few steps.

"Four, five, six, seven hundred. Right, we're here."

At the top of the stairs was a fire door. Kat pushed down on the metal bar and released streaks of bright daylight into the dark stairwell. They both stepped through and Paul found himself stood on the roof of the hospital. The air snapped with cold, and Paul wrapped the dressing gown tightly around his body. They both walked across the roof towards the edge that looked out over the mountains.

"How's that for a change?" Kat asked.

There were four layers to the landscape – each positioned as though planned by the hand of a divine artist. At the bottom, brown trees provided the base of the image. Then came the lush green fields intersected by hedgerows and the odd road. Above that lay the haphazard grey and brown formations of the Snowdonia mountains. At their peaks were white dustings of snow. Then, finally, the light blue top layer of the sky extended the image into infinity.

"It'll do," Paul said. He turned to face Kat.

"How did you find this place?"

"I was exploring one day."

Paul inhaled the cool, fresh air. It was cold but felt good going in and out of the lungs by comparison to the warm antiseptic air of the ward. He walked up to the wall at the edge of the roof, looked down and stepped back as he felt dizzy. He focused on the mountains once again.

"Quite a place to grow up," he said.

"If you like mountains." Kat leaned on the wall overlooking the landscape.

"You don't?"

"It's great for goats…" She stepped up onto the wall.

"Whoa, what are you doing?"

"…But I'm a bird." Kat stretched out her arms. "And all I want is to spread these wings and fly away."

Paul bit his lip and reached out his hand, ready to pull her down.

"Just come down from there, will you?"

"I can't fly yet," she said. "They keep telling me it's not time…" She looked at the ground below and her head tilted forwards.

"Please, get down, will you?" Paul said again.

"…But that time will soon come," she said glancing over at Paul.

He signalled for her to step down.

"Fine." She turned around and sat down facing Paul with her back against the wall.

Paul shivered and rubbed his chin. "Who's telling you it isn't time to fly?"

"What? Oh, no one. Forget about it."

"Okay." He looked at her and narrowed his eyes.

She saw him looking. "What?"

"I desperately wanted to get away when I was your age."

"Oh, here we go," she said. "Go on then, give me your pep talk, old man."

"Huh?" Paul crossed his arms.

"I can see it in your eyes. You want to tell me to be patient, that the world is my oyster, and that I have my whole life ahead to be free."

"Is that what you want to hear?"

"No, but it's what older people like to do, isn't it? Give the kids advice so they can learn from their mistakes."

"You'd learn nothing from me," Paul said as he sat down next to Kat. "I got married and joined the army. I made decisions that I thought would help me to escape. But things went to shit and rather than setting me free, my choices left me trapped. There was no escaping my destiny."

"What happened in the army?"

"I was stationed in Northern Ireland during the Troubles. Got caught in the wrong place at the wrong time."

Kat frowned. "Do you believe in fate?"

Paul closed his eyes. "Whatever has come to be has already been named, and it is known what man is, and that he is not able to dispute with one stronger than he."

"Yes or no would have sufficed."

"It's from the Bible."

"Oh."

"It means that everything has already been decided. Everything, including what each person would be. So, there's no use arguing with God about your destiny."

"I'll take that as a yes then?"

"I guess I used to," Paul said. "It's what I was taught to believe from a young age. But now, after this Revelation, I have no idea what I believe."

"It's a headfuck alright."

Paul laughed and it became a cough. He settled his breathing and then thought about himself at Kat's age. "Instead of waiting for this old guy's advice, you tell me – who do you want to be? Where do you want to go?"

"I do want to be a bird. I want to fly high in the sky away from this place. Away from all the bullshit. I want all the stupid people in my life to be the size of ants, miles below me. I want to be free of it all."

"Then don't leave that to fate. Be brave and take control of your destiny. It's what I'm coming to realise that I should've done. I used fate as my excuse for what happened. But the truth was I didn't have the guts."

"It's not too late, you know. I know you're old and everything, but you must have a year or two left at least to make it matter." Her tone was the same but for a moment, Paul thought he could see a smile in her eyes.

"Thanks." Paul nodded his appreciation.

"Seriously though. Maybe the Revelation gives you a second chance. Think of it as a reset. You're no longer under the control of that big, bearded man in the sky. Now it's all on you to mess up your own life."

Paul grinned but she had a point.

ELEVEN

That night when the lights went out, Paul stared at the window and gazed as the rain fell against it. Small drops glinted as they clung to the glass before succumbing to gravity and trailing down. Their paths appeared chaotic and unplanned, yet on they continued with determination along their own unique route.

He fought sleep but knew it was a battle he was destined to lose. He watched as his chest lifted and then dropped and considered what the night's encounter would bring. He was so tired that he felt ill, and he gave up on trying to evade his destiny. Tonight, he would accept whatever fate – Eve – had planned for him. He decided to close his eyes and wait for her to come.

"Welcome to my home." She was here. But where was here? He saw nothing but darkness. Paul reached up and touched his face. His eyes were open, but he could see nothing. He was surrounded by the night.

"Where am I?" he asked.

"This is where we all go when we are done."

"There's nothing here. We are nowhere."

"Exactly. We are nothing and we are nowhere."

"How can this be?"

"Don't worry, you're not alone, Paul."

"What?"

"Some of your old friends are here as well."

"It's such a shame you brought us here, Paul." Another voice – Michaels.

"We've been here a while," spoke a younger male voice. Jesus, was that Jimmy?

"I didn't want to come." A young child's voice – the girl? Why would she be here?

"This is where I ended up," Eve said. "As a nothing in nowhere. Maybe if it's all too much out there, you should stay here with us. There's no pain. No worry. No memory. There is nothing."

"No, I don't want to be here," Paul said. His breathing became harder. He started gasping for air. He couldn't see what was happening to him, but something was stopping him from getting air.

"Stop fighting, Paul," Eve said. "You've been a nothing all your life anyway. Come and be a nothing in nowhere. It's the natural next step for you."

"No." Paul turned his head looking for an escape route, but all he saw was darkness. The only thing he could do was keep fighting. Keep breathing – that was the way out.

"Join us, Paul." They all spoke in unison. "Join us. You made us. You join us."

"No," he said again. He closed his eyes and gritted his teeth – pulling hard on air and resisting the attack. He would not join them. He would not become a nothing in nowhere. Fight. Resist. Breathe.

Paul gasped for air as he awoke on his bed and found the pillow on his face – with both his hands on it. He pulled it off and threw it to the ground. Soaked in sweat and out of breath, he looked around the room. The voices had gone and the only company he had were the occupants of the other beds. The rest of the night was quiet.

*

After breakfast, Paul looked through his holdall for a change of underwear and there in the bottom of his bag he saw his mobile phone. He hadn't packed his charger and the phone had been dead for over a week. Given its age, he didn't expect to have access to a charger but upon enquiring at the nurse's station, it seemed that they had a collection amongst other items left by patients at the ward. Surprised, he discovered they did have the one he needed, so he connected it to the mains in the corner of the room next to the bed. Within thirty seconds, he heard a series of pings and saw multiple text messages arrive. All were from Karl. He opened the first and read the message.

WHERE THE HELL R U DICKHEAD?

He scanned through the others – all were of a similar vein. Karl wasn't normally so attentive – what was going on? Paul sighed and walked over to the window where he looked out over the mountains of Snowdonia. He thought about one night he and Karl had spent together many years ago.

It was the mid-eighties. Paul and Karl were at a house party in Salford. They stood in a smoke-filled living room.

Coloured party lights rotated and lit up the walls making the room feel like a merry-go-round. In the corner, 'Billie Jean' played on a ghetto blaster. Karl had a rolled-up cigarette in his mouth and a can of SKOL in his hand. His usually narrow eyes were thinner than usual as he looked across the room and swayed in time to the music.

"That girl keeps looking at you, dickhead."

"Who?"

"Her with the brown hair." He signalled with his cigarette making no attempt to be subtle.

"Oh, that's what's-her-name from school. She's in my form."

"She's into you, mate. Hasn't stopped staring since you came back from the khazi."

"Oh right. What should I do?"

"Go talk to her."

"What, now?" Paul shook his beer can. "I think I need another drink first."

"Jesus, mate, you must've had enough of the Dutch courage by now, surely?"

Paul rubbed his chin. "I don't know. I need to go home soon. Mum'll go mental if I'm late again."

"Seriously, man. Think about all that bollocks you keep telling me about finding your path and what's meant to be? What if that young lady there is your destiny?"

Paul peered through the crowd trying to see her face.

"Bollocks?" Paul said. "I thought good Catholic boys followed the will of God."

"Ha, good Catholic boy, yeah right. I never understood predestination. Maybe if I'd spent less time running away from priests…"

Paul turned to face Karl. "Okay, I'll go. What will you do?"

"I'll be alright. I'll talk to one of these idiots."

Paul nodded to Karl and made his way across the room to the girl. She saw that he was walking towards her and she turned away from her friends.

"Alright? You're in English with me. You're Esther, right?"

"Eve."

She tilted her head and smiled. From behind, Paul heard shouting, and he turned his head to see Karl squaring up to one of the lads that had been stood nearby. He looked back at Eve.

"Eve, yeah right, like the first woman. It's a nice name."

"Maybe you'll remember it next time. Is your friend okay?"

"Yeah, best to leave him to it when he gets like that."

"He likes to pick fights?"

"Everyone needs a hobby, right?"

Eve tilted her head back and laughed and at that moment Paul knew he was exactly where he was meant to be.

*

Paul returned to his bed and tried to stretch his body as best he could. There was some pain in his arm, but it paled in comparison to the desperate suffering it caused just a few days earlier. He checked the time on his phone. Ten twenty-nine.

"Knock knock." And there she was, as regular as clockwork. Kat poked her head around the side of the door.

"Who's there?" he replied.

"Ima," she said.

"Ima who?"

"Ima psychiatrist. I'm here because you won't open up."

Paul shook his head. "You really need to work on your delivery. The tone lets you down."

"So I'm told." She walked in, as always with that empty look on her face. What was it that went on beneath the surface, Paul wondered? Her words were full of spirit and wit, but the sound of her voice and the look on her face made it seem like she cared for nothing.

"Still pretending to be ill then?" Kat asked.

"I play the role well."

Kat sat down in the plastic chair next to Paul's bed.

He tried to look into her eyes, but she looked away.

"Does your mother ever come to visit your dad?" he asked.

She was wearing her denim jacket and some brightly coloured jogging pants.

"We come at different times. We don't really get on."

"Doesn't she like your jokes?"

"Everyone likes my jokes. She's a tough nut to crack."

"Serious lady?"

"Not always and not with everyone." She paused. "I don't think she likes me."

"You really think that?"

"She's said as much a few times." Kat changed the tone of her voice to a higher pitch and spoke with a strong Welsh accent. "Now loving you is something I am obliged to do as your mother, but I'm not sure I will ever be able to like you." The impersonation could have been funny had the subject matter not been so tragic.

"I had a tricky relationship with my mother as well," Paul said. "Born and raised in Manchester but strong Irish blood."

"What about your father?"

"He disappeared when I was little. When he left, I became the focus of her *attention*."

"Sounds familiar," Kat muttered. "My father is a good man though. He's always been there for us. I have no idea how he puts up with her. He is an ocean of patience and kindness."

"When will he be able to go home?"

Her hands were fidgeting. "They're not sure yet. He may need more surgery."

"Oh right. His legs must have been hurt pretty badly in the crash."

"Yeah, they were a mess. At the start we thought they'd be lost completely. Both needed pins and metal plates to keep them together."

"I guess he was lucky to have survived."

"That's true. Had he been alone then he'd likely have bled to death. It was the middle of the night and we were on a country road outside of Bangor."

"We?"

"I was with him. Somehow was unhurt. They think he lost control driving through ice. Car spun around and the driver's side was scrunched up like an old tissue."

"And you were okay after the—" Paul was interrupted by a beeping sound from the corner next to his bed. Kat looked over at his charging phone.

"Holy Anne Frank, is that your phone?"

"Yes."

"Wow, that thing is a historical item. Where did you find it – in an archaeological dig?"

Paul looked at her, stern-faced.

"Did you uncover it in the sand as you were searching for artefacts?" She looked down and used her fingers to mimic the action of someone excavating a site. "There's a fossil, there's an Egyptian mummy, there's a Roman spear, ooh hang on, is that a mobile phone from the nineties? I'm having that."

"Hey, it does what I need it to. I can phone and text."

"No apps then?"

"I have a calendar, and this game, snake. Is that what you mean?"

"You never access news sites or social media platforms?"

"Should I?"

"Okay, boomer, how else do you know what's happening in the world?"

"Like everyone else – newspapers, radio, television."

"Right, well look. Using these apps, I can see and hear what people around the world are thinking and doing right now." She lifted her phone to show Paul. All he saw were a bunch of square images on the screen.

"From arsehole celebrities to interesting outsiders. The world is your virtual oyster."

Paul rubbed his face. "Go on then. Tell me something I don't know."

She rubbed the back of her head. "Okay, well, after your man there lost it about the External Force on Tuesday, I did a bit more reading about the Witnesses. Aside from all the big talk online, there's actually some discussion about them taking direct action, and that their members may be behind some of the attacks that have been happening."

Paul sat up. "Attacks?"

"Attacks against religious people and buildings and stuff."

Paul's heart started racing.

"Where has that happened?"

"It's been happening everywhere. Here and abroad."

"And you can find out all that using your phone?"

"You really haven't got a c-clue, have you?" There was that stutter again but Paul didn't care.

"Can you look something up for me?"

"What?"

"St Luke's Church in Salford – see if it says what happened there on the night of the Revelation?"

"Right, just give me a second." Paul heard the keys of a typewriter as Kat did something on her phone.

"Yes, here it is, *Church burnt down, Pastor and family found dead*. Sad story."

Paul sat back on his bed. Yes, it had really happened.

"Wait, there's more," Kat said. Paul looked up at her. "The pastor and his family didn't die in the fire. They were killed beforehand."

His jaw dropped.

"It says they probably died from knife wounds. The bodies were badly burnt but absence of smoke in the lungs shows they were definitely dead before the fire started."

"Let me see that." Paul grabbed her phone. He read the information. It was true – he wasn't responsible for the deaths of Father Michaels and his family. The article said that both the murders and the arson attack remained unsolved. Paul handed the phone back to Kat and then stared straight ahead before dropping his head. He held it in his hands and remained still.

"P-Paul, are you okay? What is it – d-did you know them?"

"Just give me a minute, will you?" Paul turned on his side and pulled the blanket over his head.

"P-P-Paul?"

Through the thin bedding he could make out Kat's figure. She put her phone away in her pocket and then turned her head. She got up and walked away awkwardly, hesitating at the door briefly and glancing back before leaving.

Paul was stunned but couldn't place the emotions – were they relief or sadness, anger or guilt? How could they have been dead already? Somebody had got into the church and murdered the whole family one by one. In what order had it happened? Father, mother, then four-year-old son? Who could have done that? Why would they have done that? The Revelation had turned Paul into an arsonist, but it had turned someone else into a murderer.

TWELVE

Paul lay on his bed running through the events of the night of the Revelation. He became aware of the strange sound effects from the cartoon. Someone had turned up the volume and it was blasting across the room.

"For goodness' sake." Paul got up from his bed and stormed over to the television. He reached up and ran his fingers along the side of the set until he found a button that changed the channel. Someone in the room started decrying his actions. Another person was laughing. He pressed once and the cartoons were replaced by a black-and-white cowboy movie. He pressed another couple of times and a news channel appeared. The protesting behind him became louder. It was George – from the bed next to his – who hadn't spoken a word since Paul arrived in the ward.

Paul turned around. "What is it? We're not fucking children. Can we not for once watch something about the real world?"

George started shaking his head. "Not this – no, no," he repeated.

Beneath the television, Mal watched and laughed. On the news channel, a female reporter appeared to be talking to the prime minister about recent events.

"Turn that bastard off," Mr Phillips yelled from behind the curtains. "That idiot has no place in charge in times like these. We need leadership – not the rantings of an overweight man-child."

"No, no, no." George sounded like a malfunctioning robot.

Mal rocked backwards and forwards laughing and clapping.

"Turn it off," yelled Mr Phillips. "Turn it off. Turn the bloody thing off."

"Oh, dear Lord," Paul muttered as he watched the spectacle. Anwen rushed in with a remote control and switched the channel back to the cartoon. She gave Paul a stern look.

"That's why we don't change it, Paul."

"I need to get out of this place," he said. "I can't take another minute."

"Okay, let me talk to the doctor."

Paul watched as the nurse went to speak with her colleagues. He returned to his bed and sat down in his chair. It was time to leave, he thought, time to finish the journey he'd started over a week earlier with Eve.

Anwen came back and told Paul that both the infectious disease consultant and the psychiatrist would need to sign off on his case before he could leave. He sighed but agreed to wait. And wait he did for a good couple of hours. Dr Jarvis was happy for him to go, explaining that he was pleased with Paul's recovery. He gave him a course of antibiotics to continue taking for another week and warned about the residual effects he might experience.

By the time Dr Khan arrived it was early evening.

"You do feel ready, Paul?"

"Yes, it's time, I think."

"Very well."

She asked about his current state of mind. Paul told her he was fine. He did, however, agree not to leave until the next morning. It was late in the day and the thought of walking through the Welsh countryside on a cold, wet February night was not appealing.

*

That night, Paul was dead to the world and he slept without any disturbance.

*

He awoke early and washed, fed, and readied himself to go. Before he would leave the hospital, he needed to say goodbye to Kat. He opened his curtains and lay on the bed while he watched the first cartoons of the day.

Paul looked at his clock – it was now ten forty-three. For the first time, Kat was late. He thought about getting up and going to look for her but then there she was. Right away, he knew something was different. Her entrance was slow and cumbersome – no jokes or frenetic energy.

"You're off then?"

"Yes, if I stay any longer in this nuthouse, I will go crazy." He grinned.

"Don't blame you."

"Are you okay? You don't seem… yourself."

"Don't seem myself? Some days I don't know who I am, P-Paul. So, I'm not sure how anyone else could know."

"I wasn't being funny with you…" Paul trailed off as he saw her gaze drop to the floor.

"I waited to leave so that I could say goodbye to you. That was important to me."

"So kind of you – thanks."

Paul was taken aback by her words. He sat up on the bed. "Okay then. Time I was on my way."

"P-Paul," she said, closing her eyes shut. "I'm sorry. I'm just struggling today." There was something in her voice that Paul had not heard before. Sincerity. Vulnerability.

"Have you been to see your dad yet?"

"My dad?" She hesitated. "Not yet. Are you leaving now?"

"Yes."

"And you're still planning on walking to that village on Anglesey?"

"Yes, if I can."

She looked away and bit her lower lip. Paul wondered what she was thinking about.

"I'm ready," she said under her breath before looking up. "Give me ten minutes and I'll walk with you some of the way. I can show you a nice route to the bridge."

"Okay. That would be good."

Kat went off while Paul gathered his things in his bag and went to thank and say goodbye to the nurses. They met in the corridor and made their way out through the main entrance.

Paul was seeing the place with fresh eyes. Barely conscious when he'd arrived, the journey from the beach to the hospital was missing from his memory. They walked out of the car park and through the outskirts of the city of Bangor.

"Feels good to be out of that place," Paul said. "I bet you'll be glad when your dad is home, and you won't have to go there so frequently."

Kat said nothing.

"Is this the way to your house? Do you walk this way every day?"

"I normally take the bus." Her voice cracked and she cleared her throat.

They headed up a steep hill and Paul had to slow down as he became breathless.

"Take my arm," Kat said, and she helped him on the way. They stopped halfway up and sat at a bus stop for a few minutes.

"You'll be walking all day to where you're going. You should take the bus."

"I'll be alright." He did feel weak, but he felt compelled to end the journey on foot – like he'd started.

"Come on, let's keep going," he said.

They reached the top of the incline and had a clear view of the small city.

"How much longer are you going to stay with me?" Paul asked. "You know, I'll be okay if you need to get home. I don't need you to guide me all of the way."

"I wasn't planning to."

They came down the other side of the hill and out of the city area. Beyond a green verge, Paul could see water.

"Menai Strait?"

"Yes. That's Beaumaris on the other side and further down is the first of two bridges where we'll cross."

They followed the road along the strait and the sun shone on the other side of the bridge while on their side they remained in the shadow of the hill.

As they got closer to their crossing point, Paul could see the looming suspension bridge grow to fill the landscape. Its imposing grey stone and chains looked like they were holding the two lands together. Before they stepped onto the bridge, Kat stopped.

"See that village on the other side? That's Menai Bridge. *Porthaethwy* in Welsh. That is where my house is."

"Nice."

"Do you see that row of houses by the water? The middle one there – the one with the darker-coloured slate roof, that is where I've lived all my life. Number thirty-five, Bridge Street. It has a red door."

"Right."

"Let's go," she said.

As they walked across the bridge, he felt her reach for his hand, and she grabbed it tight. He looked at her pretty young face and smiled. On the other side, he saw the drop to the water through the railings; it was a hundred feet or so at least.

They reached midway across and stopped. She turned towards the road and pointed into the distance. "Can you see the other bridge? That's Britannia Bridge. If you look closely there are two stone lions on either end."

She pushed Paul further into the middle and directed him where to look.

"Keep looking," she said, stepping away. "Just there – that's right. There's a poem about them: *Four fat lions, without any hair, two on this side and two over there.*" Her voice quivered, and he turned to see that she had climbed over the bridge rail and was hanging high over the water. At first, Paul thought it was one of her games but then he processed the look on her face and her intentions became clear. He lunged over to the railing. "No, stop. Don't."

He tried to climb over, but he didn't have the strength. He tried pushing his hands through the bars to grab on to her clothes or fingers or anything. His fingertips pinched hold of her denim sleeve and – desperately – he tried to pull on the material.

"Let go, P-Paul." She stuttered and twisted her arm. He lost his grip and tried to pinch her fingers but all he could do was gently stroke her skin.

"Don't, please." His eyes welled up as he pleaded. "Stop this. You've got your life ahead of you. Come on, don't do this. Just don't."

She had tears in her eyes. "I have to, Paul. I need to be free."

"This isn't freedom."

"You don't know me. It's the only way I'll be free." She put her finger to her mouth and hushed him. "Be quiet. Be quiet, P-Paul." She raised her voice to drown out his pleading.

"Do me one thing. Take the letter in your pocket to my mother. Remember, number thirty-five, red door. It's time I was a bird."

As she pushed herself away from the bars she yelled, "I'm coming." She stretched out her arms like they were wings and began to drop. Her face was serene as she fell.

Paul raised his head and wailed into the sky. Behind him, a car screeched to a stop. He looked down and tried to see where she had fallen but there was no sign of her. She had disappeared into the cold and rocky waters of the strait.

THIRTEEN

Traffic over the bridge had been stopped. The police questioned Paul and those who had been passing in vehicles when the young woman launched herself off the bridge. Paul sat at the side watching the scene play out. In his hands was a pink envelope with *Margaret* handwritten across it in big blocky text.

He'd explained it all to the police – the walk from the hospital, her name and apparent address, and the way she'd distracted him. The police gave no sense of doubting his account. There were a few witnesses who'd stopped their cars when it happened.

Some of the drivers were now frustrated at being stuck on the bridge, unable to move forward or reverse back due to the single lane of traffic on each side of the road. Paul heard one of the policemen speaking to a young officer.

"That's the fourth from this bridge since last summer. You'd think they'd raise the rails or put spikes on them or something. We should have been expecting it after the madness of last week."

Paul's head fell into his hands. He rubbed his eyes and sighed. He felt useless and looked at the envelope in his hand. There was still one thing he could do. He stood up and went over to the police officer.

"Can you tell me if someone has gone to her house to inform the family?"

"Yes sir, we've just had officers over there talking to the mother."

"Can I go then, or do you need me for anything else?"

"No," she said. "We have everything we need for now. We'll be in touch if there is anything else."

Paul nodded, and turned to leave.

"Will you be okay, sir?" she called to him as he walked away. "Do you want us to take you anywhere?"

He glanced back to acknowledge her concern. "I'll be fine."

He continued over the bridge and reached the other side. There, he turned back to face the mainland and his eyes followed their route across the bridge. At the spot where it happened, a woman now stood in a green dress. Eve was still with him, but she was keeping her distance. He gazed at the first of the two towers and then along the chain that suspended the whole structure. On the second tower someone had painted the words, *WE ARE ALL WITNESSES NOW*.

"We certainly are," he muttered before walking away. He followed the road as it wound its way into the village of Menai Bridge. He saw the fronts of buildings and examined the doors, tracking the numbers until – there it was – a red door with 35. Paul reached into his pocket and touched the envelope. He took a few deep breaths before knocking. At first, there was no answer. He knocked harder – until his knuckles were sore. The curtains in the window shook and the door was finally opened by a well-dressed, middle-aged lady with straight silver hair and circular glasses. She wasn't smiling. This had to be Margaret.

"You don't know me," he said, "but—"

"You were the one with her, weren't you?"

"Yes," he replied.

"You better come in."

Margaret led Paul into the living room.

"Take a seat," she said. "Would you like a cup of tea?"

"No, I'm fine thanks." Paul was slightly taken aback by the hospitality of this woman who had not long before been informed of the death of her daughter. *She must be in shock*, he thought. He looked around the very clean and tidy room. The window looked out over the waters of the Menai Strait.

"Go on then. What do you need to tell me?" Margaret asked.

"Sorry, what?"

"I know that girl would never have done anything like this without some final dramatic gesture."

"Well, I did need to…" Paul stopped, lost for words. "Are you okay?" he asked.

"I'm fine."

"Have you told your husband yet?"

Margaret tilted her head and gave him a puzzled look; then she began to nod.

"You met her at the hospital, didn't you?"

"Yes, she came to visit me every day after seeing her father."

Margaret shook her head. "Her father – my husband – has been dead for three years. Katherine was going to the hospital each day as an outpatient. She had schizophrenia."

Paul's jaw dropped but then a few things started to make sense.

"She'd been fine for months until this thing happened last week. It knocked her sideways – off her medication. She started talking about her father again. She could see him. She said he talked to her; told her she wasn't to blame for his death."

Paul could do nothing but listen.

"I told her to keep seeing her doctor until things improved. So off she'd go each day to the hospital. She'd return and tell me she'd spent time with her father. She said they'd laughed together and talked about things like life when she was a little girl. And always that he didn't blame her for his death."

"Why would he blame her?"

"Because she was to blame. She killed him. Didn't mean to, of course. But it was her fault."

Paul sat up. "How?"

"Before she was diagnosed with her condition, she went off the rails; drugs, drinking and who knows what else. One night we got a call from one of her friends' parents saying she was drunk at their house and that somebody needed to go pick her up. I had no patience with the girl but her father, Bill, well he was different."

Paul looked to the window and out over the water.

"On the way back, she became argumentative and tried to open the door to get out as the car sped along. He tried to stop her but lost control of the vehicle and ended up crushed against a stone wall. She told me all this, of course. He died instantly. Sometimes I wish it had been the other side of the car that had been destroyed by that rock."

"You don't mean that."

"Don't I? That girl was always trouble – damaged on arrival. We gave her all we could and in return she tried to ruin our lives. Eventually, she managed it. So yes, she was to blame. And I blamed her every day of her life after she killed my husband. And now I continue to blame her, even though she's gone."

Paul felt the hairs on the back of his neck stand up. It reminded him of something in his own past, something unsettling buried deep in a dark corner of his mind.

"I'm sorry, I shouldn't have come." He sat up and readied himself to leave.

"It's fine," she said. "But why is it you're here? You must have a message to deliver to me. One final insult maybe? What was it she wanted you to tell me?"

Paul reached into his pocket and took out the envelope.

"A letter, of course. Give it to me."

Paul looked at it for a second then reached over and handed it to Margaret. She just placed it on the arm of her chair.

"I only knew her for a short time, but she seemed like a really nice girl. She made me laugh at a time when I really didn't want to."

"She was good at wrapping men around her little finger. Particularly older men."

"I think you're being unfair. Your daughter was thoughtful and kind."

"My daughter left a trail of destruction wherever she went. It was only a carefully balanced mixture of pills that stopped her from ruining the lives of others or – for that matter – taking her own any sooner."

"But falling out of balance because of the Revelation wasn't her fault." Paul rubbed the back of his neck. "That event was unnatural – it messed with the heads of a lot of people. That hospital on the other side of the bridge is full of them."

"That may be true, but my dear Katherine was a time bomb waiting to go off. If it wasn't the Revelation, then it would've been something else. She was always destined for a tragic ending. At least this way no one else was hurt."

Paul couldn't take any more. He stood up; Margaret remained seated.

"Right, I'm going to go. I'm very sorry for your loss and I do hope you find some peace."

Margaret stared at him. Paul saw a pen on the window frame and reached for it. He took an old receipt from his pocket and started to write his name and number on it.

"If and when you do hear anything, do please call me." He dropped the piece of paper onto the sofa where he had sat.

"I'll show myself out." Before he opened the front door, he zipped up his coat and looked at a framed photograph on the wall. A family portrait – two parents and a happy little girl. As he reached for the door handle, he heard a noise from the living room – the slow tearing of paper.

Further along the street, Paul found a gap between the houses where a narrow path took him down to the water's edge. He clumsily crossed a pebble beach that was covered in stones the size of his hand and crouched next to the water. He lifted a long oval rock and smashed it down against a larger piece of stone. He repeated the motion a few times until his arm became tired.

He sighed and shook his head. How could that woman be so cold about the death of her child? Kat was sick and her mother was unable to accept that or forgive her for what happened to her husband.

As he watched the fast-moving water of the strait, his breathing calmed. A fishing boat passed, and he caught a glimpse of someone stood on the deck. Was it Eve? He turned his head, but he couldn't see her. Had she disappeared? It wouldn't have been the first time. The boat slowed next to a small pier, not far from where he sat. It moored up and two fishermen started bringing in plastic boxes filled with silver-skinned fish.

Paul thought about his own mother and a memory came to him. He was eight or maybe nine. His father had been out of the picture for quite some time. It was a Sunday afternoon on a warm summer's day. Paul was pretending to be a wizard. He had made a hat out of an old newspaper. His mother's dressing gown became his wizard's robe. He was in his bedroom pretending to prepare potions when he realised what he really needed was a book of spells. Then it came to him – use the old book that sat on the table next to his mum's bed. It looked just like a book of spells – with its old leather cover and weathered pages full of strange words. He'd peeked inside it once, but he dared not move it. It had belonged to his father and he knew it was very important to his mother. But this was a Sunday, and his mother was downstairs doing the same as she did every Sunday. After their lunch, she would sit in her chair in the living room and watch her programme on television, while he played.

He listened at the top of the landing and heard the noise of the television from downstairs. He tiptoed into his parents' room and picked up the old book from the side of the bed. It surprised him how heavy it was. As he tried to tread slowly and quietly back to his bedroom, the edge of his mother's robe became caught under his foot, and he tripped next to the landing at the top of the stairs. The Bible slipped from his arms and bounced, tumbling, and banging down the steps. As he lay on his front at the top of the stairs, frozen, the television was switched off. The door at the bottom of the staircase opened, and his mother peeked around the corner. She looked up at Paul and then down at the floor. When she saw the Bible lying at the bottom of the stairs, she rushed over to it and crouched down.

"No, no, that shouldn't be there. No, that won't do at all."

She picked up the book, dusted it off then wrapped her arms around it and rocked it from side to side. She gazed at Paul and her eyes narrowed. "Why would you treat your father's book like this? What is wrong with you?"

She shook her head and started backing into the living room.

"He left because of you. He knew you were trouble."

She held the Bible in her arms like a child, whilst her real boy lay at the top of the stairs – stunned – with tears in his eyes.

"Someday you'll see," she said. "We reap what we sow. The trouble you cause will not be rewarded with kindness. It's horror you'll face, my boy."

*

Paul sat on the beach with his face in his hands. He felt disorientated and shocked. Nothing made sense anymore. He looked around at the landscape and then reached his fingers into the sand beneath the pebbles. The cold touch gave him brief comfort; right there, at that moment, there was nothing that could harm him. He pulled his sandy hands to his face and tried to fight the tears. Inside, a scared little boy was crying out. All he needed was some reassurance. He lay down on his back and looked at the thick clouds moving across the sky. Layered against the vibrant blue, the flocculent masses drifted through each other's paths, paying little attention to one another.

He got to his feet and dusted the sand off his clothes and wiped his face. It was time to carry on.

He returned up the narrow path to Bridge Street and saw a bus stop across the road. He considered his options. Physically, he was uncertain whether he could continue by foot for another seven hours. Mentally, he doubted he had the momentum to push his body forward through the physical pain and weakness. He crossed the road and saw that the 62 would take him around the island to Llanffug.

The journey was about forty minutes and took him along country lanes near the sea, in and out of villages and through the odd town. Asides from the driver, only two other individuals boarded the bus. After the town of Amlwch, the route opened out to an expanse of green fields on one side and sea on the other. The coast was rocky and exposed, and the waves erupted into the sky as they crashed against the land. On his left, they passed a small mountain, which had a red colouration that made its rocky terrain look like the surface of Mars. There were wind turbines that added a strange alien tone to the already unique landscape. The bus came down a steep hill and then turned right up another incline where they passed an old boat resting on a grassy verge. It was filled with flowers and had the words *Croeso i Llanffug – Welcome to Llanffug* written on the side.

This was it, the physical destination he had been battling towards for the last week and a half. But a place he had meant to come back to for a lot longer; the setting of a scene that he had held in his memory for over three decades. The bus came up over a small hill that overlooked the village, which was set out around a sandy bay and separated into two main beaches by a small harbour with a stone pier and a collection of sailing boats and yachts. The bus followed a twisting road which overlooked the bigger of the two beaches and the harbour and then drove over a bridge where a river on one side appeared to undulate through a wooded park to meet the sea at the harbour. Paul alighted the bus in the middle of the village. It was a picturesque collection of brightly coloured houses plus a few shops and a couple of old-fashioned pubs. He didn't remember it so well but having just seen a bird's-eye view of the village from the hill, he was able to orientate himself. He walked back to the bridge then turned down towards the larger beach. The skies had now clouded over, the air had cooled and the horizon was grey. It was a stark contrast to his glossy memory of bright colours and warm hues. He walked through a small car park and passed a closed ice-cream shop, and then down a few steps onto the sandy beach. He looked around and tried to find the spot where he'd sat with Eve so many years ago. He stopped at the most likely position and then surveyed the full expanse of his field of vision. To his right, the green headland emerging from the sea with a church and its tower silhouetted against the cloudy sky. Directly in front of him was a bright yellow sand layered against a cold blue sea surrounded on three sides by the bay. To his left, the harbour – filled with boats bobbing in the water – and the surrounding village. So here he was, at the terminus of his journey, in the paradise he had dreamt of for so long. He looked around, expecting to find something but what was it? A person? A message? An answer?

The tide was midway in across the beach, and he walked over to the water and crouched down, touching it with his fingers. This was the same icy cold medium that cradled Kat's young body. He turned his head from side to side trying to shake the images that were coming to him. He walked back to the spot on the beach and sat down clumsily in the sand.

He held out his hands and called out towards the sea, "I'm here, so now what? Tell me, what comes next?"

FOURTEEN

"Are you okay down there?" A woman called to him from above. Paul looked up and saw two big brown eyes peering down at him.

"Fine," he said. "Just leave me, will you?"

"Right," she said, and the head disappeared.

But she didn't leave him, and Paul heard someone approaching down the stone steps to the beach. Before he could see her, he could hear her voice.

"I would of course be very happy to leave you alone. But, you know, since the Revelation, we keep receiving visits from loners looking for something; lost souls with the same looks on their faces. It's difficult to ignore them – especially when you hear them calling out to the sea for answers."

She stood at the bottom of the steps. Paul was struck by her bright round eyes. Seemingly aware of his gaze, she smiled and looked to the ground, pushing her long chestnut-coloured hair over her ear. She wore a yellow waterproof coat and green wellies and held the end of a lead in her hand. An elderly black-and-white sheepdog followed behind her down the path.

Paul bit his lip and turned away. "Just leave me alone, please. That's all I ask."

"Okay, if that's what you want." She looked to the old dog. "Come on, Ben."

She ambled across the beach and released the dog from the lead. A younger dog would have leapt away, but the old boy trotted over to the water's edge, all the while keeping an eye on his master. The woman glanced over at Paul. She walked on to the furthest reaches of the sand where the dog sniffed at dried seaweed and barked at something it encountered in a rock pool.

Would it be some unsuspecting dog walker out for a stroll who would find Kat's body, he wondered? What would her young face look like after days or even weeks in the sea? He rubbed his forehead. Why couldn't he have stopped her? Too easily distracted as always. He was nothing more than a spectator to the child's death.

He could make no sense in any of it. The universe had taken aim at one of its brighter, shinier constituents and extinguished it for ever.

He sighed.

"Why did you bring me here?" he said expecting someone to respond but no answer came. The woman was too far away to hear him.

"There must be some reason. I'm not going back until I know."

He wasn't ready to return to the city. He felt weak and needed somewhere to rest and recuperate.

The woman returned with the old dog plodding along behind her. She looked over at him but seemed less willing to engage in conversation.

"I'm sorry I yelled," he said, half smiling. "Just another lost soul looking for answers."

"At least you didn't go looking for them in the water."

"What?" Paul said before noticing her smile. There was no way she could know about the day he'd had.

"Do you know of any cheap guest houses around here?"

"I know of one guest house that is reasonably priced, gets great reviews, and currently has plenty of rooms."

"Your place?"

"Yes, indeed. Not that we get many visitors at this time of year anyway, but recent circumstances have led to the few reservations we had being cancelled."

"Good, and you have rooms ready right now?"

"Oh absolutely. Come with me."

Paul stood up and felt light-headed.

"You okay there?"

"Yes, just got up… a little fast."

The woman held out her hand. "Sarah," she said.

He grabbed it and shook it. "Paul. Nice to meet you. After you."

He followed Sarah back up the road the bus had travelled down until they reached a large, detached house with wide windows that overlooked the bay. On the gate, the sign said, *Golygfa Môr*.

Sarah pointed to it. "It's Welsh for Sea View."

The house appeared a little run-down from the outside. Paul smiled as she opened the front door to let him in before leaving him and going down the side of the building to take the dog in through the back entrance. He walked inside and saw a bright living room with three large sofas and walls covered in maritime memorabilia. There was a loud and prominent grandfather clock in the corner of the room. The broad bay window he'd seen from the outside had a perfect view of the beach.

A bronze vintage telescope had been placed so the sight looked out beyond the sand and over the sea; someone evidently liked to watch the passing ships. As he turned away from the window, he almost jumped when he saw an old man sat in a dark leather armchair. The man silently looked out at the landscape. He was well dressed in a jacket and shirt, but his head of wild grey hair and thick, dark-framed glasses gave him the appearance of a mad scientist. He frowned like he was deeply concentrating on something.

"Sorry, didn't see you there."

The old man did not respond – nor did he appear to acknowledge Paul's presence.

Behind him, he heard footsteps and then Sarah's voice.

"So, you've met my father?"

"Not one for conversation, is he?"

Sarah pulled Paul away from the old man and turned her head towards his ear.

"Before the Revelation you wouldn't have been able to shut him up. But since then, he's been in this state – won't say a word and he won't interact with anyone."

As they stepped further away from the window, she spoke a bit louder, but her eyes remained focused on her father.

"He was a lay preacher and a local councillor after retiring." Her voice began to tremble. "Before that, a philosophy professor at Bangor University. He enjoyed nothing more than a debate about the classics – always happiest in that ancient world." She frowned and put her hand to her mouth.

"Where he is now, I don't know."

"Was he taken to the hospital?" Paul asked.

"Of course. He was there for six days or so, but there was nothing they could do. *Catatonic Symptomatic Revelation*, they said. A long made-up name for something they didn't understand. I got tired of the toing and froing from the hospital each day. I thought he'd benefit more from being back here at home."

"You take care of him by yourself?"

"Oh no, Julie from the village comes twice a day to help out. She'd left just before we returned."

She signalled with her hand for Paul to follow her.

"Let's get you checked in and set up with your room."

In an office area next to the dining room, she took his details and arranged the payment. He didn't specify how long he would stay. At this point, he didn't know. She took him up two flights of stairs to the third floor and opened a door.

"Here you go," she said, entering the room. Paul raised his eyebrows as he looked around and saw the king-sized bed and the wide window overlooking the sea.

"Do all your guests get a room like this?"

"You're the only occupant right now and you're getting a pretty good deal." She had a broad smile on her face.

He walked over to the window and looked out. It was a view he'd seen in his mind's eye a thousand times, but the elevation gave him a different angle on the familiar scene. Sarah left him and he lay down on the bed and looked at the plaster shapes in the ceiling. It felt homely, which was good, and at that moment he felt in no rush to go anywhere else.

His mother's old house would be fine; he had no job to worry about; and his friends, were they really friends at all? The bed felt comfortable, and he felt at ease.

*

He opened his eyes to daylight. He got up – sipped from a bottle of water – and looked out across the bay. The skies were clear – aside from a few wispy threads of cloud that hung near the horizon like a cobweb. He decided to get some fresh air so put on his coat and went out to the front of the house where he sat down on a bench.

Down the side path he heard footsteps, and Sarah appeared carrying a large plant pot.

"I thought I heard the door," she said. "Are you settling in okay?"

"Yes, fine thanks."

Paul stood up and stepped towards her. "Can I help you with that?"

"Oh well, I suppose now you're here… yes, thank you. It's going over there."

The pot was full of soil and heavier than he expected but he took it from her and huffed his way over to the corner of the grass where he put it down as carefully as he could manage.

Sarah stood and watched with a gentle smile on her face. "What happened to your arm?"

Paul looked down and saw that the sleeve of his coat had been pushed up as he carried the plant pot.

"I put it through a glass window. Accidentally."

"Ouch."

"Yeah. Did some harm. Got infected and had to go to hospital with blood poisoning."

"Oh God, when did you get out?"

"This morning."

"Bloody hell. You should be resting – not helping me with the gardening."

"Feels good to be active."

"Well, that was the last of it anyway. I was thinking of having a cheeky gin and tonic out here now the sun is out. Would you like one?"

Paul gave her a restrained nod. Sarah headed back inside and he sat down on the bench. He looked up towards the headland where the church sat. It no longer had the crucifix on the roof – at least he couldn't see it from his current position. Otherwise, it looked the same as he remembered.

Sarah returned with two filled glasses in her hands.

"There you go. Sorry if it's a little strong. I like it to have a bit of a kick."

Paul glanced back at the house. "Is your dad okay?"

"He's fine. Pretty low maintenance most of the time." Sarah half-smiled.

"Cheers," she said, and they clinked their glasses. Paul gritted his teeth and grimaced. She hadn't lied about liking it strong.

"You sound like you're from Manchester," she said as they both looked out over the bay.

"Salford actually."

"Ah, the second city. I lived in Withington for twenty years."

"But you're from here originally?"

"Yes. I went to university there and stayed on afterwards." She glanced over at Paul. "They say it was bad in the cities last week. How was Manchester?"

"Like a war zone. But I left the next day." He saw the burning church and heard sirens. He blinked and turned to face Sarah.

"Twenty years?" he said. "What brought you back here?"

"A mixture of reasons." She sighed. "Failing marriage and Mam's health being the main. She was the one who really ran this place. Coming back here gave me a fresh start and an opportunity to keep an eye on Dad." She leaned forward and peeked through the window. "Even before the Revelation, he wasn't the best at taking care of himself. What about you – what brought you here?"

"A mixture of reasons."

She smiled. "Which hospital did you come from this morning?"

"The one in Bangor."

"Ysbyty Gwynedd? Oh, you were just up the road. I was there every day last week."

"I bet it was rammed after the Revelation."

"Oh, it was. They were beyond capacity. Full of injured people. This thing has done so much harm…"

She trailed off.

"It's been quite a battle, hasn't it?" he said as something caught his eye. In the sky beyond Sarah's head, a single seagull flew in the direction of the sea. Paul watched as it circled the beach rising and falling on the breeze. It flew with no restraints or hindrances – free to go wherever it wanted. Sarah tried to see what he was staring at. Paul's lower lip began trembling and he felt his eyes well up with tears. He looked to the ground and tried to hold it back – but he couldn't. With his hand on his forehead he began to sob.

"Paul, what is it? What's wrong?"

"I – er – sorry, I need to go."

Paul placed the half-empty glass on the chair and bolted inside and up into his room. He sat on his bed and cried until the sorrow faded, and a quiet calm fell upon him as the sky over the bay reddened and the sun set on a strange day.

FIFTEEN

Paul opened the curtains and surveyed the scenery. To the far right of the landscape, the sun rose above the headland. He stared at the church before getting dressed and grabbing his room keys and heading out through the empty house. He looked out from the gate onto the road and his eyes mapped out the route, down towards the beach and then up the hill on the other side. The air was cool, and the sky was bright. A crescent moon was fading from view as the sunlight grew in strength. The sound of the waves was refreshing. He walked past the spot where he'd sat on the beach the day before, then through the car park and up the road towards the church. The hill left him panting, but he was making progress and he had far more energy in each step than he'd had the day before.

Nearer the church, the road narrowed, and on both sides, he saw healthy green pastures and thick hedgerows. The wind picked up as he reached the exposed plateau and he turned to see the whole of the bay and the village positioned in the middle.

A stone wall enclosed the church and its gardens. At the nearest end, it separated the gardens from a boulder-filled field. At the other, it marked the edge of the graveyard, which was only accessible through a small iron gate. Opposite to the road was the sea. Paul couldn't be certain from his current position, but it did appear that the church was quite near the edge of the clifftop, and it made for a magnificent sight. Paul stopped by the gate and studied the landscape like a painter preparing to recreate the image on canvas. The positioning of this ancient building next to the raw elements of the ocean and the sky left him in awe.

He entered the gardens that surrounded the church through a rickety old gate that screeched one sound as he opened it and then another as he closed it. The gardens were wild and overgrown and had not been taken care of in recent years. The church itself was in an even worse state. Slates from the roof were scattered on the ground, the windows were smashed, and one of the doors hung off its hinges. The old walls still held up though; what storms those rocks had weathered, Paul thought. He approached the building carefully, stepping around the broken pieces of roofing. The path from the gate was short and took him straight to the entrance of the church. Paul stroked the walls and placed his cheek against the cold stone.

Visiting the church had made less of an impact on him all those years before when he stayed in Llanffug with Eve. Yes, his memory on the beach had haunted him for decades, but for some reason the ancient building had not affected him much at the time. The distractions of youth and love he supposed.

He peered through the gap under the door that hung off the frame. The inside of the church was a jumbled mess. Broken church pews were everywhere. The exposed floors were covered in water and a small tree appeared to be growing where the altar should have been. Paul pushed the door and it opened in a diagonal fashion allowing him some space to crawl through. Seeing the building like this made him feel sad. He reminded himself that God did not exist, and the faith experienced by all of those who had attended this building was a lie. But there was a power in the old walls; something he couldn't explain.

He treaded through the debris; the air was musty. Through the holes in the roof, he could hear seagulls and when he looked up, he could see the birds flying in the air. A large timber crucifix covered in cobwebs hung on the wall and Paul stared at it.

He left the building through the same hole as he had entered. Outside, an elderly man in a baseball cap walked towards him with a bundle of sticks in his arms. He shook his head.

"You be careful around that place. Not safe."

"What happened to it?"

"Neglect, mostly. The last service here was in the seventies."

"Shame." Paul turned his head and looked at it again.

"Popular spot though since this Revolution."

Paul looked at the man. "What? Oh, you mean the Revelation."

"That's what I said."

"Right. How so?"

"Lots of travellers coming here. I've seen a few of them."

"Why do they come here?"

"Don't know. They say there's always been something special about this place. The church was founded by some saint who was shipwrecked here." He pointed to the sea. "There's a magic well somewhere near the cliff that can heal people."

"Where?"

"Never seen it. Would've used it for my bad back if I had."

The man started to walk away. "Just be careful. Special or not, those slates will cause some damage if they fall on your head."

Paul followed the path on the near side of the church – up to the wall next to the sea. It was only three feet high or so. He leaned over and saw a narrow grassy verge on the other side. Beyond that, a steep cliff edge dropped down to the water where huge waves battered the rocks. He looked either way along the clifftop. Where could the well be, he wondered? There were no obvious sources of fresh water. Perhaps it was in a cave or an opening in the cliff face.

He went up to the graveyard and examined the crypts and tombs that filled the small green space. Most were either slate or marble. There were three or four at the furthest end that were made of some other type of stone, granite perhaps. A few of the graves were from recent deaths but most were over fifty years old.

From the graveyard he saw a young stranger come through the church gates. Paul recognised the look on the man's face. He carried a rucksack and was covered from head to toe in waterproof clothing. He entered the church gardens and made his way across to the derelict building, gently touching the walls and examining the details. He looked in through the broken windows and then pushed the half door open. He took his time to experience the place and get a sense of the ancient building. Before he left, he took one last look at the church before disappearing down the hill.

Paul decided it was time he also returned to the village. As he left the gardens through the gate, he glanced at the church and did a double take. Looking back at him through a broken window was Eve; he could only see her face. She didn't smile; she didn't look angry or sad. He was about to return when he heard rustling from the hedgerow behind him. It sounded like a large animal but as he stared into the thicket, he was sure he could make out a pair of human eyes looking back at him.

"Hello?" he called out. There was no response. He moved closer and whomever it was dashed away down the hill at pace. *Odd*, he thought. He turned back to look at the church once again. Eve was gone. Although she was still with him, it was evident she had weakened since he'd left the hospital. He rubbed his forehead and carried on down the road.

*

He was greeted by the smell of fried breakfast as he entered the house. Sarah stuck her head out of the kitchen.

"Morning," she said. "I thought you might like the full breakfast options." Before he was allowed to respond, she rushed over to the dining area and started setting the table. "I also have quite a few things to use before they go off."

He sat down and she brought over a pot of tea and a plate loaded with bacon, sausages, scrambled eggs, beans, tomatoes, and mushrooms, and then a smaller plate with a heap of buttered toast. After several days of hospital food, this was a welcome sight.

She left Paul to eat his breakfast and walked over to the front door, returning moments later with the morning post.

He looked out of the window. Dark clouds were now coming in from the sea.

"About yesterday..." he said.

"It's okay." She examined the envelopes in her hands. "No need to explain. It's an emotional time for us all."

He bit his lip and nodded.

"Did you go for a walk?"

"Yes, sad to see the old church in such a state."

"Yes, well, that is a bit of a hot topic here right now."

"What do you mean?"

"Since the Revelation, it's been receiving a lot of visitors."

"So I hear, but why would that be an issue? Surely tourism is good?"

"Yes, but the building itself is a deathtrap. It's only a matter of time until someone gets hurt there."

"Right."

"Also, there are some here who don't like to see an old religious site becoming so popular. They'd be quite happy to use the safety concerns as an excuse to have it demolished."

"That's extreme."

"But not an uncommon opinion nowadays. If you're interested, you can have your say. There's a village meeting in the hall tonight to discuss it. Open to anyone, and if nothing else, fireworks are likely to fly so it's sure to be entertaining."

"Maybe I will," Paul said, before a thought came to him. "You know when I was at the church before, I could have sworn someone was watching me in the field."

Sarah stopped in her tracks. "Ha, really?" She shook her head. "I'd heard that some of them had been keeping an eye on the old place to see what type of attention it was receiving but I'm not sure if I believed it. It's odd but they're harmless."

She went back in the kitchen and left Paul to eat. The meal was simple but it was the tastiest food Paul had experienced in a while. His appetite wasn't great but he did what he could to work through the plate. Before he finished, Sarah ran through the living room. "Damn it, he's gone again."

She rushed outside, put her coat on and ran down the street. A few minutes later she returned with Ben attached to a lead. She brought him into the house and he started wagging his tail when he saw Paul. She pulled him through the living room yelling something about a hole in the fence. Paul took his empty plate into the kitchen. He placed it in the sink and smiled.

"Just what the doctor ordered." He then walked over to the window and looked outside at the fence.

"I keep putting boards in place, but he pulls them off with his scratching. He's strong for such an old boy."

Ben was eating from his bowl and looked up as though he knew she was talking about him.

"Do you have any more of those boards?" Paul asked.

"Probably. We've got all sorts out in that shed. Dad was always good at starting projects, but not so good at finishing them. Mam was always the one who fixed things."

"Right, let me see what I can do."

Paul started with the fence – replacing as much as he could of the rotten panel that was pushed aside by a persistent dog. He then turned his attention to the kitchen window frame, putting filler in a hole to stop the cold from getting in. When the rain came, he moved inside and discovered a few other jobs that needed doing. He fitted a washer in a bathroom tap. He fixed a broken light in one of the bedrooms and mended a hole in a floorboard on the stairs.

Sarah objected at first, but soon stopped battling against his doggedness and left him to it. As he finished off the floorboard, she brought over a cup of tea.

"After a bigger discount for your room, are you?"

"Just trying to help. You have your hands full with your dad."

"It's okay, I was kidding. It's much appreciated."

Paul lifted the cup and tried to sip the hot tea.

"Was this a hobby or a way of living for you in Salford?"

"Fixing things is what I've done most of my life. My wife used to say I only learnt that skill as a counterpoint to my ability to break things."

"You're married?"

"I was. She died two years ago."

"Sorry to hear that." Sarah crouched down and reached through the bannister to examine the fixed floorboard.

"What would your wife have made of recent events?" She tapped the step.

"She wouldn't have liked it but would have fared better than I have."

"You had a difficult Revelation?"

"Took me by surprise. But I'm uncertain of how bad it was. Seen people who had it better certainly, but also a few who had it much worse. You?"

"I was down at the beach with Ben. I remember reaching down to pick up his ball to throw it, and then it all went dark. The next thing I knew, there were waves lapping around me and Ben was licking my face."

Sarah walked around to the bottom of the stairs and sat down next to Paul.

"The worst part was returning to the house to find Dad collapsed on the floor. He had this empty look on his face. I couldn't get through to the emergency services. Eventually I tracked down Dr Price who came over and checked on him. He told me of the extent of what'd happened – what he knew about it, at least."

"What do you think happened?"

Sarah hesitated. "I think someone, or something, decided it was time for the training wheels to come off."

"You think people are ready for that?"

"I don't think people have a choice in the matter. How do you feel about it?"

"How do I feel?" Paul stopped and looked away. "I don't know. My faith was a crutch in recent years and before that – long before that – I was told that everything happened for a reason, according to a plan. Now I know there never was any reason nor a plan behind any of it. That's something I struggle with – the meaningless of it all."

"Maybe it's not meaningless? Maybe you've been looking for meaning in the wrong places. Think about human connection or the beauty of nature. Did you know that there are times in the year when bioluminescent plankton cause the sea here to glow in the dark? They call it the *burning of the sea*. The surf across the bay appears this magical blue colour. It's incredible."

Paul's eyes narrowed. "I'm not sure I follow."

"My point is – isn't it more powerful – more meaningful – that it all came from nature without a Creator's hand?"

"I suppose, but that also means all the bad stuff comes from nothing as well. Anything could happen tomorrow and you, me, everyone we know could all be gone."

"Bit glass half empty, Paul."

"It's where we are."

"Alright, then doesn't that make it more precious? Any moment could be our last."

"Maybe, but doesn't it give you the fear?"

"Fear of what?"

"A fear that none of it matters – the choices we make and the types of people we decide to be. It's all aimless."

"Of course it matters. The person you choose to be directly affects people around you. If you're nice to people, you can make them feel good. If you're a dick to them, then… well, you won't."

"I don't know. This idea of a universe driven by chance and free will is still something I'm getting used to."

"Sounds like you've got concerns about taking responsibility for your own decisions."

"Maybe I do."

"Why though – what is there to fear?"

"What if I make mistakes? What if I choose the wrong path?"

"What if you do? No one will judge you or punish you for it. If you make mistakes you dust yourself off and try again."

Paul had no answer this time. He nodded to her slowly and picked up the cup and sipped his tea.

"I have to get to the pharmacy before it closes," Sarah said. "Why don't you join me later at the village hall. Some distraction from country folk and villagers arguing about an old building might be good."

"Okay," he said. "Maybe you're right."

SIXTEEN

Paul sat at the dining table sipping from a bowl of soup that Sarah had prepared earlier in the evening. She was seated near the bay window trying to feed her father – who was wearing a large bib to stop the dripping soup from falling onto his shirt. Julie turned up midway through the meal and took over from Sarah who attended to a few things in the kitchen before returning and telling Paul it was time to head to the village hall.

They arrived at the building just before eight. It was full. Paul and Sarah sat near the back of the room. Ahead of them were rows upon rows of occupied chairs.

Up stepped an older, respectably dressed lady with short hair and some notes in her hand. She walked over to a podium.

"She's the chair of the community council," Sarah whispered. "The nearest thing we have to a mayor."

"Welcome friends, family and neighbours," said the councilwoman, her eyes looking around the room.

"We are living in strange days. We all have been affected by the events of the Revelation. Some of us, more so than others." She glanced in Sarah's direction.

"But here we are. The planet continues to revolve on its axis, and we continue to live our lives and attend to the things that we care about. Tonight, we have some business to discuss and that is the fate of the Llanffug Church. Now, to many of us here, it's a place that holds some significance. But since the Revelation it has started to attract more attention than we have seen in several years and this is creating some concern. Or should I say, it's creating concern for certain individuals…"

"Get to the point, Jane," shouted a man at the front.

"Bob, why don't you come up here and explain?"

"This is who was likely watching you from the field," Sarah said.

A short, stocky man in a raincoat stepped up to the podium. He held onto a handful of scruffy pieces of paper, and repeatedly pushed his glasses up the ridge of his nose as he prepared to speak.

"For the good of all mankind, our world has changed forever," he said. Sarah sighed. "The oppressive forces of the Vatican, Mecca, and Jerusalem – amongst others – have been defeated and it is time for people to take responsibility for their own actions and their own lives and realise that this right here is all there is."

He turned a page from his notes.

"We have lived under the dominion of these made-up gods, charlatans and fairy-tale stories for millennia, and what has it given us? War and genocide; suppression of women; torture of heretics; and a slew of the more terrible acts committed by humanity."

Paul looked over at Sarah with raised eyebrows. This was far more drama than he'd expected.

"Now, those oppressive powers are gone. Something *or someone* has given us all a second chance and an opportunity to start again. The shackles have been taken off and we have been told to go and live our lives as we see fit, free of their tyranny. Somewhere out there, a benevolent, External Force has liberated us."

Paul leant over to Sarah. "I feel like I'm back in church." She smiled.

Bob pushed his glasses up his nose again. His face was sombre.

"Now, despite this gift of mental clarity given to us, there are still many out there struggling with these new-found freedoms; those who are pining for their oppressors' return. These are people who've been held captive for too long. People with Stockholm syndrome. They've been kept in their dark cages for so long that they are unaware of what the daylight means. These poor people are the ones we see visiting our little village; the ones drawn to that dangerous old building that sits up on the hill overlooking the bay. They come looking for answers and for hope. They are unaware of the bright new day in which we now live. They are unable to see that the night is now over."

Jane looked unhappy and walked over and whispered something in Bob's ear. He held up his hand, appearing to tell her to back off.

"Friends, it's our duty to remove this magnet for lost souls from our proximity. This dangerous and structurally unsafe building; this relic of the past and symbol of oppression should be pulled down and destroyed. Let's help free these poor individuals who turn up here every day looking for something that no longer exists or – let's be honest – never actually existed."

Jane approached again – this time with two men who had the same unimpressed look on their faces. Bob saw that his time at the podium was almost over, and he began to speak faster.

"The graveyard is safe and will continue to be accessible of course, but the decaying deathtrap needs to be pulled down. We need it destroyed."

Bob was encouraged to sit down. He nodded, appearing content to have said his piece.

"Thank you, Bob, for your – as always – frank and thorough summary. Now typically, this is not something we would discuss like this as a village. But these are unprecedented times. Can I put this out to everyone, does anyone have any comments?"

The attendees were silent. Paul saw people across the hall looking at each other. He heard whispers.

A lady in the middle stood up and spoke. "That church has sat on that hill for more than a thousand years. Whether or not we believe in its purpose anymore, why should we be the ones to remove it?"

A man stood. "Exactly. We all know the truth about religion – there's no denying it. But that place represents our history and that is not something we can wipe away and forget about."

Bob stood up and turned towards him.

"That building is our oppressor's house. It's like having our slave owner stood at the top of the hill ready to take back control at any moment."

Another man stood up. "In Bob's defence, it is unsafe and it's only a matter of time until someone gets hurt there. The roof won't last long and the remaining window panes will fall out at some point. Whatever we do, we can't leave it as it is."

Sarah stood up, and most of the hall turned to hear what she had to say.

"What if we were to make it safe? What if we were to turn it into something that could be used by everyone?" She looked towards Bob. "Bob, surely you must see that it's better to disarm and neutralise an old enemy rather than destroy it and pretend it never existed?"

Bob shook his head and tried to respond but many yelled their thoughts. Jane called out trying to achieve order, but the chattering continued.

Someone in the back of the hall started howling like a wolf. The room fell silent, and many heads turned. Paul glanced over to Sarah with a quizzical look on his face.

"That's Jerry," she said. "He was lead singer of that eighties band, Wheel Deal."

They both listened to what he had to say.

"Thank you," he said. "Guys, here's an idea. Why don't we just do the place up and use it as a venue for events? Gigs, art exhibitions – things like that? The good stuff that people have to offer. Rather than pull it down out of fear of the past, why not turn it into a positive feature of the future? It's a lovely old building in a beautiful place. All it needs is a bit of TLC."

Many of the attendees started clapping. Jane asked everyone to be quiet.

"But that would need a lot of money," she said, "and I'm afraid to say the council doesn't have such funds for projects like that, no matter how valuable the outcome."

"Well, let's raise the money," Jerry said. "I'll do a concert here for starters. I reckon with my connections, we could get a decent audience and raise more than enough money to pay for the refurb."

"How long would that take to organise, Jerry?" someone shouted across the hall.

"A couple of weeks I reckon."

"But you're talking about quite an investment," Jane said. "Between supplies and labour costs, I'm not sure you'll be able to raise it all. I mean, who'll do the work without charging a fortune?"

Paul stood up and everyone looked over. "I'll do it."

"Sorry, who are you?" Jane asked.

"I'm one of those lost souls Bob talked about. I came here looking for something, but I also bring thirty odd years of construction and maintenance experience. I'll get the job done."

Paul looked over at Jerry who gave him a thumbs up.

"Assuming all this is possible, can we have a quick vote?" Jane asked. "Hands up, those who are in favour of Jerry's proposal – of turning our derelict church into a place that can be used by current and future generations?"

Most of the room raised their arms.

"Those against?"

Two arms went up. Bob was very vocal, but his protests were ignored.

"Right, the voting result is clear. Gentlemen, let's see what we can do."

SEVENTEEN

There was a mood of victory in the air and a few of the attendees made their way to the Pilgrim Inn on the High Street after the meeting. The journey down to the pub only took a few minutes. Paul followed Sarah and Jerry – who were in good spirits and chattering away. He had surprised himself volunteering to help renovate the old church. But somehow it all made sense. The timing of his arrival and his experience aligned perfectly. Like it was meant to be. Paul tried not to dwell on this thought for too long.

They walked into the pub and Paul immediately took to the place – there was something familiar about the slightly dated decor and the walls covered in fake wooden panelling. It was full of maritime artefacts and fixtures – old ropes and buoys, ceramic lighthouses, and the odd wooden helm. On the wall next to the entrance were a series of photographs from various boat trips. Paul examined one picture that showed Jerry playing skipper on a boat called *Patrick*. He was surrounded by a crew who were all holding wine bottles and beer cans. He recognised one of the men as Sarah's father. The man was smiling and holding a full glass of wine in his hand.

Opposite the bar was a fireplace in which a bundle of logs burned and warmed the room. Two weathered old men with the unmistakable appearance of regulars stood between the bar and the fire – putting the world to rights. Another – sat in the chair nearest the heat – diligently tended to the burning wood. He had an iron poker in his hand and rarely took his eyes away from the flames. Paul recognised him from the church – carrying sticks that were likely kindling.

"What are you both having?" Jerry asked.

Sarah ordered a wine and Paul a pint of lager.

Paul listened to the conversation of the two old men.

"A virus? From where?"

"China, Thailand. One of them places."

"They're saying a virus caused it?"

"It's no sillier than an External Force. Aliens – my arse."

Jerry turned around and handed both Paul and Sarah their drinks before raising his glass.

"Cheers, guys. That was quite a win."

They sipped and Sarah licked her lips.

"For a moment, I thought Bob's diatribe might sway everyone."

"He's a passionate nutter. I'll give him that," Jerry said.

Sarah laughed and turned to Paul.

"You're very quiet. What did you make of it?"

Paul sipped on his drink before answering. "Wanting to destroy that place so desperately… seems mad."

"These are mad times indeed," Jerry said.

*

A few drinks in and Paul sat with Jerry at a table near the window. Sarah was on the other side of the room, chatting to the man tending the fire. His name was Bedwyr, and he took his role very seriously.

"You arrived here yesterday?" Jerry asked, surprised.

"Good timing it seems," Paul said.

"It was fate – you were destined to be here." Jerry bellowed with laughter. He had a chest as big as a barrel and the noise reverberated from inside like a big drum.

Paul rubbed his chin and drank some more of his beer.

"You certainly tipped the discussion in our favour. What brought you here?"

"Needed to get away from the city and…"

"Something brought you here?"

"Something brought me back here."

"Ah, you've been here before?"

"A long time ago."

"It does have that effect. Lots of people say the same thing. I came to the island years ago to film a music video. Did you see that small mountain on the way? The one covered in red rocks?"

Paul nodded.

"It was supposed to be Mars in the video."

"The song about a spaceman?"

"That's right. 'Shanty Spaceman'. After filming we stopped off in the village for a few drinks."

Jerry lifted his pint to his eye and examined the room through the glass like it was a telescope.

"There was something about the place that stayed with me. Ten years later, after the band split up, I was going through a rough period; got into all sorts of shit. I almost died from a drug overdose – well, technically I did die for a few minutes – and when I woke up in hospital the first thought that came to me was this place. Not long afterwards, Patrick and I sold up our house in London and we came here. I got clean and never looked back."

"What was it like?" Paul said.

"What was what like, mate?"

"Being in a band. Fame. Seeing the world."

"It was a drag…" Jerry looked down at the floor.

"Really?" Paul cocked his head to the side.

"Of course not. It was bloody awesome." And he roared with laughter again.

*

Jerry brought out a guitar and sat in the corner playing a mixture of old and not-so-old songs. A small group that included Sarah had gathered around him and they sang along with each cover. Between songs there was laughter as Jerry played the entertainer.

Paul stood near the bar watching Bedwyr as he cared for the fire. He became aware of a young barmaid who came and went. She served customers on the other side of the bar while the owner – Dave – served this side. He glanced over when she went past, made eye contact with her and she smiled.

He was now on his fifth or sixth drink. He heard the clinking of glasses and noticed Dave refilling the shelves below the bar.

"Does he ever stop tending to that fire?" Paul asked.

"Bedwyr? No, never." Dave then purposefully raised his voice. "He's in here, day in, day out. Whether icy cold or scorching hot outside, in here, the fire still burns."

"I never hear you complain when your heating bill comes," Bedwyr said pointing at Dave with the red-hot poker.

"There is that, I suppose," Dave said.

"I'm doing him a favour you know," Bedwyr said. "Every day since I took early retirement I have tended to his fire. Nearly twenty years."

"It's a very good fire," Paul said.

"See," Bedwyr said, "this man recognises the quality of my work. Each morning I'm up early to collect kindling. Then I'm here for opening time to make this place warm and cosy for your customers."

He looked closely at Paul. "I saw you this morning. By the church. I was carrying driftwood back from Red Beach."

Paul nodded.

"See," Bedwyr said. "This man can attest to my addiction to this fire."

"Do you mean *dedication*, Beds?"

"That's what I said."

Dave raised his eyebrows at Paul. "You know I appreciate your work, Beds. It's just that come July when I'm in here in shorts and T-shirt and the back door is open, you're still piling the logs on."

"And the summer tourists love it. It's even busier here then."

"It's busier because it's the summer holidays, you old goon. Not because of the fire."

"Ha, what do you know? You stay on that side of the bar

and do what you know and let me stay here and do what I know."

Dave looked at Paul and shrugged his shoulders. Paul grinned.

*

The jamming session had ended after Jerry was called home by his partner. The bar had emptied as the time neared last orders. Paul nursed a large whiskey as he sat across a table from Sarah who sipped on a glass of red wine. She stared across the room at the fire. Bedwyr had now stopped tending to it and was himself now leant back with pint in hand. Paul examined her face. She was beautiful but she carried a lot of sadness. He noticed something about her left hand. "You still wear your wedding ring?"

"Not mine – this was my mother's." She started laughing. "Mine is still at the bottom of the Ashton Canal. Unless some lucky fisherman has caught it."

"Didn't end well?"

"Nope." She looked at her glass and twirled the liquid around. "Every night was like this."

"In the pub?"

"Drinking. Heavily."

"Oh."

"I bet yours was different. Before she died, I mean…"

"I wish I could say it was, but truth be told I wasn't the best husband."

She looked up.

"We married young. Before I left for the army. After three years, I returned, and things were different. I was different."

"Where did you serve?"

"Northern Ireland. Busy place in the eighties. Things happened that changed me."

"Changed how?"

"It's like it stayed with me. I may have left Belfast, but Belfast came with me."

Paul looked down and gritted his teeth.

"For a long time, I wasn't a good person. I struggled with many things. Being a husband was the thing I struggled with the most."

Paul looked up and his gaze met Sarah's eyes. The corners of her mouth were turned down. He laughed. "I don't know why I'm telling you this."

She shrugged.

He paused and his eyes scanned across the ceiling.

"The worst thing was the way it affected Eve. The first time I noticed was her birthday after I'd left the army. We'd planned to go out for a nice dinner. She'd been on about it for weeks and had made a booking at this expensive Italian in town."

He paused to try and recall the details.

"I was working on a new job at a building site and ended up going for a pint after work. One thing led to another and I didn't get home until the early hours. When I did, I found Eve asleep on the sofa. She had this green flowery dress on that I hadn't seen her wear since our honeymoon. She looked beautiful."

Paul rubbed his aching arm.

"That is what I did to her, over and over for years. Slowly but surely, I chipped away at her spirit until the woman I'd fallen in love with was no longer there."

Sarah had her hand over her mouth.

"When we found out she was ill, I didn't know what to do, and in the end, I did nothing. I faded into the shadows. I wasn't there when she needed me the most."

"But she stayed with you. There must have been something keeping you together."

"Maybe. What is it that keeps people together?" Paul cleared his throat.

From across the bar, Dave rang the bell for last orders and Sarah's eyes widened.

"God, I lost track of the time. I need to get back. Julie will be finishing up."

She looked at Paul. "Are you heading back to the house?"

"Might stay for a nightcap," he said.

"Okay, see you tomorrow." She put her coat on and left him to it.

Paul stepped over to the bar and put his empty glass down. The barmaid came over and smiled.

"Same again?" she asked.

Paul nodded. "Dave gone now?"

"He's cashing up in the back."

Paul scanned the bar. The place was almost empty. Bedwyr had gone and the fire was dying down. Two voices argued on the other side of the bar about something relating to the pool table.

"Visiting here, are you?" the woman said as she filled the glass with whiskey from the optic.

"Yeah."

"Taking a break from things after the Revelation?"

"You could say that."

She came over and placed Paul's drink on the bar then

reached for her own and took a sip. She put her hand on her hip where her short jeans skirt met a tight white T-shirt and stretched her back and groaned.

"Done for the day?" Paul asked.

"Almost, but I deserve a treat."

Paul glanced back at his empty seat where he'd sat earlier with Sarah and then leant on the bar.

"So, are you going to tell me your name?" the woman asked before downing the glass of whiskey in her hand.

"Paul. You?" He did the same.

"Jess. You like tequila?" Jess reached under the bar and opened a cupboard.

"Well, I… maybe I should… probably time…"

Before he'd responded, she pulled out a bottle of Jose Cuervo, some salt, and limes, and grabbed two shot glasses. She filled each glass to the top and then licked her wrist and shook a little salt on before licking it again and downing the tequila. She grabbed the lime and stuck it in her mouth, shutting her eyes tight as she sucked on the fruit.

Paul followed her lead and did the same.

*

Dave had not returned, and the pub was now empty apart from Paul and Jess. From either side, they both leant on the bar. Between them lay a pile of chewed up limes. Most of the lights had been turned off and all that remained of the fire were glowing embers.

"Just imagine you'd lived your whole life for a god that didn't exist," Jess said. "That's the most tragic thing."

"Yeah, tragic." Paul tried hard not to sway where he stood.

"You've eaten only food that God allows, drunk only drinks that God allows, even loved according to what God allows. You've lived a life in denial."

"Denial." Paul shook his head.

Jess turned to face Paul. "Mate, you don't look well."

"Am fine."

"Yeah, right. You want to come back to mine for a smoke?"

"Sure."

Jess made a half-hearted attempt to clean up the bar.

"Ha, Dave can do it in the morning."

They walked up the High Street arm in arm and up some stairs at the side of a flower shop.

"I live above the florist," Jess said. "I get my pick of the wasted flowers whenever I want them."

"Great."

Inside the flat, Jess led Paul into the living room. She cleared some clothes off the sofa and guided him to his seat. She put reggae music on and took her shoes off. Then she pulled out a tin and sat down next to him and started skinning up a joint. She was talking away, but Paul wasn't listening. His eyes darted around the room as he examined the space she lived in. There were posters on the wall, a small television set that balanced on an upturned milk crate, and a neon beaded door curtain that hung between the living room and the kitchen. He spotted three separate vases full of flowers that had seen better days.

Smoke appeared in front of Paul's eyes and he turned to see Jess holding a huge joint between her lips. She passed it over to him and he took a long draw. Then, another. After the third, his head began to spin, and he was forced to close his eyes and let go.

Someone was touching him. He looked down and Jess's head was bent over him and she was trying to open his flies.

"No," he mumbled.

"Come on, Paul. You want this." She clumsily tried to reach into his pants, and he could feel her fingers brush against his penis.

He shook his head and said no again but she continued to fumble. He pulled away from her over the side of the sofa and fell to the floor. Jess remained seated and looked at him, disgusted.

"What's wrong with you?"

"Not right," he slurred, and his chin trembled.

She shook her head and reached over to the ashtray and relit the joint.

He crawled away from the sofa, pulled on the door handle so he could get to his feet and then made his way out through the door. Outside, he staggered down the steps, holding the banister with both hands. He banged his left arm against the wall and groaned. On the street, he looked around at where he was to try and orientate himself. He heard the sea and turned in its direction. He recognised the road past the pub that led up the hill to the guest house. Near the beach he heard a woman chortle. He looked around him, but the street was empty.

"Ha, of course you're still there. Bet you fricking loved that, didn't you?"

The lights were off at the house. Inside, he tried as hard as he could to not make a sound. In the living room, he held onto the sofa like a rock climber edging across a crevice and in the dining area he lost his footing and almost collapsed on a table. He slipped on the stairs and crawled the rest of the way up to his bedroom where he pushed the door closed behind him with his foot before pulling himself up on to his bed and closing his eyes.

EIGHTEEN

Paul sat at the breakfast table staring at the plate of food in front of him. He felt like someone had bashed his head with a sledgehammer. He thought about Jess, took a deep, pained breath and closed his eyes. She was a child – how could he have got himself into that situation?

"You wanted it." Eve spoke but he did not expect to see her. Sarah entered from the kitchen with a pot of tea.

"Had a lock-in at the pub, did you?"

"Yeah."

"Who was there with you?"

"That barmaid – Jess – and…"

"Oh." Sarah's eyes widened and then she walked around to the other side of the table.

"What?"

"She has a bit of a reputation."

"For what?"

"Needing a father figure."

"Nothing happened. Apart from the shots."

"That's your business."

"No, seriously, listen..." Paul protested as Sarah walked out of the room.

He shuddered but decided that food is what he needed. He picked up a sausage and took a bite from the end before chewing it slowly. As he went in for the second bite, a knock came at the door. Sarah went past and he heard her talking to someone.

She walked back in and was followed by an elderly woman wearing a straw hat.

"Of course, no reservation is needed right now," Sarah said as she guided the woman around the corner to the office. The elderly lady gave Paul a wide smile.

In a short while they returned to the dining area.

"...And he's been like this ever since," Sarah said signalling to her father who was sat in his usual spot by the window.

"Oh dear." The elderly lady gave Sarah a sympathetic look.

"Paul here is our only other guest right now." Sarah looked at Paul and crossed her arms.

"Paul's a little delicate after a late night at the local." The elderly lady giggled.

"Paul, this is Agnes. She wants to visit the old church. I suggested you might show her the way."

Paul touched the back of his neck. "Er, okay. When?"

"Oh, there's no rush. Perhaps we could get going once you've finished your breakfast?"

"Alright." He looked at Agnes and then Sarah. "It's quite a steep hill that you have to walk up."

"Oh, I'll be fine, dear. Plenty of hill walking left in these old legs." She lifted her skirt a little to show her shins and

Sarah smiled. "Just get me there and I'll find my own way back, no need for you to wait for me."

*

Sarah watched from the window as they set off down the road towards the beach. Breakfast and fresh air helped a little, but he could still taste the tequila and the banging in his head continued, unabated. He glanced over at Agnes. Beneath her straw hat, she wore a shirt and a skirt, and a purple shawl draped over her shoulders. The lines on her face told the story of a character who smiled a lot. When she did, her eyes became thin, and her face broadened like a Cheshire cat.

"You came here after the Revelation as well?" Agnes asked.

"Yes."

"What brought you here?"

"Needed to get away from the city."

"But why here specifically?"

He shook his head. "Don't know."

"I bet you do know. On some level, it's as clear as day to you."

"Why are you here?"

"I've been meaning to come here all my life. I'm here to pay homage to Morwell."

At the bottom of the hill Paul ushered her to the edge of the car park to avoid a car that was leaving.

"Who?"

"You don't know about Morwell? The false saint?" She grabbed his arm and gave Paul a look of genuine surprise. "Oh goodness, stop here for a second."

She sat down on the beach wall and gestured for Paul to do the same.

"Morwell was a farmer who lived in Cornwall in the third century. One day, Vikings came and murdered his family and abducted him – intending to sell him as a slave. As they sailed along the coast, he prayed to God asking for him to be freed from his pagan kidnappers. He did this for five days straight. On the sixth day, tired of pleading for his life, he called out to the sky and said that this was God's last chance. *Free me or I will forget thee*, he yelled. There was no response. On the seventh day, a huge storm came and the ship was wrecked on these rocks." Agnes pointed towards the headland.

"Morwell was the only survivor, and he was badly injured. He managed to climb up the rocks to a spot where he found a freshwater well. He lay in this place for two days. The water sustained him long enough for him to heal. Locals found him stood on the edge of the cliff yelling curses at the sea and the sky and the elements. He had rejected God and his faith. He told those who discovered him about his experience. They were in awe. Here was a man who turned his back on God. His preaching scared people but they were also enthralled by his message – that man could stand up to the divine. The well became known for its magical properties. They said anyone who drank from it would know the entire truth of it all. His followers built a house near the well – where they could gather and listen to his teachings."

Agnes placed her hand on Paul's leg and tapped his knee.

"Now here's the funny part. Somehow, over the next few hundred years, the house is extended and becomes converted into a church. The building built to honour a man who turned his back on God. Funnier still was that as founder of the church, Morwell became St Morwell."

"This church here?" Paul said.

"This church. I guess you hadn't heard that story?"

"Only something about a saint founding the church after being shipwrecked here. And that the well had healing qualities."

Agnes leant back on the wall and guffawed as Paul looked on with curiosity.

"Everyone knows the Christian version of the story."

"But now?" Paul asked.

"Now, I don't know."

She stood up and tapped Paul's knee with her walking stick. "Anyway, let's go explore this place and see if we can find the well, shall we?"

*

As they approached the gates, Agnes started walking more quickly. She glanced at Paul and smiled.

"Oh, look at it," she said. "A glorious building in a glorious location. For so many years I dreamt of coming here."

"Why didn't you?" Paul asked, walking up behind her.

"Never had the chance. My work always kept me busy in my community."

"What did you do?"

She turned around to face Paul.

"I was a Methodist minister."

"Of course."

They strolled through the gardens and Agnes looked around at the place.

"It's a shame it was neglected like this."

"We're going to refurbish it."

"How so?"

"Turn it into a place for the community. We just need to raise the cash first."

"That is wonderful."

They both had a look inside the building then strolled along the wall and stared out at the sea. Agnes took out a book and put her reading glasses on. She examined the image on the page and compared it with the landscape.

"The north wall of the church is here. That means the well should be right about there."

Paul looked to where she pointed on the page.

"I searched all around there yesterday and could see no sign of it. On the other side there's a green verge that's about five feet wide and then it drops off into the sea."

"According to this map, it's there."

At the wall, Agnes watched as Paul climbed to the other side. On the grassy area, he peered over the side and saw nothing but sea and rocks below.

"Sorry, there is no well here."

"Look closer, will you? It may not have much flow now, but the fresh water source should still be there."

Paul got down on the ground and leant on his front to see if he could examine the cliff face. He stretched his neck as far as he could but saw no sign of what they were searching for. Then he heard something. Above the roar of the waves, there was the gentle sound of trickling water like someone had forgotten to turn off a tap. He reached his arm down and he could feel it. Beneath the grassy verge, there was a small hole in the cliff face in which he could feel a steady stream of cold water.

"It's here," he called out to Agnes.

"Excellent, take this and fill it, if you can."

Paul got up and she handed him a small plastic bottle. Back on his front he held the bottle under the flow of the water and filled it. He stepped away from the cliff edge and held out the bottle for Agnes.

"You deserve to go first, Paul."

"What do I get though – truth or healing?"

"What do you prefer?"

"I don't know." He put the bottle to his mouth and drank. It was cold and refreshing. He drank more until the bottle was empty. He filled it up again for Agnes and handed her the bottle. They both sat on the wall gazing out at the sea.

"This really is a special place," she said. Paul was silent.

"It's funny, despite being one of the oldest Christian sites in the country, it still has a history that long predates that. Pagans were drawn here and buried their dead hundreds of years before the Christians came. And now the time of Christianity has passed…"

"And people continue to come here."

"Indeed."

Agnes turned to face Paul.

"How do you feel now that you've tasted the truth?"

"Rough."

Agnes gently laughed and reached over and patted Paul on the leg.

"Yes, sometimes it can feel a bit like that."

*

When Paul arrived back at the guest house, Sarah was digging in the soil and turning over the flower bed that lined the front garden wall.

"Can I help?" he asked.

"Where's Agnes?" Sarah said.

"She wanted some time by herself at the church."

"Will she be okay?"

"She'll be fine. She's a spirited one."

Sarah leant over and continued her digging. "And how are you feeling?"

"Not as bad as I did before." Paul knelt next to her and pulled a handful of weeds from the soil.

"You know, I might take a break from the booze."

"That must be quite a hangover you had." There was some derision in her voice.

"It's not just that. This Revelation has really messed with my head. I need to…" He thought for a second, "…slow things down a bit."

Sarah took a deep breath and nodded.

"First thing you can do is grab that trowel and get digging."

Paul reached over and picked up the small tool. He pushed it deep into the soil and the cold matter felt good against his skin.

NINETEEN

The day of the fundraising concert, March tenth, had arrived. Paul sat in the living room of the guest house watching television. He'd been monitoring local news every day for any reports on bodies found in the Menai Strait. There had been two since he arrived in Llanffug, but both were men. After the local segment, the news then returned to the main feature with a report called *One Month After the Revelation*.

"So, what do we know?" a deep-voiced man said over scenes of crash sites, burning buildings and injured people in hospital.

"As a direct or indirect result of the Revelation, it is estimated that nearly two million people died across the world. Of course, the actual cause remains unknown, but the effects have been very well documented.

"Beyond the initial loss of consciousness, mental health issues followed according to the extent of pre-Revelation faith. Fervent religiousness and deep faith were associated with a strongly Symptomatic Revelation, manifesting as a mixture of psychiatric and neurological symptoms. The type of religion didn't appear to affect the nature of symptoms – although there was some indication that the three monotheistic religions were more frequently associated with severe effects. Those who were atheists prior to the event, largely experienced minimal or no symptoms.

"The full extent of Symptomatic Revelation has been difficult to ascertain but governments and healthcare systems around the world suggest that the number of those severely affected may be in the tens of millions."

Sarah walked through the living room and stopped for a second.

"Any mention of the girl from the hospital?"

Paul shook his head, and she placed her hand on his shoulder.

"What's this about?"

"They're summarising events after the Revelation, since it's one month on."

"One month only? Feels like a lifetime." Sarah left the room. From the hallway she called out to him. "We'll need to get going in a minute."

"I'm ready whenever you are."

The television now showed a male reporter stood in front of the barricaded entrance of the Vatican.

"The activity of organised religions has been put on hold. In many parts of the world, governments have intervened and taken control of all resources and wealth as senior leaders have vacated roles and abandoned their associations with various groups. Some of the major religious centres have wealth comparable to small nations. The Vatican here behind me was its own self-governing country but is now under the control of the Italian government.

"We're told they're trying to determine how best to utilise the vast wealth owned by this tiny state. Some leaders have called for the riches, investments, and treasures of religions to be shared among the poorest nations – many of which would have made major financial contributions to the various organisations over the years. But this very complex discussion will not likely be concluded in the near future."

Ben ambled over to Paul and pushed his head against his knee. Paul leaned down and rubbed his fur.

The report now switched to a woman stood in front of New Scotland Yard.

"A particularly concerning aspect of recent events has been the widespread reports of violence towards religions, their leadership and their symbols since the Revelation. Religious buildings and sites have become targets for attack. Many, such as the Kaaba in Mecca and the Tomb of Christ in Jerusalem, are now under the protection of the military.

"The United Nations has moved quickly to class any groups targeting religions as terrorists. In the UK, one such group – the Witnesses of the External Force – has been linked to many of the attacks across larger cities. Earlier this week they took responsibility for the assassination of the Archbishop of Durham and the firebombing of the cathedral. The government has put pressure on the police and security services to find the perpetrators responsible for the numerous violent crimes committed in the aftermath of the Revelation."

Paul turned the television off. It was all starting to get a little too close to home.

In the hallway he found Sarah putting her earrings in. She was wearing make-up and a low-cut dress. He watched her before realising that she could see his reflection. She smiled and he reached over to grab his coat.

Together, they left the house and made their way to the top of the hill that overlooked the beach. There they stopped. At the far end of the car park, they could see a stage surrounded by three or four kiosks, caravans and a few hundred people. Loud music was coming from the stage but there did not appear to be anyone on there playing at present.

"How was Jerry able to organise this thing in such a short space of time?" Paul asked.

"Good connections, I guess. Also, Wheel Deal are still very popular – especially for us youngsters who remember the eighties." She winked at Paul.

Full cars drove past them on their way into the car park. The two descended along the road and entered the makeshift arena. There were a few recognisable faces from the village, but the majority were outsiders.

Paul had now been in Llanffug for over two weeks. Most of that time had been spent examining the church and determining what supplies would be needed to carry out the work. Of course, the whole project was subject to the success of the concert that Jerry had organised. A few local bands and musicians were to play over the course of the evening and then Jerry and two of the other surviving members of Wheel Deal would headline later that night. Despite being a Monday, the decision to host the event on the one-month anniversary of the Revelation was appreciated by most as a positive move. A signal to – perhaps – not dwell on the darkness of the last few weeks but focus on a bright new future of hope and positivity.

"Right, I'm off to the bar for a wine," Sarah said. "Do you want a coke or a lemonade?"

Paul shook his head. He had avoided all drink since the night of the village meeting. He watched as Sarah went over to queue at the bar. He had grown quite accustomed to being around her. Most evenings, they chatted over dinner. She told him about her life in the city, about her job at the law firm and her struggles with an alcoholic husband. He told her about his childhood, his time in the army and his life with Eve. Sarah knew that he'd come to Llanffug because of Eve but did not know that she had led him along the way.

"I don't know why I didn't bring my own wine," Sarah said as she returned. "Five quid each for these tiny bottles!"

"I suppose the mark-up is going to a worthy cause." Paul examined the large schedule next to the stage. "Do you know any of these other bands?"

"No, and I doubt they'll be my cup of tea."

Paul shivered slightly and buttoned up his coat. Sarah rubbed his arm and smiled at him.

"It's cooling now," he said. "Need to keep moving."

They walked around the site and then stopped at a van selling T-shirts.

"What was the name of that one song they did?" Paul asked. "The really popular one."

"Do you mean 'Keep Each Other Shining'?"

"Yeah, that's the one. God, I remember when it was in the charts."

"I think I was in primary school."

"Do you ever feel like looking back at memories is like trying to find a particular moment on a video?"

"Video? Paul, you are old-fashioned. What do you mean?"

"It's like looking through a mixture of images and some appear fast in front of your eyes, then some appear slower, and what you really want is to find that moment you liked but it seems that it went too fast and you have to go back and try and find it again."

"I guess," Sarah said. "But I'm still not sure of where you're going with this."

"I just feel that sometimes when I look back at my life, there are times, maybe years of my life, that appear to me as a blur, and I don't remember them so well. Like I'm fast-forwarding through them. Maybe I don't want to remember them. But then there are these moments that are crystal clear – like they're happening in slow motion and it feels like I can jump back into each scene and walk around and interact with all the details. These memories to me – I suppose – are the important ones."

"Okay."

"I guess what I'm saying is that I feel like these last couple of weeks in the village, and the time I've spent here with you has been a bit like that. It's been special and the best that I can remember for quite a while. I want to remember every detail."

Sarah pulled him close and wrapped her arms around him.

"Now maybe I understand," she whispered in his ear. Paul looked up.

"Hey, there's Jerry."

Sarah took a long sip of wine. "Let's go say hello to the rock star."

Jerry wore a Parka and jeans, and – despite the grey March evening – also had an expensive pair of sunglasses on. His partner – Patrick – stood next to him. He was a few years younger than Jerry and had a thick black beard and carefully styled hair. There were a few others hovering around Jerry but when he saw Sarah and Paul, he welcomed them over and hugged them both.

"So, the comeback starts here?" Sarah asked.

"Well, what better place is there?" Jerry replied.

"It's a great turnout," she said.

"Yes, it is. Although concerningly I have heard that some people here do want to hear genuine eighties hits and may not really care about a third-century Welsh church."

"You are kidding." Sarah laughed.

"Seriously though," Jerry said, "between ticket sales and any cash we can prise away from these vendors, we may have raised thirty grand or so for our project. What do you think, Paul – will that get us what we need to do the old place up?"

"I'm sure we can make it work."

"It certainly helps that Paul is not charging the village for his labour costs," Sarah said.

"It's good of you, man," Jerry said. "More gestures of kindness and positivity are what humanity needs right now. It may just be an old building but for people round here and the lonely travellers who come searching for answers, it's an oasis of hope in these uncertain times."

"Babe, you sound pissed already," Patrick said. "Are you going to be alright going on stage?"

"Patty, you know me. I can perform just as well after a bottle of whiskey. A couple of beers will barely touch the sides." Jerry bent over and kissed Patrick on the lips. Sarah looked over at Paul and rolled her eyes.

A loud noise came from the stage and they all turned their heads.

"Jesus, what does he want?" Jerry said.

Stood by the microphone was Bob. Paul could see the young sound engineer at the side of the stage panicking. Bob had his eye on the two security guards climbing up on either side of the stage.

"I don't have long, but you should all know that what you're doing here today is wrong. You're supporting something that is against the direction of human progress. We're now free of the oppression of the church and to try and save that old building – that prison – is wrong of you."

The two security guards were now on either side of him and he held up the microphone stand and waved it towards both of them.

"I ask you not to do this. I ask you to leave and—"

Before he finished his sentence, one of the security guards had rugby-tackled him. The other then pounced and there was a struggle – during which Bob was able to speak a few further words.

"You will… regret… this."

Then the sound was cut, and he was taken away. The crowd cheered and Dave walked onto the stage clapping and pointing to the guards. He made a joke about Bob being unable to leave anywhere without being escorted away and the crowd laughed. He introduced the first band – a young group of local lads with guitars who came on and made quite a bit of noise.

The evening progressed and a mixture of musicians took to the stage. As darkness fell, so did the temperature but spirts remained high. Paul looked around at the crowd and saw that people needed this. Maybe this was the way forward. The way people would heal after the madness of the Revelation. Sarah was now a few wines down the road; she danced away at each beat that came from the stage – no matter how toneless the singer or how bland the music sounded.

"Aren't you going to dance with me?" Sarah shouted in his ear.

Paul smiled and shook his head – he felt very sober.

"It feels great to be here, doesn't it?" she said. "Be around people having fun for once and just letting go."

"Yeah," he replied, and he grinned at her.

It was getting late, and it was time for Wheel Deal to come on for their headline act. Dave stumbled onto the stage once again.

"Right, everyone, here's the moment you've been waiting for. I'm proud to welcome onto the stage my friend and regular at the Pilgrim Inn pub on the High Street in the village, which – by the way – is open for another hour after this gig has finished." He took a breath, looked at the ground then spoke the next words slowly.

"Here… is… Wheel… Deal."

The band walked on like they'd done it a million times before, and the audience screamed and made more noise than Paul had heard all evening. Sarah put her arm around him and gave him a kiss on the cheek.

Wheel Deal's first song hit the crowd like a wave. This was a band with a great deal more experience than all the others that had played on the stage that evening. Paul stood and watched as everyone around him moved and yelled.

After the first song, Jerry spoke. "How are you all doing?" he yelled and the crowd yelled back at him.

"It's great to have you all here tonight. This has been a crazy month, hasn't it? But here we are, rocking this beautiful location, which has been my home for the last twenty-five years. Anyway, you don't want to hear me preaching. I just wanted to say thank you for being here and being part of the day. We're trying to save a special place that we hope can help people who've found these last few weeks to be a battle. But also, to have a place where we can come together and do more shit like this. Are you with me?"

The crowd roared their agreement.

The set progressed and each song was received with equal enthusiasm. Paul thought he recognised one or two, but it wasn't until the final song that he felt real excitement. The first few chords of guitar played and then the riff and the bass kicked in, followed by the drums. Suddenly his body came to life and he found himself moving along to the music in a way that he hadn't done in a long time.

Paul grabbed Sarah and they danced around together and joined the rest of the crowd with a loud singalong of the chorus.

"Gotta' live your life, like the brightest of lights, shining on through the darkest of nights. Stick with me baby, I'll show you the way. We'll keep each other shining, we'll never fade away."

Sarah pulled him close and kissed him, and for a moment, Paul was lost in her lips. But then dismay caught up with him. An explosion of panic and guilt erupted, and he felt the world closing in around him. He frantically pulled away from her and looked around expecting to see... and there she was. Eve was stood next to Jerry on the stage; she had her arms crossed and she gazed directly at Paul. Her face did not have the anger he was used to seeing – she looked sad; disappointed.

"What's wrong?" Sarah appeared shocked.

Paul mumbled something and then shook his head and he turned and left. He refused to look back as he rushed through the wild audience. He walked up the hill and stopped to breathe, hearing the band continue to play and the crowd continue to scream. He carried on towards the guest house. By the gate, he stopped and tried to understand what had just happened. But then he saw a figure that had followed him up the hill. Sarah looked concerned.

"Did I do something wrong?"

"No, Sarah. It's me. It's a situation I'm not familiar with."

"I thought you were enjoying yourself."

"I was but it's not that simple."

"And what you said earlier made it sound like you were happy here. Happy with me."

"I am happy. At least I think I am."

"What else is there?"

"I wasn't completely honest with you about the Revelation and the effect it had on me."

Sarah stepped closer and leaned on the wall next to him. "What do you mean?"

He took a couple of deep breaths before speaking.

"What I'm about to tell you, I haven't said to anyone else. You may think I'm crazy."

Her eyes didn't lose contact from his and she took his hand.

"These are not normal days for any of us," she said.

"Okay. After the Revelation, I started seeing my dead wife again."

Sarah's eyebrows rose. "What? Where?"

"Everywhere. For a while anyway. But it wasn't her as I remembered her before she died. She looked like the woman I fell for over thirty years ago, wearing the same dress as the time we were on this beach on that summer's day – the one I told you about."

Sarah did not speak but her grip on his hand became tighter.

"But it's more than that. She's the one who guided me here. On the morning after the Revelation, when I awoke, she was there, and I knew I had to pack a bag and follow her on a journey. That journey brought me here."

"And you saw her again tonight?"

"Yes, for the first time, clearly that is, since I was in hospital. After that, it's only been glimpses here and there. Until tonight. When we kissed, I saw her fully again."

"I take it you didn't mention this to the doctors when you were at the hospital?"

"No, they just treated the infection."

"Do you see her now?"

"No."

"How does she make you feel when you see her?"

"I don't know. Guilty, ashamed, sad…"

"She's real, you know."

Paul cocked his head to the side.

"I mean what you see is not your dead wife. Her spirit is not haunting you. She's part of you. A part of you that has unresolved matters. The guilt, the shame, the sadness, those are things you own. It's your brain trying to cope with these things in light of the Revelation and the effect that has had on you."

"You're probably right. I'm sorry about tonight. I meant what I said before. Being here with you over the last two weeks has been amazing. But I think I may need some time."

"It's okay, I think we all need some time to get used to this new world."

"You're not concerned about me staying here, are you? I can go elsewhere…"

She grabbed his hand again and patted it with hers. "It's fine. Besides, I still need you to fix that fence properly. Ben keeps getting out."

They both chuckled.

A light switched on behind them and they both turned around.

"That's odd," Sarah said. "Julie texted me to say she'd left after putting Dad to bed."

Sarah walked up the path, followed closely by Paul. The living room light in the house was on and the curtains were wide open. As they entered through the front door, they could hear clattering coming from the back. They both glanced at each other before tiptoeing through the living room into the kitchen. There, in his pyjamas, stood Sarah's father. He was frying some eggs on the stove.

"Hello, Sarah. I woke up feeling famished." He pointed the spatula at Paul. "Who's this?"

It was the first time Paul had heard the man's deep Welsh-accented voice. Sarah gave Paul a look of shock and then she rushed over to her father and hugged him. He seemed glad although somewhat confused by her reaction.

TWENTY

They were back in the village hall two days after the fundraising concert. The event had been a resounding success by all accounts – raising more than enough money to renovate the old church. Ahead of the meeting, Paul had finalised his costing plan, which set out what materials would be needed to turn the derelict building into something that was safe and usable.

Paul, Jerry and Sarah were sat along one side of a long table. On the other side sat Jane, Gwyn the butcher, Geraint and Manon who – along with Gwilym – were the current councillors. Another member, Myfanwy, had not been heard from since the Revelation. The story was that she had gone to live with her son in Wrexham. An election would be needed in the coming weeks to replace her as local regulations dictated that the council was to always have a chair and five other members.

"Is your dad joining us?" Jane asked Sarah.

"Yes, he should be here. I don't know what's taking him so long. Maybe we should get started."

Sarah had spent most of her time since the concert with her father. He'd been checked out by the local GP and was seemingly in good health for a man of his age. He was booked in to undergo tests at the hospital in Bangor in due course – but at present – the impact of the Revelation and the month-long catatonic state had not left him with any obvious long-term ill effects.

"Right," said Jane. "On the back of the success we had on Monday," she gave Jerry a thumbs up, "we now have a sizable pot to fund our renovation project. Thank you, Paul, for the detailed quote. I think we're all agreed it makes sense and covers the necessary improvements, so I propose we don't spend too much time discussing that this evening. What we do need to discuss though is some of the aesthetic considerations, with particular reference to how the building will be used."

Geraint's large frame leant forward over the table with his hands crossed and everyone turned to face him.

"Manon and I have some thoughts about this," he said. "We think we should return the building to its original appearance. It was built as a church and we think it should be made to look as it was initially intended again. The place has history, and we should demonstrate that history when we bring the old building back to life."

"You mean renovate the place back to its original appearance as a church?"

"Yes."

"But that wasn't its original purpose." A voice spoke from the far end of the hall. Gwilym had arrived. He walked over to the table and sat down in the one empty chair. Paul looked to Sarah; her smile spoke volumes. He hadn't had the opportunity yet to speak with Gwilym at length but there were things about the man that intrigued him.

"The place was a church for nearly a millennium and a half, Gwilym. That was its primary use." Manon spoke in a delicate, hushed tone.

"Poppycock," Gwilym said, and Jane raised her eyebrows. "It was originally built by Morwell's followers as a tribute to a man who turned his back on God. That was before the early Christians reinvented the place and rebranded Morwell."

"There's no evidence for that," Geraint said.

"There's enough," Gwilym batted back.

"What's your proposal, Gwilym?" Jane asked.

Gwilym put his head down, exhaled loudly and looked around at everyone.

"You all know what happened to me," he said. "I was gone from this world for one month – from the instant the Revelation hit to Monday evening. But what you may not know is that for me it was only a few minutes."

"Where did you go then, Gwil?" Gwyn asked.

"For those brief moments I was up on the headland looking out at the water, and I wasn't alone."

"Dad, you didn't tell me this."

Gwilym shrugged.

"Morwell stood next to me and he spoke. He said, *my child, you're finally free. Take these truths and illuminate the darkness.* As he spoke, I heard bells chiming. Not like church bells – more like an old clock."

Paul leaned forwards and clasped his hands.

"I turned my head and saw that the church building was now there but there was something different about it and as I walked around to the entrance, there were dazzling lights emanating from each window. They were so dazzling in fact that I had to cover my eyes. I got to the door and pushed it open…"

Gwilym stopped and looked around at everyone. They were hanging on his every word.

"…And what I saw inside was a bright room filled with people of every age and every ethnicity. Some were smiling and some were frowning. Some were laughing and some were crying. An old man close to death held a newborn baby. There were loving couples embracing. Young people debated their views about the world. Old friends consoled each other about loss. There was no fear or bitterness. There was only acceptance in the truth of it all. Honest and open humility about who we are and who we may be. It was beautiful." His eyes were welling up with tears as he spoke.

"You saw all this inside the church?" Geraint asked.

"It was that building, yes. But it wasn't a church. There were no crucifixes or Christian symbols. The walls were white, and the decor was simple. The place was full of light; there were no shadows or dark corners."

"You propose we decorate the place like that?" Jerry asked.

"More than that, the location and the building are special. We should make it a home for the community – for people to come together to celebrate and to better understand life and what it is to be human. I'd like to run a regular meeting there for this purpose. It would be open to everyone."

"Who would attend?" Geraint asked.

"My suspicion is that a lot of people would want to – if we cover the right subject matter."

"It should be available for other uses as well," Manon said. "For whoever wants to book it."

"Of course, I'm only thinking of one hour a week." Gwilym sat back and looked over at Jane.

"It makes sense to me," she said. "Simple clean decor – no longer a church but a community house. Councillors, shall we vote on it?"

The result was unanimous, and the plan was set for the Llanffug Community House.

*

Later that night, Paul and Sarah sat together watching television after dinner. Paul looked over at Gwilym who was in his chair with a glass of wine in his hand. He was reading the Bible. Curious, Paul approached the old man and signalled to his reading material.

"Bit out of date now?"

"This? Oh, there's still plenty we can take from it – from many religions actually."

Paul crossed his arms.

"I know you may feel sceptical right now. But if you put aside all the paranormal guff, control and guilt, blind fanaticism, persecution, ignorance and the rest of the negative nonsense, you'll see there's some good stuff in there as well."

Paul sat down cross-legged on the floor next to the old man's chair.

"For a time, the church was my life," he said. "I needed it."

"It was a comfort blanket for many. Perhaps for too long and for the wrong reasons. But what it was good at was bringing people together, creating community through rituals and shared experiences, and helping people navigate the more challenging times of life."

"Sarah told me you were a lay preacher after retirement."

"Yes. Before the Revelation, my faith was important to me. But I also found religions deeply interesting in terms of their role in society and human development. Perhaps I was more of an anthropologist than a theologian."

Paul looked out over the sea again. The sun was setting fast, and it would soon be dark.

"You know I heard bells chime as well – just before my Revelation. I thought I was hearing things."

"Perhaps it was more of a shared experience than we know?"

"What was your Revelation like? In the meeting today you told us about your experience afterwards, but what exactly took you there in the first place?"

Gwilym closed the book and took a sip from his glass of wine.

"I was on my way out of the house. I stood here looking out of the window. I remember rubbing my eyes after seeing an aura dancing over the sea. Then I was hit by this light-headedness and waves of unexpected emotions – sadness, guilt, loneliness. I thought I was having a stroke. But then rather than fall to the ground, I remember feeling like something was holding me up in the air; that I was being pulled upwards. I remember thinking that this was it – the end of everything."

"Perhaps it was in some way," Paul said. "I thought it was the rapture. I thought I was about to be taken up to heaven. To be honest, I was ready for it."

Gwilym cleared his throat. "And then we who are alive and remain shall be caught up together with them in the clouds, to meet the Lord in the air, and so shall we ever be with the Lord."

He chuckled, shook his head and patted Paul on his shoulder.

"They pulled the wool over all our eyes, son."

"Mmm." Paul looked up at the old man and gave him a wry smile.

TWENTY-ONE

The church started looking less like it had been abandoned. The skip on the road was filled with old timber, broken glass panes and smashed pieces of slate. Inside, it was empty. Paul stood near the east end of the building sizing up a large oak crucifix that hung on the wall. It was firmly fixed in place, but after some experimentation, he realised that it could be moved by pushing up from directly underneath. It was heavy, but he managed to lift it away from the hooks on the wall and it toppled onto the stone floor making a loud clattering sound that echoed across the empty building. It was around six or seven feet in length and four feet or so across, but Paul was able to lift it up onto his shoulders and pull it out into the gardens. As he dragged it across the grass, he left a deep furrow behind him. He continued along the path and through the gate, past the skip and down the road. Paul realised the potential spectacle it would present to anyone he passed but the timber was too good to throw away when it could be put to good use.

In the beach car park, he rested the crucifix against the wall so that he could catch his breath. He rubbed his shoulders and rotated his neck. A couple walking on the beach stopped and peered at him. The man said something and the woman laughed.

Slightly refreshed, Paul lifted the heavy end again and walked up the hill that curved around to the guest house. As he approached the gate at the side of the house, Gwilym came out. He was dressed in his standard light-blue shirt, burgundy cardigan, and navy-blue trousers.

"Thank goodness, our Lord and Saviour has returned." He had a wide smile on his face. Paul nodded – out of breath – before dropping the crucifix on the floor so that he could open the side gate to the backyard.

"Is Ben inside?" he asked.

"He and Sarah have gone for a walk along the river." Gwilym came down the steps and examined the crucifix. "I don't think we have room for this in the house."

"It's not for the house. I'm going to cut it and use it to replace that rotting post in the fence so we can finally fix that hole."

"We're using this old thing for that?"

"Yes, it's perfect. It's some of the best wood you can find for this type of job. It has so much lacquer on it that it will probably outlast the rest of the fence. It even matches the appearance."

"Yes, of course."

Gwilym crouched down and ran his fingers along the crucifix; his smile dropped.

"I remember going to that church for Christmas services as a child and it always fascinated me to see this old piece of wood hanging on the wall. Such a simple shape, yet a symbol with huge significance."

"A symbol of lies and control," Paul said.

"Yes, that was the ultimate truth of it, I suppose, although I'm not sure it was always the intention." Gwilym straightened his back and sighed. "It'll be good to turn that old building into something worthwhile."

Paul nodded then lifted the crucifix and took it through the gates into the yard before returning to Gwilym.

"Are you going back up there now?" Gwilym asked.

"Yes. I can't do much here. All the tools are at the church."

"Then if you don't mind, I'll come with you for a walk?"

"Of course."

The old man went into the house and came back out wearing a coat and a flat cap.

"How much more work is there left to do?" Gwilym asked as they strode along side by side.

"Quite a bit really. I've finished clearing out the inside. This afternoon I'm expecting a slate delivery that will allow me to finish off the roof repairs. That should stop the rain getting in. Later this week, the new windows will be arriving. Then there are the doors that need replacing and the wiring will need to be sorted before we do the plastering and painting. And don't get me started on the flooring."

"What about the furniture?"

"Early next week."

"And we'll have everything we need to run the meetings?"

"Should do."

"That's good. I've already started planning. I want our meetings to be welcome events where people can come together to celebrate the good in life, share experiences and learn."

Paul nodded and they started up the hill.

"You and my daughter have become quite close, haven't you?"

"She has been very kind to me. I guess we've become good friends."

"Just friends? You know as well as I that she wants more."

Paul bit his lip.

"Don't worry. I have no intention of interfering. For what it's worth I think you're a good man. But I do suspect there are many layers and complexities to you and that you – like many of us – are trying hard to make sense of these very strange times we are living in."

Gwilym stopped and grabbed Paul's arm.

"All that I ask is that you be mindful of Sarah in this situation. She lived and suffered with a very difficult and troubled man for many years. Another man of layers and complexities who found himself in a situation that he was unable to escape from. My daughter persisted with that relationship for far longer than was good for either of them and it took its toll."

They stood quietly and stared out across the fields at the sea.

"Despite how grateful you may be to Sarah for her support since you arrived here, do please be honest with her about your feelings, whatever they may be. It will serve you both better at the end of it all."

Paul's gaze dropped and he nodded.

They carried on to the top of the hill and in through the church garden gates. They entered the building and Paul showed Gwilym the progress he had made so far.

"Thank you, Paul, for doing this." Gwilym looked around at the empty building. "I think this place will be important for us going forwards. Somewhere where people can flourish. Not dwell on our sins or place our hopes on the doctrines and dogma of texts written millennia ago, but to recognise the honest goodness in humanity, and build bridges from our fears to reason, humility, kindness and, ultimately, other people."

Paul acknowledged Gwilym's words with a nod and a benign smile.

"When do you think you'll be finished?" Gwilym asked.

"In two weeks or so. I'm waiting on some deliveries, so we need everything to come on time."

"Two weeks, you say? Right then, I better get back to the house. There's work to be done. Perhaps I will see you back there for dinner afterwards?"

"Maybe. If the delivery comes this afternoon, then I want to get the roofing done before the end of the day so that we stop the flooding that happens every time it rains."

Gwilym said goodbye and left Paul to his work.

Paul checked his phone. It was now quarter past two and there was still no sign of the delivery from the roofing company. He popped the phone in his pocket and made sure it was on the loud setting so that he could hear it, should they get lost on their way and need to call. He walked outside and decided to go up on the roof and see if there was anything further that could be done in preparation. He climbed the ladder attached to the scaffold. He always enjoyed reaching the top. The view in each direction up and down the coastline was spectacular.

He crawled along re-examining locations where broken or damaged slates had already been removed. He checked other sections, pushing and pulling on slates trying to identify any other weak points. The current roof was over eighty years old. As he manoeuvred his way around, he was careful to ensure his footing was stable.

As he examined one corner of the roof, he heard his phone ring. *Finally*, he thought.

"Hello? Have you got the slates?"

A woman's voice replied. "Sorry, slates? Is that Paul?"

Paul stopped what he was doing. "Yes, this is Paul."

"Paul, this is Margaret Roberts."

"Sorry, who?"

"Margaret Roberts," she said again. "You came to visit me a few weeks ago. I was Katherine's mother."

"Sorry, who are you?"

"Kat's mother."

Paul's stomach sank. "Oh no." He paused. "They found her, didn't they?"

"Yes, they found her. Her body had travelled quite far out to sea and was discovered on the other side of Caernarfon."

Body. He didn't know what to say. "I'm really sorry for your loss."

"Thank you, Paul."

"Poor girl."

There was a sigh at the other end of the phone.

"Yes, but it was her own choice. She always made decisions without much regard for others."

Paul's hand trembled as it held the phone. He bit his lip before speaking.

"When is the funeral?"

"Oh, I'm sorry. That was last week. I came upon the piece of paper with your number on it when I was cleaning before.

It was down the side of the chair where you sat when you visited. I remember thinking that you seemed like a nice man so I thought I would call you."

Paul put his hand to his forehead.

"Well, thank you for calling. I hope you can find peace with what happened. She was a good child."

"Thank you, Paul. All the best to you also."

She hung up and Paul immediately leant over the side of the roof and threw up. He sat up and panted as the retching stopped. He needed to lie down. When he turned, he saw that Eve was crouched in front of him looking him straight in the eyes. Paul felt her hands push against his chest and he fell from the roof.

The next moment he was sat in the living room of his mother's house in Salford. She was in the chair opposite him facing the television. This was not the room as it had been in recent times; this was as it was decades ago.

"Mum, I need to tell you something."

"Not now, you know this is when I need to be left alone to watch my programmes."

"Mum, listen to me. It's important."

"For goodness' sake." His mother got up and walked over to the television to turn down the volume. "What is it?"

"I'm leaving."

She sat back down in her chair, her face ashen.

"What do you mean, you're leaving?"

"I'm leaving. I've joined the army and I'll be going on basic training at the end of the summer."

She cackled. "You, join the army?"

"It's a good opportunity. Lots of things I can learn and get experience from."

"You won't last a minute there. You're weak, just like your father. It's just an excuse to leave me, isn't it?"

"No, of course not. There are no opportunities around here. At least in the army, I'll learn to do something useful. Here, I'll be nothing."

"Here, you'll be with your mother – your only family. Your father did nothing for you. He left when you were young. I was the one to keep you in clothes, food, and schooling. And now you're going to repay me by doing what – leaving at the time when I need you the most, as I get old, and need your support?"

"Mum, I'll earn decent money in the army. And after a few years of service, I'll get a good job and I can move on and do something else."

She took her time to respond, slowly examining his face.

"Wait," she said. "There's more, isn't there? Where does your little Jezebel fit into this plan? Surely you're not going to leave her here alone while you go off to play soldier boy?"

"I was coming to that. Eve and I are engaged. We want to get married as soon as we can."

"Boy, you're sixteen years old – you know nothing. Your father and I were married when we were sixteen and look at what happened there."

Paul's awareness grew. He knew he was watching this scene play out like an old repeat on the television. He knew every word was set in stone and every movement pre-recorded, but observation did not make it painless. Immersion made it feel very real.

"Mum, whatever mistakes you and Dad made were yours."

"Mistakes? We loved each other and things were good until you came. When you arrived, it became too much for your father. That is when he left us. He left because of you. And now you're going to leave me alone as well."

"I'm leaving because I have to find my path. I think I can do well in the army. For a few years at least. And then, when I return, Eve and I will get a house together."

"You're ready to spend the rest of your life with this girl after a few months of teenage love?"

"It's not like that – it's serious. We're ready for this."

His mother laughed. "My dear boy, you're as stupid and naïve as your father."

She turned away from him. "God does not look fondly on those who abandon their loved ones. Leaving for the army is one stupid thing but leaving and betraying me for that empty-headed harlot is treachery."

Paul stood up but his mother remained seated.

"How dare you say that about her."

His mother's expression became serious, and she put her hands over her eyes. She seemed to be crying.

"You're such a…" He stopped. "For fuck's sake," he yelled, before kneeling next to her.

"Mum, it's alright. I'm doing the right thing for all of us. I know I am. Please don't be upset. I'm not leaving you because I want to. I need to find my way in life – for me and Eve and the family we want in the future. There's nothing here for me that I'm good at. I need to try and get away and do something different."

His mother began sobbing.

"You're leaving me, Paul. I haven't done enough for you to stay. Your father left because of you and I always tried to defend you from it, but that was the reality. It's alright, I respect what you need to do. I just wasn't good enough to fill the hole your father left."

"Mum, you did all that you could – an amazing job, in fact. But this isn't about that. This is about me taking the next steps in my life. This is about me stretching my wings and flying from the nest. It's the natural progression in any family."

Paul's mother lifted her head; her eyes were red and filled with tears.

"Just go, Paul. Go and do what you need to. Leave me. I did all I could for you after your father left. It just wasn't enough. Go with your lady friend. See where it takes you. See how faithful she is when you're away. See how happy you are when you're away. Go my son, go. See where life takes you and how you are judged by God."

Paul patted his mother on her arm then got to his feet. He turned away from her and she started calling after him. He walked out of the room and then out of the house. But somehow, he still heard her call his name. He felt like an invisible cord kept him tethered to her. It took all his strength to get away. Outside, he turned back and took one more look at his house before finally feeling like he was free. But he never was truly free.

*

The scene faded and Paul felt pain throughout his body. He was on his back in the church gardens of Llanffug again.

"Mate, are you okay?" A big pale face was looking down at him. Paul raised his head and then sat up.

"Er – yes, thanks. Think I took a funny turn."

"You want me to call an ambulance?"

Paul slowly stood up feeling quite a bit of soreness around his back.

"No, I'll be fine. Sorry, who are you?"

"Just dropping off the slates for your project here. You're Paul, aren't you? Sorry for the delay. We're a bit short-staffed today."

"Yeah, okay. Just leave them there, please."

As the delivery man drove away, Paul glanced at the clock on his phone. It was just after half four. He stepped over to the slates, placed a few under his arm and climbed the ladder. He felt twinges of pain in his back but tried to shake it off. When he got to the roof, he looked around and cleared his throat. "You keep trying but I won't let you stop me." He lifted his head to the sky and roared in defiance.

TWENTY-TWO

Paul had put up posters all around Llanffug – on lamp posts, at the entrance of the Pilgrim Inn, in the window of the butcher's shop, and at the two bus shelters on either end of the village. As he pinned the last copy onto the community noticeboard next to the public toilets on the High Street, he stopped and read the text one last time.

Confused by recent events? The Llanffug Community Truth and Trust Coalition invites you to a weekly meeting to learn more about the Revelation and what it means to our lives. Join us for an honest and open discussion in a safe and friendly environment. Share in the experiences of others so that we can adapt to this new normal together! One and all are welcome. Sundays, 6pm at the Community House.

When he got back to the guesthouse, he could hear Gwilym upstairs in his bedroom practising his oration.

"He's been at it all day." Sarah walked into the living room followed by Ben. She carried a bottle of red wine in her hand and had a dishcloth hanging over her shoulder.

"He's taking it very seriously." Paul reached down and stroked the old dog.

"I'm not sure what he's expecting," Sarah said. "Even with all those posters up, will people really want to spend an hour each week talking about this stuff?"

"There was a bit of interest from passers-by."

"Of course, the whole thing is a bit out there, isn't it?"

Paul studied her and scratched the side of his jaw.

"You're getting very worked up about this meeting."

"Not as much as Dad is."

"Does it bother you?"

"Dad woke up from that state saying all sorts. It inspired him to plan out these meetings and set up the group. He believes he's on a mission to save people."

"What's wrong with that?"

"I just…" She paused. "I don't want to see him disappointed."

"He's a grown man."

"He's an elderly man who's been through a traumatic event. He should be taking it easy – not working himself up into a frenzy like this."

"I think you underestimate your father. He's passionate about what he's doing."

"It just worries me that he's setting himself up for a fall. What if this thing fails? What if I lose him again?"

"You won't, Sarah *bach*." Gwilym walked into the room from the hallway. He had a big smile on his face. He put his hand on his daughter's shoulder.

"I'm not leaving you again. This is just something I have to do."

Sarah's eyes moved between the two men. She handed

her father the bottle of wine and sighed.

"Dinner will be half an hour." She turned on her heels and left.

Gwilym examined the bottle and a look of disappointment fell on his face.

"I'll never get used to screw-cap bottles."

He went over to the sideboard, picked up a glass and then walked over to his seat near the window. There was now a second chair next to Gwilym's, where Paul would join him. Gwilym poured himself a large glass of red and placed it on the windowsill. Paul sat down next to him.

"Are you ready for tomorrow's meeting?" Paul asked.

"As ready as I ever will be."

"So, what's the plan?"

With a wide grin on his face, he turned to face Paul.

"You know I won't spoil the surprise."

Paul smiled and nodded.

"Not even a taster?"

"Let me tell you one thing. What I want people to think about is that the Revelation was a gift."

"A gift?"

"A gift. A second chance to reassess priorities. The clarity that your time is all you have is the greatest gift anyone could ever receive. It puts you in absolute control. Without higher power, your fate and destiny are in your own hands. That is true freedom." He reached for his glass and took a long sip.

"That is still something I struggle with."

Gwilym narrowed his eyes. "Even after the Revelation?"

"The Lord preserves all who love him…"

"…but all the wicked he will destroy." Gwilym finished the sentence.

"Those words hung in a frame near our dinner table. I was four when Dad left us. Mum said he left because of me. Because of my wicked behaviour. Those words haunted me. I was to blame for him leaving and as such I would always be a bad person in God's eyes. I could never be good."

"Ah, indoctrination – a staple of so many religions. This belief stayed with you?"

"It faded over time. But after I served in Belfast, it came back. Stronger."

Gwilym leaned forward in his chair and clasped his hands on his lap. Paul could almost feel the old man's gaze on his skin.

"Paul, you've mentioned Belfast a few times these last few nights. Is there something you'd like to talk about?"

Paul rubbed his hands together like he was washing them under a tap.

"Yes, I think there is. But it's hard for me to tell you. Not many know what really happened there."

"I will not pressure you, but it might help to share your experience."

Paul nodded his head slowly up and down. He sighed and looked to the ground – his hands were knotted into fists that pushed down on his thighs.

"There was a pub near the base called The Duke of York. We went there every Friday night. It was run by an old protestant couple so was friendly for Brits. One night in July of eighty-seven, me and the boys headed over as usual. It'd been a really tense week with Orange Order parades."

His mouth felt dry, and he reached for his glass of water.

"When we got to the pub, the doors were locked, and the lights were off. Around the back we found the landlord talking to a plumber. Seems a broken pipe in the toilet had flooded most of the place.

"Some of the lads decided to go drink beers in the mess hall, but I was keen to find somewhere else. The others were uncertain, so I suggested we flip a coin. I said that fate would choose how our night would go. They agreed. Heads, we would go back to the barracks. Tails, we would carry on and find another pub. It landed on tails and off we went. Being young and cocky, we didn't pay much attention to the warnings and we found a busy pub near Falls Road."

"The Catholic area?"

Paul nodded.

"After a few beers, I went to call my wife. I did it every Friday night. The payphone in the pub was broken so I used the phone box across the road. It was the usual type of call. Love you, miss you. You're drunk, let me watch my programme."

Paul stopped smiling and he felt his cheeks drop.

"I was so focused that I hadn't realised the pub was emptying. I put the phone down and dashed back. I couldn't see my friends in the crowd. An old man grabbed my arm. He didn't say anything. He just gave me this strange, sad look and shook his head. I pulled away and pushed past him. I made my way around the side of the building. Through the window I saw all three of them on their knees in front of the bar with their hands behind their heads."

Gwilym put his hand to his mouth.

"Around them were five armed men in ski masks. One was talking and pacing like he was delivering a speech. Another one glanced towards the window and saw me. And I…"

Paul exhaled and looked out at the sea.

"...I ran away, as fast as I could, back to the base where I told a guard what had happened. Troops were sent out straight away, but it was too late. The place was empty, apart from the landlord – who they found unconscious."

"And what happened to your friends?"

"Two of them were found in a field near the South Armagh border. Both had been shot in the head. The third – Jimmy – as far as I'm aware, he was never found."

Both sat in silence. Gwilym reached over and put his hand on Paul's arm.

"Oh Paul. Those poor boys."

Gwilym reached for his glass and quaffed the wine. Paul sat silently stroking his cheeks.

"What happened then? You weren't in the army for very long after that, were you?"

"No, I couldn't live with myself. Got into all sorts of trouble and a year later they kicked me out. Back home, I lost all passion as a husband and struggled to keep a job. My path into the darkness was set."

Gwilym swirled the wine in his glass around.

"Do you still feel like the universe has it in for you?"

"I'm in control of my own destiny, right?" Paul pursed his lips and blew.

Something dropped to the floor behind the two and Paul turned to see Sarah stood by the dining table. She had her arms crossed and had her hand over her mouth.

*

The clock chimed as it reached six. Paul turned his head to see a handful of familiar faces from the village. Earlier in the day, he had laid out a hundred and twenty plastic seats. In rows of twelve they comfortably filled the Community House. The number of attendees – however – didn't even fill one row. He made eye contact with Sarah – who sat almost directly behind him. She refused to sit in the front row, but Paul insisted he should in case Gwilym needed help. Next to Paul was Jerry, who Paul knew was to play some role in the meeting.

Gwilym stood at the front, waiting. He shuffled his papers on the podium and looked up. Paul could see his eyes darting around the room. He straightened his tie and bit his lower lip. Paul scanned the inside of the building. The white paint – barely dry – looked good on the rough stone of the walls. The remaining stained glass that he was able to salvage in the west-wall window projected coloured lights onto the stone slabs of the floor. The rest of the windows had to be replaced – most of the glass having been smashed and the surrounding wooden frames had become rotten. All the chairs faced the east wall and the space where the altar used to occupy. The large crucifix was long gone and the wall would now be used as a screen for the projector, which sat on a small table with a laptop next to the podium. In the corner, an acoustic guitar stood on a stand. While on the outside, the building and its proximity to a graveyard still made it look like a church, on the inside it was a comfortable community space. All remaining evidence of its previous history had been removed to create a simple, functional area.

Gwilym cleared his throat.

"Let's get started. Welcome, everyone. I hope you've all managed to find a seat."

Jerry tittered.

"Why are we here, you ask? Let me begin by telling you about myself. I am seventy-six years old. Before the Revelation I was a passionate advocate for my faith. It gave me strength and hope." He walked around the podium and tapped it with his left hand. "The Revelation hit me hard. It left me fearful about my own life and my own existence. It made me realise that I would never see my Angharad again and that one day in the future there would come a time when I wouldn't be around for my daughter. How much time I have left in my existence is an answer I do not have but I do intend to spend my remaining days – not fearful about non-existence – but thankful for my life. I want to help others to see things the way I do.

"Here we are, just over two months into a new world. For many, adjusting to the way of things after the Revelation has been hard. But as the dust continues to settle following the events of February tenth, we can start to see this Revelation as what it really is – a gift. We can begin to see that we have lived our lives like scared children unable to see the realities of our existence. We've speculated about what lies in the shadows, the monsters under our bed and ghosts in the wardrobe. The gift of the Revelation is a shining light that enables us to see that there are no monsters or ghosts hiding away – we are in this room alone. I say alone, but we are of course not alone. We have each other."

Paul looked around at those few individuals in the Community House that day and saw smiles.

"Now, we have come together as a community to make this old place usable again and set up this group to run these meetings each week. But let me tell you what I want to achieve. I want these meetings to be a platform for our community to come together. Now I know there are some who want to demonise religions and hold them to account for what they did to humans over thousands of years. I don't want to do that. What is done is done and rather than focus on the past, what I think is most important is that we move forward, as a people, together. There are big questions – many of which in the past were plugged up by religious belief and faith but now are like open, gaping wounds. I want us to look at those questions and try and find an answer based on our new rational view of the world and ourselves. These answers won't be simple, easy solutions like those offered by faith. We cannot excuse this life because we'll have a better existence in the next; this is all we have.

"What I can bring to the discussion is the perspective of thinkers who pondered many of the big questions thousands of years ago. I taught and researched philosophy for many years before I retired."

He lifted his hands up into the air. "Don't worry though, these meetings won't be just an old man lecturing about thinkers from the ancient world. They'll be a celebration of life – the good stuff that makes us laugh and cry. We'll talk about art and science. We'll explore the human mind and what makes us tick. We'll examine the impact of the Revelation and consider how some beliefs may be more difficult to shed – even after the passing of faith." Gwilym glanced over at Paul.

"Right, after that hefty intro, let's have some music, shall we? Jerry – our resident rock star – will lead us all in a singsong. I think we're going to start with a Bob Dylan song. Jerry?"

"That's right, Gwil."

Jerry strode over to the guitar in the corner of the room. Paul turned and gave Sarah a look. He raised his eyebrows; she nodded and shrugged. It was a good start.

TWENTY-THREE

Over the following month, the number of attendees grew each Sunday. Gwilym continued to lead discussions – interspersed with the very popular musical interludes by Jerry and invited guests with a mixture of backgrounds. During the second meeting, a retired astronomy lecturer spoke about the universe. In the third meeting, a psychiatrist from Conwy discussed mental health challenges in the wake of the Revelation. The week after, a local artist did a presentation on modern art. The topics and themes for each meeting were varied. Every session was planned by Gwilym in detail, and he drew on his academic knowledge and deep fascination with the bigger questions.

By the fifth meeting, on a balmy evening in late May, nearly three quarters of the chairs in the Community House were occupied. After the meeting, Sarah and Paul sat on the wall of the church gardens and watched as the attendees emptied the Community House and were greeted by Gwilym. Paul wore a short-sleeve shirt and Sarah a summer dress.

"Even more this week. We'll have a full house soon," Sarah said.

"Your dad really connects with people."

"He was born for this kind of role."

They both watched as Manon from the community council approached Gwilym and embraced him. Then she broke down in his arms and started sobbing.

"Manon objected to these meetings at first and now look at her," Sarah said.

"I'd say she's a convert."

"It's crazy."

"Incredible is what it is," Paul said. "He's touching people on a very deep level."

"You've clearly drunk the Kool-Aid." Sarah smiled at Paul.

"You really don't see what's happening here?"

"I see my dad playing the charmer. That's always been a skill of his."

Paul dropped his hands to his sides. "Are you kidding? Look at the people attending and how they react to his words."

A noise from behind distracted Paul and he looked to the hedge on the other side of the road. There was someone there. As he gazed, he could see the person had a device in their hands. They were filming.

"That little shit," Paul said, baring his teeth.

"What?" Sarah said, watching as he jogged across the road.

The person made a run for it down the hill on the other side of the hedge. Paul followed along on the road until he saw a gap in the hedgerow that was only filled by a fence.

He climbed over and leapt into the field. It was Bob and he was ahead by a minute or so, but he was a stocky man and Paul fancied his chances. The ground was dry, which meant his footing was firm and he was able to run faster. He wore an old pair of Gwilym's shoes, which had become worn over the years and lacked any grip underneath. Nonetheless, he was running downhill and picking up pace. Bob reached the bottom and started crossing a kissing gate that took him into another field. This one was full of sheep and as he entered, scores of the creatures scattered in all directions.

Paul reached the gate and could see that Bob was slowing down. He'd soon catch him if he kept up this pace. Where was he going? His car must be parked somewhere in the village. Bob's house was a couple of miles outside, and he came and went in an old Ford Cortina. He'd probably parked it in the beach car park. That is where would make most sense. Leave the car there then sneak up to the Community House through the fields.

As he got closer to the hedgerow at the end, Bob began to slow considerably. Paul's lungs were on fire, but the fury pushed him through the pain. When he caught up with Bob, the chubby man was barely jogging. Paul flew into him and knocked him to the ground. Bob's glasses went flying from his face and he tried to crawl away, but Paul leapt on top of him and started hitting him with closed fists.

"No, please," Bob pleaded and tried to shield his face from the barrage of punches. Paul's knuckles cycled against the man's head. He shrieked as left, right, left, right, he swung at Bob's skull until his fists were raw. His tired arms continued as blood streamed across the swollen, cut face of the man and his protests became mumbled slurs.

A seagull landed directly in Paul's line of vision. No more than five yards away, it stood on the grass staring at him. Paul and the bird made eye contact and he stopped. Panting, he leant back, looked at Bob and then examined the back of his hands.

"Don't film us," he said.

"What the hell's wrong with you?" Bob spat the words from the side of his mouth like it was the only part he could move.

Paul stood up and shook out his hands.

"Leave us alone."

Bob sat up slowly. He groaned and wiped bloody dribble from his chin.

"You're sick." He coughed and rubbed his arm against his mouth.

As Paul stood, the bird flew up and his eyes followed it across the sky. He turned away from Bob and shuffled towards the gate at the corner of the field. His knuckles ached but he felt calm. The bird called out as it flew, and Paul let out a huge breath.

"You'll regret what you did," Bob said. "The External Force gave us the Revelation. You and your people, you're blocking progress. The External Force won't stand for it. We won't stand for it."

Paul reached the gate and rested both arms on it. Before he began to climb, he turned back to look at Bob. Bob now had his glasses back on his battered face. His eyes widened and mouth opened when Paul turned, like a child who'd been poking a beehive only to be surprised when the bees were released.

"We'll see," Paul said.

Sarah came over with a bag of frozen peas.

"Put this on your hands. It'll help with the swelling."

Paul abided by the direction. The cold felt good against his swollen hands.

"Where's your dad?"

"He went to the pub after the meeting. Good thing really – he wouldn't be happy about this. I can't believe Bob attacked you."

Paul bit his lip. "I must have startled him. He'll think twice about doing that in future."

"Where did he hit you?"

"He caught me a couple of times on the side of the head."

"It looks like you got some punches in."

"One or two."

"It's odd that he was filming." Sarah looked away and stroked her hair.

"I don't think it's anything to worry about."

"I'm not worried. Not about him, anyway. But who's he sharing these videos with?"

"More of his odd friends?" He forced a smile. "Doesn't matter, anyway. He won't be back in a hurry. And if he does then I'll be waiting for him."

Sarah narrowed her eyes.

"You'll be waiting for him? What are you – our head of security now?"

"I just don't want you to worry." Paul sat up and puffed out his chest. "I'll make sure we're safe."

"Okay, fine." Sarah shrugged and walked away.

"Look," she said, "I need to talk to you about something

else." She went over into the office and then returned with a piece of paper in her hand.

"What?" Paul asked.

"Your last cheque bounced."

"Ah okay, I'd been expecting that."

"You could have just told me."

"It's not an easy conversation." Paul rubbed his eyes and then looked directly at Sarah. "I'm skint."

"You have nothing?"

Paul shook his head.

"No savings?"

"I have my mother's old house. But that's it."

Sarah paced around the room.

"What was your plan? To stay here until you ran out of money?"

"I didn't have a plan."

"But you did all that work on the church for free."

"I'm glad I could."

Sarah stopped in front of Paul and placed her hands on her hips.

"You know you could do more of that type of work here around the village. People have seen what you can do. Getting work wouldn't be difficult."

"And what about paying you?"

Sarah sat down in the chair opposite Paul and leant over.

"You could do the same here. You could do all the maintenance and help with the cleaning. In return I give you bed and board."

"I wouldn't want to put you out."

"No, it could work well. I need all the help I can get –

especially as the summer season starts." She put her hand on his knee.

"We'd need to downsize your room though. I think we'd need to save the master suite for paying customers."

"And I'd be in the broom cupboard?"

"I was thinking you could share Ben's kennel." Sarah grinned. Paul rubbed his aching knuckles.

TWENTY-FOUR

Paul found himself somewhere he hadn't seen for a while – the Duke of York pub in Belfast. The place was full. Many of the faces he recognised from the barracks. He was there but he wasn't. He was an observer. No one paid any attention to him and he paid no attention to them. He couldn't – the chatter that surrounded him was like a wall of noise. The people weren't real; they were shadows like silhouettes behind frosted glass. They were ghosts. He sat at a round table with two friends he knew less intimately. The others he had lost a few weeks earlier – taken away and executed by a paramilitary group. Things had returned to normal now. Only they hadn't, and they would never be normal again. He was back in the pub and enjoying a drink with these two other lads from his company. The ghosts paid no attention to Paul apart from one. He was a tall Welsh lad from the valleys called Powell. He didn't appear like a shadow. He was solid and real, and he gazed at Paul as he tried to drink his pint. Paul got up and walked over to Powell.

"Why are you staring at me?" The words coming from Paul's mouth emerged in slow motion; slurred and deep.

"Cos I'm wondering what it feels like," Powell said.

"How what feels like?"

"To have allowed your brothers to die."

Paul looked at the ghosts around him. They paid him no attention, yet this tall man was staring straight at him and he was growing. He was now a giant and his gaze was trying to break through Paul's skull and into his brain. He wanted more than to be told how it felt – he wanted to see the thoughts reflected in Paul's mind.

"You ran away like a coward and left them to be murdered. How does that feel?" Powell turned his head from side to side as though trying to find a better vantage point. He was looking for vulnerability.

"Imagine what their final moments were like. Crying and pleading for their lives. How does it feel to know you left them to that?"

Paul looked down and felt something hard inside his clenched hand. He opened it and saw a pebble resting on his palm. In the other was a leather sling.

"One of them was never found. Jimmy was your favourite, and he just disappeared. How does it feel to know that?"

Powell's voice echoed over the chatter and Paul stared at him. His tone was full of mocking judgement and derision. Paul placed the pebble in the sling and swung it around his head. It grew in speed until it moved like a helicopter rotor. He released the sling and the pebble crashed into Powell's head. The giant fell to the ground like a huge, felled tree. When he struck the ground, Paul leapt onto him and started hitting him in his face with his bloody and bruised fists. He stepped up onto the giant's face and pummelled him with all the violence he could muster. He broke through the skin and opened a dark hole. He continued to hit the man and pieces of his face shattered into the hole. Paul lost his footing and fell into it himself. He tumbled and spun in the cold darkness of space and screamed until he was awake and back in his single bed in the guest house. His sheets were soaked, and he was panting.

He looked around the small room and got up out of his bed. He opened the curtains and looked out across the fields. He missed the view of the bay but reminded himself that he was lucky to have a place to stay. A shadow in the corner of the room caught his eye and he thought he saw someone. No one was there, yet he heard her voice.

"Belfast again?" Eve whispered, like she was stood behind him speaking into his ear. "You've been back almost every night since you beat the shit out of that fat pig."

He turned expecting to see someone there, but he was alone.

"Time to visit the church – sorry, the Community House – now, isn't it?"

She was right. He would get dressed and go check on the Community House. He needed to know it was safe.

*

The skies were clear and countless specks of glimmering light hung in the darkness. Night was a pleasant time to venture out. There was no one around and the village was silent. The sea was invisible in the darkness and were it not for the crashing of the waves, it would be easy to forget that it was there at all. Paul did not, however, feel completely alone.

"Made you feel vulnerable, didn't he? The fat oaf."

Paul shook his head and tried to ignore her.

"Scared enough to visit this place most nights. What are you expecting – to find it all ablaze?"

"I just need to make sure it's all secure," Paul said.

"I thought you weren't speaking to me."

"Show yourself and I'll speak to you."

"You know I can't do that. I need a bit more from you to really show myself. You're suffering – I know – but not enough for my needs."

"Then shut the hell up."

The silence and darkness continued at the gates to the Community House gardens. Paul's tired eyes stared across at the grounds and then he turned his head to look at Bob's usual hiding spot behind the hedge.

"See? Everything's fine."

Paul followed the path to the building and pushed on the door to check it was still locked. He walked around the side and peered through the window.

"Just you and me here."

"Just me," Paul said.

He walked over to the wall near the cliff and sat down on the soft, mossy grass.

"So, now what? You stay here until dawn… again?"

"I'll rest here for a bit."

Paul closed his eyes and he thought about the Duke of York pub. He remembered the heat of the room, the stink of sweat and cigarettes, and the cacophony of off-duty soldiers trying to engage in R&R.

"This was your dream tonight." Eve's voice was loud and prominent like the narrator of a story. "This is always a favourite."

Paul sat at a small round table with Chris and Wormsley. Three beer-filled pint glasses rested on the table.

"These were the only two who would speak to you after what happened. The rest of them treated you like scum."

The pub was full of squaddies and the odd officer. He knew Powell from his early days in basic training. They were now stationed together.

"Big guy. What were you thinking?"

"He kept looking at me."

Powell stood near the bar with a bunch of other lads from the company. He had a long flat nose and heavy brows that gave him the look of a caveman. Paul examined everyone in the room and peered at where each person's eyes were directed.

"Seems to me you were looking for a fight."

"I wasn't. I thought they were all talking about me. Like they were judging me for what happened."

Paul made eye contact with a moustached man near the window.

"What?" Paul called out. "Are you looking for something, mate?"

"Leave it, Paul," Chris said. "He's not after anything."

"Maybe you've had enough, eh, Paul?" Wormsley said.

"I'm still standing, aren't I? You'll know when I've had enough because I won't be."

"Where did this Paul go?" Eve said. "He had so much spirit."

"He had so much rage."

Near the bar, Powell's head fell back, and he bellowed with laughter. Then as he turned his head, he glanced over at Paul and their eyes connected.

"That's it." Paul got up and rushed over to the tall man, launching his pint glass at the man's face. Powell yelped and staggered backwards with his head in his hands.

"Don't you fucking judge me." Paul thrust his knuckles into the man's gut and then did the same again and again, until someone behind him pulled him away. Hands pulled on his shoulders and his waist. Voices around him urged him to stop. Someone landed a punch near his ear. He turned his head and then the next landed on his cheekbone.

"He's mine." Powell grabbed him by the front of his shirt and Paul turned to see the bloodshot whites of the big man's eyes. His face was covered in blood, but he could see clearly enough to direct his huge fist into Paul's jaw – knocking him to the floor and into darkness. He opened his eyes and he saw the church gardens around him. His night vision was somewhat enhanced, and he could see the shapes of the gravestones in more detail.

"So that's what dishonourable discharge looks like?" Eve said.

"It was the last straw."

"You picked a fight with a man twice your size. How stupid were you?"

Paul looked around again, expecting to see someone there.

"No more stupid than I am now. But I was desperate."

"Desperate to have the shit kicked out of you?"

"For relief. For quiet. For peace. I believed it was all my fault and I couldn't cope."

"Believed? It was your fault."

"Maybe it wasn't. Shit happens."

Paul got up and looked to the east where a thin strip of

light was growing on the horizon. He walked over to the Community House building and lay his hands on the wall.

"Enough," he said. "I'm done here." Paul turned and left.

His walk back to the guest house was quiet. When he got in, Sarah was stood in the kitchen wearing a dressing gown and sipping a cup of coffee. She gave him a smile and nodded to the pot on the side.

"Couldn't sleep again?" she asked.

"I woke up and there was no going back," Paul said.

"You went for a walk?"

"Yeah."

"You really need a break from that place, Paul."

"Yeah, well I…"

"Actually, I may have the medicine you need. Jerry's arranged a boat trip for Saturday, and we're all invited."

"A boat trip?"

"They're informally known as Jerry's booze cruises. They're a blast."

Paul sipped on the black bitter coffee and licked his lips.

"Do you some good to let your hair down."

"Let my hair down," Paul said. "Yeah, maybe."

TWENTY-FIVE

It was a bright Saturday morning in June and Paul, Sarah and Gwilym were on their way to the harbour to board Jerry's fishing boat for a trip along the coast.

"I did tell you why it's called Jerry's booze cruise, didn't I?" Sarah wore sunglasses and a garland around her neck.

"I kind of guessed," Paul said.

"Don't scare the man," Gwilym said. "They're good fun. You'll get to see the place from a different perspective."

"Why the rule about no phones?" Paul said.

"He likes to make sure the trips are uninterrupted. That everyone is present in the here and now – not distracted by the wider world."

"Right."

"His boat. His rules."

At the harbour they found Jerry loading his boat from the pier. He walked up and down a stone stairwell. The boat had been moved from its usual position – further in the enclave where it was protected from storms during the winter months. The boat was all white – apart from a blue strip that marked the lower half of the hull. In a bold, black fancy font, at the front of the boat, the name *Patrick* was written.

As they got closer, Jerry came up the steps.

"Ahoy there, maties." He wore a captain's hat and saluted the three.

"Nice day for it," Sarah said.

"Forecast looking grim later," Jerry said. "But I reckon we should have a nice few hours out on the water before the storm comes."

"Need any help?" Paul asked.

"Think we have everything now," Jerry said. "Get yourself comfy on board."

Down the steps they saw Dave sprawled on the seats at the back of the boat next to Patrick. He had a can of beer in his hand, and Patrick had a plastic glass half filled with wine. Out of the cabin came Jess and Jane – each holding a drink. Paul turned to Jerry who was on his way down behind him huffing and puffing with a box on his shoulder. "Quite a mixed crowd today."

"A special group for a special celebration," Jerry said.

Jerry instructed everyone to find a seat and ensure they had a drink in hand. Paul looked around and realised he was the only one with a soft drink.

"Before we set off," he said, "I wanted to raise a glass and celebrate the recent successes of the Truth and Trust Coalition. Our meetings have grown from strength to strength. Last week we had a full house for the first time. Tomorrow we've got a news crew from the IBC News Channel coming to do a report on our meetings."

There were looks at each other and a few raised glasses. Paul glanced over at Gwilym who for once didn't have much to say. He sat in the corner grinning like a Cheshire cat.

"Everyone here today has played their part, so I say congratulations to you all and thank you for doing something so worthwhile."

There were smiles and laughter all around. Paul made eye contact with Jess and immediately looked down.

The boat set off – Jerry the skipper with beer in hand guiding his vessel firstly out of the harbour and then down the centre of the bay and out into the open seas. Patrick and Jess stood either side of Jerry. The boat headed east – past Morwell's headland and the Community House. Paul examined the wall of rock where the headland met the sea. From the beach, it appeared more like a slope that emerged and grew from the water but from this angle it looked like a sheer cliff face.

"Can you see the well?" Gwilym asked.

Paul struggled and then shook his head.

"Yes, it's difficult to see it from down here. Lord knows how Morwell found it."

Paul reached his hand out as far as he could over the side and felt water splash against it. The sea was a little choppy and waves thrust the boat up and down in quick succession.

"I hope no one here gets seasick," Dave said.

Gwilym made a face and filled his cheeks with air.

Sarah was very quiet. She was looking at Jess.

"You okay?" Paul asked.

"Yes, just enjoying the sea air."

"Look," Jane called out. She pointed behind them and they turned to see the smooth grey features of a pod of dolphins following the boat. Sarah grabbed Paul's hand and they watched the dolphins like excited children. He looked down and released his grip and stroked Sarah's arm.

"Come on, Flipper," Dave said. "Let's see some tricks."

"Don't be an idiot, Dave." Jess slapped him on the arm.

Paul stepped into the cockpit and joined Jerry as the others watched the dolphins.

"How long have you had *Patrick*?" he said.

"Oh, we've been together for nearly thirty years."

"I meant the boat."

Jerry snickered and poked Paul in the stomach.

"I'm just messing with you. Since the late nineties, I suppose."

"How far are we going?"

"We're heading to the Nose. A small island just over an hour up to the north-east."

"What's there?"

"Might see a few puffins and some seals if we're lucky."

*

By the time they reached the Nose, the volume of noise on the boat had drastically increased. Paul looked over at the bow where Dave was stood urinating over the side.

"Dave, man. What are you doing?" Jerry called to him. "There's a toilet below."

"Occupied," Dave yelled back.

There wasn't much to the Nose. It was barely three times the length of the boat and was home to one seal and a couple of seagulls.

"Now how would I claim this island as my own?" Sarah said.

"Well, you'd need a flag for starters," Jane replied. "But what would you do with it?"

"Dunno. Have a house here maybe. That seal and I could be friends." She started laughing and Jane joined in.

Paul was sat with Gwilym on the other side of the boat.

"Are you happy how it's progressing?" Paul asked. "All these new people coming to the meetings?"

"Yes, of course. But numbers don't matter. What matters is the effect we're having on each person. Are these meetings helping people?"

Paul thought about this. "I think they are."

"Are they helping you, Paul?"

"They help me to find the words for my questions."

"And what about finding the answers?"

"We'll see."

There was a splash from the other side of the boat followed by screaming.

"Dave," Jess yelled.

Paul jumped up and rushed around to see what had happened.

"Jesus, Dave. You're a liability, mate." Jerry threw a life ring over to Dave who was treading water.

"It's freezing in here."

"Idiot," Jess said.

Holding on to the life ring, he swam to the back of the vessel where both Jerry and Paul helped him out of the water.

"How did you manage to fall in?" Jane asked.

"I must've slipped," Dave said, shivering.

"I saw you, Mr Landlord," Sarah said. "You were stood on the bow doing the Rose and Jack thing from *Titanic*." She stretched out her arms and made a serious face.

They all laughed.

"Hilarious," Dave said.

"Come on, mate, let me find you some dry clothes." Jerry took Dave down into the cabin.

As Sarah and Patrick went to find more wine, Jane went to sit with Gwilym on the far side of the boat and Paul was face to face with Jess.

"We haven't had a chance to speak yet, have we?" she said.

"Er – speak about what?" Paul was drying his hands on a towel and repeatedly rubbed his fingers on the cloth.

"That night you ran from my flat."

"Oh. I wasn't sure if you'd remembered."

"That's not a reaction you easily forget."

"I'm sorry, you just caught me by surprise. I was wasted and not in a good place and…"

Jess lifted her hand up to him. "It's fine. I'm the one who stuck my hand down your pants."

Paul looked over at the Nose and scratched his chin.

"Okay, okay, we're good then."

She cocked her head to the side and tried to make eye contact with him. "You haven't drunk anything since that night, have you?"

Paul shook his head.

"Wow. Good effort." She patted Paul on the arm and entered the cockpit to pour herself a glass of wine from the bottle Patrick had opened.

*

After a half hour at the Nose, the boat circled the small island and then slowly made its way back towards the bay. Paul sat at the front of the bow enjoying the feel of the sea air as it rushed past his face.

"Mind if I join you?" Sarah was making her way along the gunwale, holding the rail tightly.

"Sure." Paul signalled to her to sit down.

Sarah closed her eyes and took a deep breath.

"I do like being out here. It feels so calm."

"For now," Paul said. "Have you seen those clouds coming in?"

"Storms are always coming, Paul. You have to enjoy the calm when you can."

"I try."

Both were silent. Sarah leant closer and Paul could smell the wine on her breath.

"Can I ask you something?" she said.

"What?"

"What you said about Belfast… after that, did you ever get any help?"

"What do you mean by help?"

"Did they treat you for PTSD?"

"No. That wasn't a term they used back then. Usually, it was shell shock or cowardice if you were unlucky. They recognised when someone was in trouble and going off the rails, like I was. But there was no grand name for it. You were just messed up and on your own."

"You know you can still get help for it. Have you thought about that?"

"I wouldn't know where to start. Right now, there are more pressing concerns."

"Right." Sarah tapped her fingers on the deck.

"So you still see her?"

"Not for a while now."

"And how are you feeling?"

"I'm okay."

"I'm glad." Sarah placed her hand onto Paul's, and she kissed him on the cheek. He turned away and squeezed her hand before releasing it. Her expression turned from a gentle smile to a frown. Paul was about to say something but he became distracted when the boat engine stopped and he heard Jerry cursing. They both looked back into the cockpit.

"What's wrong?" Dave shouted.

"It's dead," Jerry replied. "It's all dead. Nothing is working. Must be an electrical fault."

Jerry entered the cabin, and everyone looked at each other. Paul examined the land. They were adjacent to Red Beach, to the east of the headland.

"Damn it. All the power's out," Jerry said. "Can't see anything wrong."

"Is there no backup power supply?" Jane asked.

"No, this type of thing shouldn't happen. The battery's only a few weeks old."

"What do we do, babe?" Patrick asked.

"Have you got any oars?" Dave said.

"Always so funny," Jess said.

"Wasn't a joke," he replied.

"Can we use the radio?" Patrick asked.

"No, all the power's gone," Jerry said. "Let me have another look and see if there's anything I can do."

Jerry disappeared back into the cabin and this time was followed by Dave and Patrick.

"Those clouds look ominous," Gwilym said. Everyone looked up. A dark and heavy front was coming in from the north.

"This really isn't a good place to sit out a storm," Sarah said. "Look. We're right next to those rocks."

"Oh, you idiot." Patrick was yelling in the cabin. He came out with an angry look on his face.

"Our dear skipper has just informed me that the box with the life vests and the flares was left at the harbour. He took it out while clearing space for the beer cooler."

Sarah dropped her head and sat down.

Jess looked around at everyone. "Did anyone break his rule about bringing their phone?"

Paul shook his head and looked around at the others.

"I did," Dave said emerging from the cabin. "Can't be away from the pub without them being able to contact me…"

"Great, then you can call for help if we need to," Jane said.

"I didn't finish. I would if it were working but because of my dip in the Irish Sea before, said phone is buggered."

"Oh dear," Gwilym said.

Jerry and Patrick came out of the cabin.

"Yeah, I have no idea what's going on. I need a boat mechanic."

"So what do we do?" Sarah asked.

"Well, we can put down the anchor and try and wait it out. We're not short of supplies and someone will come looking for us eventually."

"You fancy our chances against that?" Jess asked, pointing to the dark clouds moving in overhead.

Jerry looked around at the sea and the land. "It's not the best place really. We're pretty exposed and if the tide takes us against those rocks, it won't be good."

"Won't the anchor keep us stationary?" Gwilym asked.

"Not if the waves are strong enough to carry us along, which often they are."

"So, what do we do?" Dave asked.

"Well…" Jerry started.

"Someone needs to swim to the land," Jane said.

"Don't we have any other options?" Sarah asked. She looked to Jerry and then Jane. Both were lost for words.

"But who?" Jess asked.

"I'll do it," Paul said. "It has to be me. You've all been drinking."

"Paul, no," Sarah said. The others were silent.

"It's fine." He looked over at the beach. "What is it… five hundred feet or so?"

"It's very cold, man," Dave said.

"You can attach yourself to the life ring at least," Patrick said. "Hang on, where is it?"

"It was just here," Dave said pointing to the back of the boat.

"Bloody hell," Patrick said. "Don't tell me we've lost that as well?"

"It's okay," Paul said, half smiling. "I learnt to swim in the River Mersey. That current was deadly."

Without further protest, Paul started to remove his shoes. He stripped down to his pants and vest. The others sat down – most of them looked uneasy. Dave cracked open a beer.

"What?" he said. "It's helping with my nerves."

"When you get to shore, your best bet is to leg it back to the village and knock on Bill, the harbour master's door." Jerry said. "He'll come out on his boat and give us a tow. It's strong enough – I've seen him do it before."

Paul stepped over to the side of the boat. He glanced back at his companions and saw worried faces. Sarah bit her nails.

"You're going to drown," someone said. He turned to reply before realising who had spoken.

"Not today," he said. "See you in a bit." He plunged into the water below and the shock of the cold snapped all the air from his chest, and he yelped as the sea took him.

"Go on, Paul," a voice called out from the boat.

Instinct kicked in and he oriented himself towards land and started crawling through the water, his arms cycling, one after the other. He kicked hard with his legs. As he moved through the sea, he felt the waves lift and then drop him. He turned back to look at the boat. He was getting further away from it, but the beach still felt like miles away. On he pushed. His body was tiring. He hadn't swum in the River Mersey – or any water for that matter – in decades. He now had the fitness of a relatively active middle-aged man. He stopped again and now struggled to see the boat. His heart was racing – he was surrounded by cold, deep water. As he carried on, his arms burned with exhaustion. They felt heavy. His foot cramped and he needed to stop again. He shook it off and swallowed big gulps of air into his lungs. He lost track of the beach and couldn't tell whether he was swimming in the right direction. A wave lifted him enough so that he was able to see. The headland was visible, and next to it, his destination at Red Beach. He pushed on, breathing heavily, and choking and retching each time he received a mouthful of salty water. Tiredness took hold and he struggled to keep the momentum going. Staying at the surface was a battle for survival. He punched and kicked at the sea, but the water was bigger and stronger than him and he increasingly felt like this was a battle he could not win. Down he dropped in the water before urging himself back into the air. His body was cold, and he was tired. Sleeping below the surface was the easy option, and survival, a burden. He dropped and then raised his head again out of the water. The last time his head went under, he thought that would be the end of it. He had given it his best shot, but the cold and the exhaustion had overcome him. As he slipped beneath, his feet hit something. Pebbles. The ground. He was close to land. He pushed himself from the bottom of the water and up to the surface one last time before stretching out one arm after the other, pulling himself along until a wave came and thrust his body over and down onto a sandy surface.

Paul lay face down in the surf coughing and trying to catch his breath. He remembered his job was not yet finished. He pushed on the soft sand and got onto his knees and then up on his feet. He turned around and waved his hands in the air. He could just about make out the cheers and claps. He punched the air as elation kicked in. He had done right by his new community – he had done right by his new family.

The clouds were much nearer, and Paul ran across the beach and up the path to the headland and from there down to the village. Soaking wet and wearing only vest and pants, he saw a few raised eyebrows on his journey. When he got to the harbour, his run had slowed to a walk. Out of breath and cold, he felt great relief when the harbour master answered the door. He told Bill what happened and before he'd finished his story, the man was on his way down to his boat. Paul returned to the guest house and was let in by a very surprised Julie. He had a hot shower and quickly changed so that he could return to the harbour in time for their arrival. He struggled to shake off the cold and wore two sweaters under his coat.

As the boats arrived, the wind was picking up and the rain had finally come. Bill's boat towed *Patrick* into the harbour. The passengers stood on the deck and began cheering as they saw Paul. He couldn't stop shaking from the cold, but he didn't mind. He grinned and whooped and thrust his fists into the air.

TWENTY-SIX

Paul groaned as he stretched to clean cobwebs from an upper corner of the bedroom. The guests had left after breakfast and he and Sarah were tasked with turnover.

"What's wrong?" she asked as she changed the bedding.

"Shoulder is sore after all that swimming yesterday." He rubbed his upper arm and rotated it at the joint.

"The hero is suffering, is he?" She grinned, dropped the pillowcase, and pulled Paul over to the bed where she seated him and began massaging his shoulders.

"I seem to be always playing your nurse right now."

"You're very good at it," he smiled up at her and their eyes connected. He swiftly looked away and bit his lip.

"I'm surprised you're not rough this morning after all that excitement," he said.

"Excitement – ha. I drank a lot of water after we returned. Besides, this work has to be done before the new guests arrive this afternoon."

"Business is starting to pick up now it seems?"

"Yes, the Revelation hasn't dampened people's need for a summer holiday. It's good – we need it."

"Have you got Julie doing more hours?"

"She will be – yes. Especially when we get into July."

"Does your dad get involved?"

"Very little. Given his new focus I doubt we'll get any of his attention going forwards."

"Yes, he's already up there, rehearsing for tonight."

"This one will be televised so it's a big deal. Any idea what's on the agenda?"

"You know he won't tell me."

"But you spend so much time with him."

"We talk about all sorts. He has very interesting thoughts about the new way of things."

Her hands were gripping his shoulders more firmly.

"I like that you two are getting on. But we don't get to spend much time together without him."

Paul pulled away from her grips.

"I'm just trying to help him," he said. "What he's doing is really important."

"Yes but – you know – it's his way. I love him very much, but he's a man that demands attention – always trying to lead people forward with his ideas and thoughts about improving the world."

"Why is that an issue? Doesn't the world need more people like that?"

"The world might. But I'm not sure if we do."

She leant forward and looked into his eyes, grabbed his hand with both of hers, and squeezed it tight before letting go and walking out of the room.

*

Paul arrived late and out of breath at the Community House after finishing his chores. He opened the doors to see that all the seats were taken, and extra attendees stood along the sides and at the back of the room. Sarah raised her arm and flagged that she had saved a chair for him.

"Excuse me. Sorry. Can I just get past you there?"

He navigated his way down the side to reach his seat. He heard whispers all around him.

"The place is buzzing," he said to Sarah. "Who are we expecting on stage – your dad or Elvis?"

"We do have a rock star here," she said. "Also, the TV crew are over there." She nodded over to the other side of the room where a scruffy-looking cameraman stood with his filming equipment. Next to him stood a young woman holding a microphone and a notebook. Paul looked over at Gwilym, who was leant against the laptop table. His fingers batted his thighs, and he watched the audience settling like a teacher about to begin his class. He walked over to the podium and spoke up.

"Good evening and welcome, friends, new and old. Tonight, we have some guests with us from the IBC News Channel. They're running a report later this week on our community meetings. They've asked me to tell you to please act normally and ignore their presence. They will be filming throughout and probably talking to some of you outside after the meeting."

He stepped out from behind the podium, clasped his hands together and grinned.

"Right, so that's that sorted. Now, before I explain the

theme for tonight's meeting, we will begin with a short performance by Chris here, who's a member of the Anglesey Amateur Dramatics Society."

He signalled with his open palm to a middle-aged man who had been sat in the front row of the audience.

"Chris, please take it away when you're ready."

The man stood up and turned to face the west-wall window. He raised his hand and frowned.

"To be, or not to be, that is the question. Whether 'tis nobler in the mind to suffer the slings and arrows of outrageous fortune, or to take arms against a sea of troubles, and by opposing end them. To die, to sleep."

Paul and Sarah exchanged glances and the performance lasted a further few minutes. At times he became overly animated, and the strange facial expressions drew chortles from the audience but he continued unphased. When he finished, Gwilym stepped forwards with a big smile on his face and placed his hand on the amateur actor's shoulder.

"Chris, that was excellent. What a wonderful performance of the bard and one of his finest pieces."

Chris nodded and sat down back in his chair.

"Don't worry, folks, tonight will not be an English literature lesson. Tonight, I want to talk about a subject that for many is very much top of our minds right now." Gwilym paused, probably for dramatic effect. "Death."

Paul scanned the faces around him. There were raised eyebrows, smiles and a few shared glances.

"Now does anyone here want to explain to me what that soliloquy by Hamlet actually means?"

Chris raised his hand.

"Not you, Chris." The audience laughed.

Someone in the middle of the room yelled out. "He's thinking about offing himself."

"Who said that?" Gwilym asked. "It doesn't matter but yes, that's more or less the gist of it."

He smiled.

"Hamlet is going through a difficult time and in this soliloquy, he is considering whether he should end it all. He refers to the experience of living as the *slings and arrows of outrageous fortune*. To be or not to be. To exist or not to exist.

"What stops him though is, upon consideration of death, the frightening uncertainty of what comes afterwards. He refers to death as the *undiscovered country from whose bourn, no traveller returns*. So ultimately, he chooses not to commit suicide because of the fear that the afterlife may actually be worse than his current life."

Gwilym paused to take a sip of water. Paul saw Kat's face on the bridge, and he wondered when she'd made her decision.

"The idea of an afterlife has shaped our behaviour since the dawn of man. For millennia, it affected the way people lived their lives. Like Hamlet, people were uncertain of what the afterlife would bring so they lived their life in its shadow. For many, this meant not fully valuing their current and only time of existence." He paused.

"So, consider this: we are the lucky ones. Since the Revelation, we are in the privileged position of knowing there is no afterlife."

Gwilym stepped behind the laptop table and pressed a key on the computer. An image of a marble statue appeared on the wall behind him – a bearded man in robes.

"An ancient Greek philosopher by the name of Epicurus said that a person can only be harmed when they exist, and because death is the end of their existence then death cannot harm them. Death, therefore, is not something that should be feared.

"Curiously, might this knowledge have changed Hamlet's decision?"

He pressed the key again and a different bearded man's stone head appeared.

"Another ancient thinker – this time a Roman poet called Lucretius – proposed an idea that has become known as the symmetry argument. Think about the time before your birth. No harm came to you then because you did not exist. And of course, because of that, there is no concern about it. In the same way, after our death, we no longer exist. We return to a state of non-existence. No harm can come to us after our death and like the time before our birth, to worry about it or fear it is irrational."

Gwilym clapped his hands together and Gwyn the butcher – sat two rows ahead of Paul – jumped in his seat.

"Here we are, alive and aware that this life is all we have; that our existence is not a test in which our behaviours are judged by some higher power to decide our fate for an eternity in the afterlife. This existence and these moments are all there are. The question is what can we do to improve matters so that we are able to better cope with the *slings and arrows of outrageous fortune*? What can we do to not just make existence bearable but a worthwhile and meaningful experience? That is a question that the Revelation gave us. Life is precious and the time we have on this planet in the company of our loved ones decreases from one moment to the next.

"I will leave you with this thought as we end this segment of the discussion."

Gwilym pressed a key on the computer, and this time words were projected against the ancient wall.

They lose the day in expectation of the night, and the night in fear of the dawn. – Seneca

The room was silent. Paul glanced around and saw hands reaching for other hands. Loved ones were making themselves known to each other. The news reporter turned to her cameraman and gave him a thumbs up.

"Right. On that light note, I think it's time for a singsong." Gwilym crossed his arms. "Jerry, is your guitar tuned up this time?"

There was a titter in the audience.

*

The reporter talked to the camera with a mic in her hand as the attendees exited the building. Paul stepped a little closer – trying not to loiter in the background. He could hear snippets of her discussion. She described how the church was converted into a communal space. She talked about the Llanffug Community Truth and Trust Coalition and the meetings they ran each week to a full house. She then asked a few attendees to be interviewed and questioned for the news report. Jerry went first. Jane was also interviewed. Paul was invited but declined. When it came to Gwilym's turn, he took his time. He spoke about his Revelation and how the experience inspired him to set up the group. He described their aims and the purpose of the meetings.

Paul stood behind, watching. Sarah joined him.

"I was wondering where Dad had gone but I should've known he'd be here."

Paul turned to look at Sarah.

"How did you find the meeting?" he asked.

"Good, I think. Not the lightest subject matter. But it seems like people want to hear about this stuff. What did you think?"

"Your father has a voice that people want to hear right now." He looked around at the people gathered outside the Community House. "He's helping these folks make sense of this crazy stuff. You should be proud of him. He is an inspiration."

"Well, he's certainly receiving a lot of attention," she said. "I just hope he doesn't end up on the radar of the wrong types."

"What do you mean?"

"Well, look around you. People are dressed up in their formal wear to attend a weekly meeting in an old church."

"And?"

"And there are people out there who are targeting these kinds of groups and meetings. People like Bob."

"I told you – you don't need to worry about Bob."

"I don't just mean him. This group is now receiving nationwide attention. Who knows which other looneys will take an interest?"

"Maybe."

"Anyway, I'm going back. I still have some things to finish off ahead of tomorrow. Are you coming with me?"

"I think I might stick around here in case your dad needs help with anything."

"Fine. I'll leave you with your friend." Sarah strode away in the direction of the road. Paul gazed after her and rubbed the back of his neck. Then his attention returned to the interview.

"Many would say that what you're doing here is no different to the pre-Revelation church services and similar religious gatherings," the reporter commented.

"Well, of course," Gwilym replied. "There are many components of religions that we can steal. They have existed for thousands of years and evolved over time to meet the existential needs of humans, helping us through the difficult times and guiding us to answers on the challenging questions that arise in everyday life."

"But critics say that meetings like these just continue the tradition of old men standing in old buildings telling people how to live their lives."

"I'm not that old," Gwilym said, and the reporter chuckled. "Though seriously, what we are tapping into here is the fact that humans do respond to community, rituals, traditions and storytelling. There is none of the paranormal stuff or the dogma or doctrines. I have no intention of telling anyone how to live. I am trying to help people ask the bigger questions about themselves and their existence. Humans have a desperate need to find meaning in their lives. We are trying to help members of this group to find meaning in reason and in our own human story."

The reporter looked at the cameraman. "I think we have enough now?"

"Plenty." He nodded.

"So, you'll edit the various bits of footage together?" Gwilym asked.

"That's right," the reporter said. "We'll edit it together and then the full segment will be shown later this week."

"You won't misrepresent us, will you?" Gwilym asked with a slight smile.

"Oh, most certainly not. We've got some good stuff here – all very authentic. The final piece should be quite powerful. It'll generate a lot of interest."

*

After all the attendees had left, Paul helped Gwilym to lock away the laptop and projector and tidy up the space.

"Sarah is concerned this coverage on the news will draw the wrong kind of attention." Paul closed the cupboard doors and locked them.

"That girl likes to worry," Gwilym said.

Paul sat down in a chair. "Can I ask you something?"

Gwilym nodded and sat down next to him.

"What you said before about finding meaning, how would you explain it? All the bad stuff, that is. All the suffering that happens in the world. How do we make sense of it?"

"I'm glad you were listening," Gwilym said. "The way I see it, it's a matter of perspective. Yes, humans desperately need meaning. They like to place events in the context of an overarching narrative or master plan. Even now, after the Revelation, it's hard for many to accept the truth that the universe – nature – all of it is random and driven by chance."

"So how do we tackle this question of meaning?" Paul asked. "Good things happen. Bad things. We just have to accept it?"

"Perhaps it will take time," Gwilym said. "The Revelation opened our eyes to the truth. So maybe we can find meaning and purpose elsewhere? For me, it's about connecting with ourselves and others. Focusing on the narrative we can control – kindness and compassion; honesty and reason; well-being and mindfulness.

"Think about what I said earlier. When people believed in an afterlife, it meant their lives could be overshadowed by the next leg of the journey. They were more willing to accept injustice and suffering because there was this potential for a better existence.

"With what we know now, wouldn't it be great if people started to focus on this moment in time to make it better for all – to fight injustice and ease suffering where we can? That would be how – in my view – we could take control of our own stories and establish an existence full of meaning and purpose."

Paul looked down at the stone-flagged flooring and saw a ten-pence piece that must've fallen from someone's pocket during the meeting.

"But what about those who are unable to overcome the suffering?" he asked. "Do we try and stop them from returning to non-existence? If death is not to be feared, then why not allow them?"

"That is an interesting question. In some extreme situations then death may be a kindness, but I'd like to think that in most cases people can do a great deal more to take care of each other. There is so much needless suffering in this world. What I hope is that communities like ours here and many groups like it can help turn the tide for humanity and we can take the gift of the Revelation as an opportunity to make the world a better place."

Gwilym stood up and groaned as he stretched his back. "Anyway," he said, "we should think about heading back before I start singing 'Kumbaya'. We can talk more after dinner if you like. I hope that answers some of your questions – for now at least?"

"I suppose," he said before reaching down and picking up the coin. As the old man gathered his belongings together, Paul placed the coin on his thumb and flipped it in the air. He caught it on the back of his hand, covering it with his other hand. He held it there for a moment and considered lifting his hand to see which side faced upwards.

"Not yet," he whispered, and he took it off the back of his hand and placed it in his pocket.

TWENTY-SEVEN

Paul did the dishes after breakfast at the guest house. Most of the residents had finished and Julie cleared the dining area while he supported in the kitchen. He heard the front door close and Sarah's voice in the living room.

"Sarah's in a foul mood this morning." Julie stormed into the kitchen with a tray of dirty plates and cutlery.

"What do you mean?"

"Bit short. Not our usual Sarah."

"What did she say?"

"Something about running into Jess on the High Street. No details though."

"Oh."

"Says she's got a headache and has gone to lie down. She asks if you can take that package on her desk to the post office. First class delivery."

"Right. Will do."

It was good to get out after most of the morning spent in the kitchen. The recent surge in visitors had led to a very noticeable increase in chores and Paul started feeling like he was earning his keep at the guest house.

On the High Street, Geraint walked towards him and greeted him with a big smile. They both stopped outside the butcher's shop.

"Meeting looked good on the news last night. I bet the TV star is glowing this morning."

Paul grinned. "Yes, it did come up once or twice over breakfast."

"Does this mean the group meetings are going on tour?"

"I hope not. We're booked up for the summer and we need all the help we can get."

"I expect we'll be receiving more visitors after all this attention."

"And what do you reckon the people here will think of that?"

"Oh, we're quite used to the place getting busy in the summer months. Some will grumble of course but the truth is we need the tourists. After the Revelation there was concern this summer would be a write-off, but things are looking a lot more hopeful now."

"Gwilym's talking about setting up a humanist retreat so that the benefits of the meetings can be shared with visitors."

"I wouldn't put it past him. Anyway, better be off. See you on Sunday."

"Bye."

Paul turned towards the butcher's shop and he noticed Gwyn serving a customer. They made eye contact and Paul nodded. As he did, the package slipped from under his arm and fell to the floor. He bent over to pick it up and became aware of someone close by.

"Not a breakable, I hope?"

Paul recognised the voice and looked up.

"Alright, dickhead?"

He lifted the box and straightened his back without taking his eyes off Karl.

"What are you doing here?" Paul asked.

"Well, very nice to see you too."

"I didn't expect—"

"So, this is where you've been hiding, eh? Not a bad spot, not a bad spot indeed."

"How did you know I was here?"

"I saw you on the news. You were in the background in a report about some new age cult. As it happens, I was staying nearby with some friends."

"Quite a coincidence."

"You're telling me. I thought I was hallucinating. Last time I saw you was outside the pub in Salford." Karl's eyes narrowed. "Eventful night that, wasn't it?"

Paul cleared his throat. "You could say that."

"Why don't we go and catch up somewhere? That pub near the harbour looks like a decent spot."

"Okay. Just give me five minutes to go and deal with this."

At the post office, Paul stood in line waiting to be served. He had a sick feeling in his stomach.

"Cult," he whispered and he grinded his teeth.

The person ahead of him in the queue finished and Paul stepped forwards. Paul saw that Betty was serving today.

"Oh hello, Paul. How's Gwilym doing after his television performance?"

"He's alright."

"Those news people did a great job, didn't they?"

Paul nodded and lifted the package up.

"Right, just put it on the scales, please." Betty hit some keys on the cash register. "Made the meetings look very important. Like we'd started something special here. Would you like first or second class for the parcel?"

"First."

She looked something up on a laminated sheet of paper and Paul tapped on the counter with his fingers.

"Right, that will be three pounds seventy-one, please."

Paul placed a five-pound note onto the counter. Betty printed off a sticker and then stuck it to the parcel before picking it up and placing it behind her.

"Will there be any changes to the meetings in light of the increased interest?" She picked up the five-pound note and pressed her keys again. The till opened and she counted out the change.

"Don't think so."

"We may need more chairs in the Community House at least." She handed Paul the coins and gave him a wide smile. He raised his cheeks pulling the corners of his mouth upwards and nodded to the woman before leaving the shop.

His steps to the Pilgrim Inn were careful and deliberate. He took his hands from his coat pockets as he felt his palms become moist with sweat. Before entering, he stopped outside and took a couple of deep breaths.

"There he is," Karl called out from the corner where Jerry normally sat with his guitar. "Got you a pint."

"Thanks, but I don't drink anymore." Paul dropped his coat on an empty chair and sat down.

"Back on the wagon, eh? Is that linked to your cult thing?"

"What do you want, Karl?"

"Hey, can't an old pal come and visit you without suspicion?"

Paul stared at him.

"Do your cult friends know about your fire-starting skills?"

Paul's jaw dropped.

"You were watching me."

"Of course I was. You had such an interesting look in your eyes. Like you'd be capable of anything."

"It was a terrible, stupid thing. My head was a complete mess."

"And the poor pastor and his family…"

"That wasn't my doing."

"I bet you thought that at the start though, didn't you? I bet that's why you ran, isn't it?"

"I didn't run. I just needed to get away from the city."

"Don't stress, man, I'm just busting your balls. I don't care what you did. We've all done lots of crazy shit since the Revelation."

"Right."

"The Revelation," Karl said sipping his pint. "What a name, eh? I told you it was big. Biggest, most important thing we'll ever live through. Someone somewhere really did call time on religion. They decided we grown-ups needed to stop believing in fairy tales."

"Yeah."

"Anyway, on that note, what's the deal with you and the Branch Davidians? On telly, it looked like you were well and truly part of the gang."

"It's not a cult, Karl. It's a community. People trying to help each other out."

"Sounds like a cult to me, mate. To be honest I kind of expected you to get involved in something like that. You never did well at being alone, did you?"

Paul pursed his lips and blew. He looked around the bar. Despite the warmer weather, Bedwyr was in his usual position tending to the fire.

"But you know, I tried getting hold of you a few times after you left. I called and texted. Didn't know if that shitty old phone of yours still worked."

"Why were you trying to call me?"

"I wondered where you disappeared to after the fire. Just concerned, you know."

"Right." Paul sat back in his chair. "So what have you been up to?"

"I made new friends."

"New friends?"

"Let's say, like-minded individuals."

"New drinking buddies, eh?"

"Not exactly. People who shared a particular view about the Revelation."

"View?"

"How it was a victory over religion. An insurrection against a false master."

"You make it sound like we were at war."

"We were. We didn't realise it, but we were."

"So, what now?"

"Now, we do all we can to ensure the master does not return to enslave us again."

"How could it? Faith, religious belief – it's all gone."

"It was man who created God and man can do it again."

Karl stared at Paul without blinking or breaking his gaze.

Under the table, both of Paul's legs shook.

"Sorry," Karl said, his face brightening. "I get so passionate about this stuff." He stroked the side of his glass. "So, the head of your cult is your girlfriend's dad?"

"What? I didn't mention any of that."

"Must have been something I saw on the news."

Paul tilted his head. Karl took a long sip on his beer.

"Man, you remember that night I got us on the guest list for the Hacienda?"

Paul nodded. "You told the bouncers we were the next big thing in Manchester."

"Yeah, our band was called Fat Lip. I was looking at someone on their way out who'd just been smacked and it came to me."

"Did the job."

"We had so many legendary nights, mate."

"Yeah."

"We were like brothers."

"At one stage."

"Why did we grow apart?"

"I couldn't keep going like you did."

"That's when I lost you to the church."

"It was my only way out."

"The church isn't there anymore."

"I know."

"So why don't we saddle up together again, my old amigo?" Karl sat back and stretched his arms along the back of the chair. "You can come join me. I'll introduce you to some new people. These are different times. We can have some laughs and make new stories. Come be my brother again."

"I can't go back to that, Karl."

"I'm not talking about going back. I'm talking about going forwards to something new."

"Whatever direction it is – the answer is no. I'm alright here. I feel like I'm part of something. Part of a family."

Paul got to his feet and picked up his coat.

"What are you doing?" Karl's face changed again.

"Mate, it was good to see you. Take care of yourself."

"You're serious? This is what you want? To be an errand boy for some egomaniac cult leader in a shitty little Welsh village?"

Paul put his coat on and turned to leave.

"Don't you be turning your back on me. Get back here right now."

Paul stopped. He glanced over at his old friend sat in the corner of the pub.

"Stay away from me, Karl. Just stay away. Okay?"

Karl muttered something as Paul exited the pub. He swiftly turned down a side path that ran along the river in the direction of the harbour. There, he waited for a couple of minutes and kept his eyes fixed on the corner of the pub near the entrance. There was no sign of Karl, so he headed back to the guest house. He felt uneasy. Karl knew too much, and he wasn't one to take no for an answer.

TWENTY-EIGHT

Paul and Sarah strolled on the beach as Ben dashed around on his old legs sniffing at the wet sand that emerged from the retreating tide. The sky was overcast, and rain was near. Paul had told her about Karl's visit. Not everything – but enough. Sarah had asked Paul to join her on the walk so they could have a chat. He did not expect an easy discussion.

"Did your dad come back?" he asked.

"I haven't seen him since this morning."

"He's been at the Community House all day?"

"Seems like it. He's taken the whole thing up a notch after the news coverage."

"Are you still concerned about the attention it received?"

"I don't know. Seems well received so far but we'll see. Anyway, that's not what I wanted to talk to you about."

Here it came.

"Then what is it?"

"Paul, where are we going?"

"We're following the dog." Paul tried to smile.

"Funny. But seriously, where do you think our relationship is going?"

"Who knows, but we're happy together, aren't we?"

"Are we? We're getting on, yes. We're spending time together, yes. Hell, we're even working together. But is there more than that? I don't know."

"What do you want?"

"What I want is to know why there's no passion between us. No intimacy. We're getting on like an elderly couple. Like old friends who live together and work together but nothing more. I feel like we've bypassed a key part of the relationship."

She stopped and looked him in the eyes. "Are you not attracted to me? Is that what this is? You can be honest."

Paul looked down at the floor. "Yes, of course I am, it's not that at all."

"It's just that I know something happened between you and Jess."

Paul's eyes widened. "Nothing at all happened between Jess and me."

"Really?"

"Honestly. Look, I appreciate how patient you've been with me. As I told you before, the Revelation left me feeling…" He tried to think of an appropriate word. "Haunted."

"But that was over four months ago. Are you telling me she still appears to you?"

"Not for a while now."

"Well good, I guess. Now listen, I want to be here for you, but if you're still troubled by that event and its effects are still holding you back from life then maybe you should try and get help. You're not the only person who was badly affected by it. Dad was catatonic for a month – and look at him now."

"I just wouldn't know where to start. It all seems so crazy."

"It is, Paul. It really is. But you're not alone in the madness. There's a lot of people who are here for you. I'm here for you."

"Not for long it seems."

"I just get frustrated. It feels like nothing is changing between us. I've seen you and my father become so close. I hear you each night after dinner sat by the window talking about anything and everything."

"He's been helping me to make sense of things. You're lucky to have a father like him – I barely remember mine."

"No, don't get me wrong, it's nice and I'm glad that he can help you. But don't you see? Your relationship with him is growing and strengthening. I just wish ours was evolving as well."

Paul sighed. "I do try. I just feel like there's an invisible wall between us, and I don't know how to get around it."

Sarah appeared distracted. She kept looking past Paul – into the distance towards the car park.

"Sarah, are you listening to me? What's wrong?"

"It's that man. He keeps watching us. I think he's coming over."

Paul turned his head and felt a cold shiver down his spine.

"Oh no, he's back."

"That's Karl?"

Paul's heart started racing.

"I didn't think I'd see you again."

"Good day to you too, dickhead." He turned his attention to Sarah. "Now aren't you going to introduce me?"

"Sarah, this is Karl. The friend from home I mentioned."

"Very nice to meet you, madam," Karl said with a broad smile on his face.

"You disappeared quickly yesterday," Karl said. "I wanted to make sure I wasn't leaving on bad terms."

He was up to something.

"Sarah, it's getting on a bit," Paul said. "Why don't you and Ben head back and let me have a few minutes with Karl?"

"Okay," she said. "Maybe we can finish that conversation later."

"Oh, I do hope I wasn't interrupting anything important," Karl said.

"Yes, let's do that," Paul replied to Sarah, but his gaze remained on Karl.

Both men watched as Sarah walked away. She called for Ben and attached the lead to his collar.

"I told you yesterday I didn't want to join you."

"I know but see my people really want to meet you. When I told them about what you did at St Luke's, they were very impressed."

"It was stupid."

"Oh no it wasn't. It was a good thing to destroy that place. In fact, it inspired us. We talked about doing more of that kind of thing."

"Burning down churches?"

"And the rest."

Karl's words sounded familiar.

"Your people – are these the ones who've been targeting innocents since the Revelation?"

Karl shrugged his shoulders.

"They're terrorists, Karl. Bastard murdering terrorists."

Karl grinned. "Come on, mate. These *innocents* as you call them knew what they were doing. They just couldn't keep doing it once the curtains had been pulled back. The

External Force did us a solid. It let us see the lies and shitty oppression for what they really were. My group wants to make certain we never go back to that world. The External Force gave us freedom and we intend to keep it."

"You're one of the Witnesses? The Witnesses of the External Force? That's the name, isn't it?"

"Me and my brothers and sisters want to make sure religion remains well and truly dead and buried."

"Surely the Revelation did that already?"

It started to rain, and Paul glanced up at the dark skies overhead.

"We can never move on until the war criminals of the old world are dealt with. Take that fucker who preyed on you."

"Father Michaels?" Paul cocked his head to the side.

"He used your sadness against you. He messed with your head for his own gains. He was a predator and you were his prey."

"Karl, the man kept me alive when I was at my lowest."

Something dawned on Paul and his jaw dropped. "Wait, was it you who…?"

Karl half smiled and looked at Paul like a child who had admitted to smashing a window.

"Yeah, you got me. Before the Witnesses of course, but it earned me my stripes."

"Oh God." Paul's legs became weak and he dropped to his knees. The lower part of his body became soaked in the cold, wet sand.

"His wife and son as well?" He put his hand to his mouth.

"Regrettably, I must admit. They turned up as I was… finishing him off. His wife fell quickly but the little boy…" Karl looked sideways at Paul.

Paul shook his head. "No. How could you?"

"Don't kid yourself, mate. Civilians always suffer in war. It was powerful – like I was doing the bidding of a higher power. But a higher power that *did* exist. The alcohol certainly helped."

"You monster." Paul got up and dove at Karl. His shoulder connected with the man's waist and knocked him to the ground. Paul scrambled on top and then reached for Karl's neck, tightly closing his hands around his throat. Before he could be subdued, Karl drove his fist into Paul's gut and he fell face first into the sand, winded and gasping.

Karl lay on his back rubbing his throat. The rain fell more heavily, and Paul wiped his wet brow to keep the drips out of his eyes.

"Listen, I get that you're angry, but this sea water is cold, and I'm already very wet from this fricking Welsh weather."

Paul sat up, panting. He looked at Karl and bared his teeth. He was ready to bury the cocky bastard's face into the ground.

"No, wait." Karl raised his hand. "I need to talk to you about something else." He spat in the sand after speaking.

"What?" Paul said, exhaling hard.

Karl stood up and wiped the wet sand from his clothes.

"I'm here to deliver a message."

"A message from who?"

"From the Witnesses. Your little cult here at the church needs to end."

"What? Why? Because people coming together are an issue for you lot?"

"Don't you see it, Paul? It starts with the meetings. Before long, you have your own rituals and beliefs. You start telling people how to live their lives. Those who follow your rules are the true believers and those who don't are your opponents – your enemies."

"That's nonsense." Paul coughed and pushed on the ground to lift himself up.

"It really isn't. It's in our DNA. We're inherently designed to be cunts. But this gift from the External Force is too much to squander."

"You and your External Force." Paul held his gut and breathed heavily as he paced around Karl. "All the violent and horrible shit you've done assumes this thing is real. But what if it isn't? What proof do you have?"

"The Revelation's our proof. It wasn't random like a natural disaster or a plague. It was targeted and had an objective. It's obvious there was intelligence behind it."

"Obvious? Really? Obvious enough to kill people in its name?"

"What we're doing is making sure the power of the External Force is recognised and the full potential of humanity is realised. We can't go backwards, Paul – the External Force has shown us the way. Think of it as progress."

The rain pounded down on the two men. Paul blinked to clear the rainwater from his eyes. He sneered. "You talk about your External Force like it's a god."

"By ancient standards, it would be a god." Karl raised his hands up in the air as he spoke. "The difference is we know it exists. Don't you see that? We know that something out there did this to us. It revealed itself through an awesome and magnificent power. Old testament shit, but real."

"Whatever the hell it is, Karl, it hasn't told us how to live our lives. That's the doing of you and your damned family.

People are scared. They have needs. They need help to understand what it is to be human. That's what we're trying to do here, help people, not kill and maim in the name of some unknown fucking power." Paul clenched his fists, ready to pounce.

"People are weak. The weak fall victim to the strong. And the strong want to control everything. It's nature. Something you… and your *community* don't seem to understand. The Revelation was a gift, but the only way to make it work is through force."

"No, no, no." Paul shook his head. "Force and fear are not how you make this work. You make it work by helping people to connect and come together. Jesus Christ, we need to heal not create more division." Paul took a few deep breaths. "You should speak to Sarah's father. He can explain all this far better than I can."

"Him, we know about." Karl faced away from Paul and put his hands in his pockets.

Paul didn't like this response. "What do you mean, *know about*?"

Karl turned his head – he had a wicked smile on his face.

"Here's the thing, mate. I'm going to need you to get your Molotov cocktail recipe out and do to your Community House what you did to St Luke's."

"What? Don't be crazy, why would I do that?"

"See, your future father-in-law has gained some attention amongst the Witnesses."

"What have you done?" Paul's stomach was turning.

"Nothing yet. But if you fail to burn down that little club house of yours, I'm afraid the old bugger will face the same sentence as the chargrilled pastor."

Paul grabbed Karl by the collar.

"You coward. You wouldn't dare."

"Paul, come on. You must know by now that I'm very capable. My brothers and sisters are also very committed and if anything happens to me then the outcome for the old man's the same. See, he's with us already. Likes to visit the Community House each day by himself, doesn't he? Really wasn't difficult – he didn't put up much of a fight."

Paul's eyes drifted to the floor in despair.

"You fucking…" He held on to Karl and reached into his pocket to get his phone.

Something struck him in his arm, and a shooting pain exploded up into his shoulder, across his torso and abdomen and beyond to all his extremities. His body rattled from whatever had struck him and he felt his head shake his brain like a marble in a tin can. Panic sprung into his mind and he lost all physical control and fell to the ground. All his muscles tightened as though his whole body was cramping. He was unable to move. He wanted to scream but his voice was lost. Karl stepped nearer and looked down at him with a taser in his hand. Paul stared at him, his face twisted, and teeth clasped.

"Sorry, mate. Had to do that." Karl kneeled next to Paul and whispered into his ear. "Couldn't have you calling the pigs, could I? Don't worry, you'll be fine in a few minutes."

Karl stood up and moved around him.

"I bet it hurts, doesn't it? Looks like it does.

"While I've got you, let me share something. You remember that care home I spent my childhood at? It was run by the church. The priest in charge – Father fucking O'Malley – was the unholiest cunt who ever walked this earth. Liked young boys. Also had friends who liked young boys."

Karl squatted next to Paul and gently spoke into his ear. "Of course, when I say like, I do mean liked to fuck. Liked to abuse. Liked to rape."

He stood up and took a few more steps around Paul, waving his arms around in the air. "I had that for years. Never said anything to anyone outside of that place. I always thought you knew. Did you know?"

Paul mumbled.

"Whatever, but see, that is what the church – religion, faith – is to me. Control, abuse, and fucking desecration of innocence. Dickhead, nothing speaks the words of God like having a sweaty, drunk priest inside you.

"What's worse is that years later, there was an investigation, but the Vatican got involved and the whole thing was closed down. The horrors of that fucking hellhole never saw the light of day."

Paul stopped fighting. Karl stopped pacing.

"I'm telling you this now because you may think I'm an absolute bastard for killing your abuser and his family, but I want you to realise that I grew up with the real face of religion. And that face was not a benevolent fucking shepherd who cares for his flock. That face was a rotten, twisted beast that feeds on the suffering of the weak."

Karl coughed and spat on the floor. "War makes us capable of anything, mate, and both sides suffer. The External Force made our victory possible. The Witnesses will ensure there's no fucking way we return to the old ways."

Karl crouched again and prodded Paul with his finger.

"Electricity does really mess you up, doesn't it?"

He stood up and stretched.

"Feels good to share. Anyway, you know the plan. If you haven't burnt down the church by dawn, tomorrow, then we do it and we'll use the old man's petrol-soaked body as a wick. That's what the other Witnesses wanted from the start. But I thought this way might be nice. At least now, you've got an important part to play as well. Obviously, tell anyone else or the fuzz, and the same thing happens. Also, I might need to tell your girlfriend about your handywork at St Luke's. Wouldn't that just add fuel to the fire?" Karl winked and stepped away.

Paul growled and fought the paralysis, but it was futile. He called out to Karl and there was no response. He called out again and again – finally realising that Karl had gone. It took a few minutes for the effects to wear off. At first, he was able to move his back, hips, and neck. Control then returned to his legs and arms, followed finally by his hands and feet. He sat up, wiped wet sand off his face and looked around. He was drenched and started to shiver. He was alone on the beach. As soon as he could, he got up to his feet and started walking – slowly at first – back across the sand. By the time he was near the house he was running.

"Have you been rolling about on the beach?" Sarah asked. She could see he was out of breath and the look on her face turned to concern. "Is something wrong?"

"Sarah, it's your father. They have him."

"What? Who has him?"

"The WEF. The goddamn Witnesses of the External Force."

"What do you mean? Is your friend one of them? I don't understand. Oh, I knew something like this would happen."

Paul sat on the floor in the kitchen, caught his breath and explained what had just happened. He held off some of the details regarding the Salford church but did explain that Karl was to be taken seriously, as were the Witnesses.

"We have to call the police."

"If we do that, they'll hurt Gwilym."

"Why like this, though? They burn down churches and synagogues, and murder priests and imams. Why demand you do it? And why take my father?"

"Karl's mind games, I think. He always liked to mess with people's heads. But he's somewhere else now. Between the Revelation and the influence of those extremists, I'm not sure what he's capable of. Also, I'm not sure the Community House is their main target."

"What do you mean?"

"From what he said, it was your father that caught their attention."

"Are you saying he's in trouble whether or not you do burn down the building?"

"I think it's possible."

"We have to go to the police – what other options do we have?"

"Not sure. At least if we knew where they were keeping him then we'd have a better idea of what to do. But they could be anywhere."

"There is one place I can think of."

"Where?"

"Bob's house."

"Right." Paul pinched the skin on his throat.

"He lives on a smallholding down a lane off the main road towards Holyhead – a couple of miles outside the village."

"He has the right type of crazy to mix with that crowd but I'm not certain if he's mad enough to support their methods." Paul rubbed his jaw. "I haven't seen him since my run-in with him."

"Even if they were there, what could we do?" Sarah asked. "It's not like we can drive over there and knock on the door."

"If there's a way I can get close enough to look, then maybe there's something I can do to help Gwilym. I don't think they'd expect that. All I'd need to do is get near to the place. Basic recon. Is there a way I could get to the house without using the road?"

"You could cross the fields from the coast. I could drop you off near the track that leads down to Kimble Beach. That route in the dark would be your best bet. But I'm not sure. It would be risky – these people are dangerous."

"I know, but this is our best option right now. At least we have some time. If Bob's place is clear, then we'll regroup and figure out what we do then."

"I just hope you're right." She put her head in her hands and began to gently sob. She lifted her head; her eyes were red, and tears streamed down her face.

"Why would they do this to an elderly man?"

Paul put his arm around her and kissed her head.

"We'll go as soon as it's dark."

TWENTY-NINE

The two were silent as they drove down the narrow lane towards Kimble Beach in Sarah's old Mini. It was late evening, and their current location was far enough from the village street lamps so that beyond the car headlights, the night was a wall of nothingness. The road had a narrow strip of grass in the middle which made a sweeping noise as the car moved over it. On either side were thick, high hedges that in the dark could be mistaken for black walls.

"How will you find your way in the dark?" Sarah asked. "You shouldn't use the torch. It might draw attention to you."

"My eyes will adapt. We used to do night manoeuvres in army training. Your eyes can see a lot in the darkness when they need to."

"Oh."

"You okay?" Paul asked.

"Just worried. Dad is seventy-six. Asides from what they might do to him, I'm concerned about how the experience will affect him."

"He's tougher than you give him credit for, you know. In the end, he came through the Revelation better than most. And he's pretty fit for a man of his age – he's been up and down that hill to the Community House every day for the last few months."

"Maybe, but he's been through so much."

There was a brief silence as a rabbit ran in front of the car.

"What do we do if they are here?" Sarah asked.

"I'm not sure yet. I haven't worked these people out yet."

"What do you mean?"

"Well, in Belfast, we came to know the various paramilitary groups – the IRA, UDA, UVF. We knew what made them tick – when to engage them and when things were a lost cause."

"Lost cause?" Sarah's voice started cracking.

"I'm not really sure what to make of these people that have taken up arms since the Revelation. They're not fighting for freedom. They're more like religious extremists. The Witnesses say they're supporting the will of the External Force. Despite the knowledge the Revelation has given us, they kill in cold blood."

Paul rolled down the window and inhaled the summer night air. "I don't know how we go up against that. It scares me."

"How did your friend end up with them?"

"Karl's another unpredictable one. He had a rough childhood; spent most of it at a care home run by the church where things were… worse than I'd ever appreciated."

He stopped and reached his arm out of the window. "He's always had an unpleasant side to him. He could be fun and charming when he wanted to be. But he could also be a nastier bastard than anyone out there."

"How close were you to him?"

"We were the best of friends as kids but in later years we became more like drinking buddies. Kindred spirits feeding off each other's misery."

"Is there no way of appealing to his good side?"

"I don't know. The Revelation and belief in the External Force has awoken something dark inside of him. Perhaps he's allowed it to take control."

"That's a frightening prospect."

Paul thought on this for a second. "You know, I always wondered whether his bitterness about my faith came from a jealousy. That he wanted some parts of what the church gave me but just couldn't come to accept it. Maybe the External Force gave him something he didn't have before – a sense of purpose and a will. He spoke of the other Witnesses like family members. Maybe it brought him love as well."

Sarah slowed the car down and turned left down an even narrower lane. This road was rough, and they both shook from side to side as the Mini's old suspensions struggled. Before long, the hedges ended, and the route opened to a small rocky clearing.

"This is the beach car park," Sarah said. "This is as far as I can take you."

"Okay." Paul reached for the door handle but then stopped. He turned to face Sarah, whose eyes were welling up.

"Call or text me as soon as you find out. Have you got everything?"

Paul took out his phone and a torch. "Yeah. Go straight home. I'll be alright."

He leant over and they embraced. He opened the door and stepped out into the dark. As Sarah drove off, he checked his pocket – he also had his penknife.

He could not see the sea, but he heard the waves and could smell it on the breeze. Paul closed his eyes, giving them time to adapt to the darkness. The first thing he noticed as he opened them were the stars above. The clear night sky was carpeted in tiny sparkling diamonds.

Paul made his way further down the small lane to the beach. He walked along the sand until he reached a rocky outcrop. There, he climbed the fence and headed inland across a field. He took his time as he moved along the edge, staying close to the hedgerow and trying to keep his head down to ensure he was unnoticed.

Paul's mind raced. A memory came to him. He was sat at the bar in the Sailor's Return with Karl, at around the time they found out that Eve was sick.

"What's the news with Eve?" Karl asked.

"Cancer. All those years of smoking have destroyed her lungs."

"Oh man… how bad is it?"

"As bad as it gets. They're going to try chemo, but the chances of it helping her are slim. The only benefit is in terms of keeping her alive. Cure was not a word they used."

"Can't they cut it out?"

"No, it's spread too far. And in both lungs. All they can do is try and shrink it."

"Shit, mate, that's grim. Is she at the hospital now?"

"No, back home. Probably sat in her armchair with a fag in her mouth."

"Then what are you doing here, dickhead?"

"I don't know what to say to her. Can't reassure her about the future. The present doesn't hold much joy. And the past, well, we can't reminisce much about that, I've been a terrible husband."

"There must be somebody who can help you with that?"

"I did think about going over to the church and talking to that pastor."

"You should fuck that thought right off, mate."

"I know you're not a fan of all that but I'm struggling here."

"You'd be perfect fodder for them. They love the desperate ones. You wait and see – as soon as they get their claws into you, there will be no release."

"I'm aware those bastards did a number on you, but they're not all like that."

"Yeah, they are, and it all comes from the same place. A need to dominate. Insecure old men preying on the vulnerable and exploiting the weak. It's what organised religions are built on. Sure, there's probably more sadists and predators in the Catholic church than anywhere else but the same need for power exists across all of them. The problem is people. We're all inherent cunts by design."

Paul's head dropped. He sighed.

"Mate, you know it doesn't take much to get me going on this stuff."

"It's just not what I need right now."

"What do you need?"

"I need someone to tell me how I can help Eve. Someone to tell me how I can give her some hope."

"I'm not sure anyone can, mate."

*

Paul hurried across the field. The sound of waves diminished as the distance from the sea grew. When he came up over a slight incline, he could see the light of the small farmhouse where Bob lived. There was smoke coming from the chimney. As he got closer, he could see the whole farm. On one side of the house was a small wooded area and on the other were two or three conjoined farm buildings. Stables. The hedge line curved around the house meaning Paul would be able to approach the property and view the buildings while remaining hidden. He walked closer and stopped as near to the farmhouse as he could. Crouched down next to the hedge, he watched carefully for a few minutes but was unable to gather any tangible evidence of whether the Witnesses were present or had been. The lights were certainly on on the ground floor but the curtains were drawn. He would need to get closer. He moved further along the hedge until he was adjacent to the wooded area. Carefully, he climbed over the barbed wire fence and moved through the shrubs and tree branches until he came out on the other side in amongst the trees. They provided cover for him to move nearer the house. As he got closer, he could see the building from another perspective. In front of it, on a concrete courtyard, were Bob's brown Ford Cortina and a white transit van. He couldn't ever remember seeing Bob with a white van like that, but still, this was not proof of anything.

He came out of the wooded area, ever mindful of his surroundings and any movement. There were no windows on the side of the house that faced the woods, so he was unable to gain any more information about the occupants.

He dashed over to the house and pressed his back against it. Still hugging the wall, he moved to the corner and looked over at the courtyard area where the van was parked. Beyond the van, he now had visibility of the group of connected stables. A light was on in the central building. Paul stretched his head further out and saw that a young man was resting on the wall outside of this building smoking. In his arms was the indistinguishable shape of an AK-47 assault rifle. His eyes opened wide and his hands knotted into fists. The Witnesses were here. Heart racing, he doubled back and dived into the trees.

He found a spot to hide and took out his phone. He stared at it for a moment. He could see Gwilym, scared, alone and tied up. Who knows what they might've done to him? He put his phone back in his pocket and hurried back to the side of the house. The young man was no longer by the door of the stable. Paul looked around; there was no sign of him. He began crawling along the ground next to the back of the house – moving underneath the windows that looked out over the field. He looked again and could see no sign of the armed man. He continued crawling across the yard until he reached the side of the stables. From there, he went into the first building. The stable was dark and stank of a mixture of manure and petrol. On the side was a bench covered in all sorts of tools and mechanical components. Paul kicked something metallic in the dark and saw that the smell of fuel was coming from a full jerrycan.

He looked out through the door – firstly at the house and the courtyard and then down towards the second building where the light was on. There was still no one around. Paul crouched down and moved as fast as he could towards the middle building. There were two saloon-bar-style doors that filled most of the entrance – one was closed and the other hung open allowing the light out. Paul pulled the open one to let himself in. The light inside was bright and he had to shut his eyes. When he opened them, the first thing he saw was a pair of feet dangling in the air. Slowly he looked up and saw Gwilym hanging from a noose tied to the stable rafters. His pale twisted face could no longer speak but the expression was of pain. Suffering. Paul fell back against the wall. He put his hand over his mouth and the world closed in on him. His chest felt tight, and he choked, unable to breathe. His body and mind froze. Wave after wave of panic and desperation hit him. He stared as his friend's body swayed in the stale summer-night air of the stable.

He couldn't stay there. His mind was screaming at him that he needed to get up, that he was in imminent danger. Run, or else you're dead. No, stand your ground. Make these fuckers suffer. He needed to do something.

From behind Gwilym's body, Eve stepped into view. She looked worried. "What are you doing, you idiot? We need to get out of here right now. We'll die if we don't go right this second. You were only meant to see if they were here."

But her appearance enabled his rage to come into focus. His fury was now pure. Distilled. Indecision was gone and he saw with clarity what he needed to do. He heard footsteps and looked around the room. In the corner he saw an axe lodged in a tree stump. He rushed over and grabbed it. Eve tried to stop him, but he pushed her out of his way. She fell to the floor and cowered where she landed. Paul stood upright against the wall next to the door with the axe held up in his arms ready to swing. The door of the stable opened and the young man with the assault rifle stepped inside. Before he could register his presence, Paul lunged forwards and swung the axe diagonally at him striking him in the neck. The axe was sharp, and it cut deep into the man's flesh – well into the bone and likely severing his windpipe. Blood began gushing out onto the floor. He made clumsy attempts to grab the axe but all he could do was paddle it with his palm. Repeatedly, he reached up and swung at it like he was swatting away a fly. He tried to vocalise but the only sounds that came from his mouth were pants and gargles. He fell to his knees. His attempts to grab the axe became more of a flailing action. Paul stepped closer and peered into the dying man's eyes. He tried to say something, but again the sounds were an incoherent clump of throaty grunts. He fell to the floor fully and was awkwardly tilted onto his side by the handle of the axe. Blood continued to pump from his neck. It sounded like a bath emptying. Paul looked to Eve to say something, but she was gone. He closed his hands into tight fists and roared like a crazed animal. He could feel the adrenalin pumping through his veins. His eyes were wide open, and he was ready for war.

Paul ran out of the stable and up to the windows by the front of the house. He peered in and saw that the curtains were open. Inside, he could see Bob sat by a dining table with a glass of something in front of him. Karl stood by the fireplace. He talked and his hands were animated. The others appeared to be listening. There were three other men and two women in the room, who Paul did not recognise. These were the Witnesses. The rage came to him again and he looked back at the stables. He wiped the spittle away from the corners of his mouth and ran over to the building nearest the field. There were chains hanging on the wall, and pieces of timber piled in the corner. Paul grabbed these, the jerrycan and a piece of piping. He then went over to the middle stable and searched the body of the young man until he found some matches. The box was drenched in blood, so he checked inside; thankfully, the matches were dry. He tore a piece of material from the man's trouser leg – seemingly the only piece of his clothing that was untouched by the blood – and took the rifle.

Paul tried as hard as he could to be quiet as he rushed back to the house. Firstly, he went to the back door and examined the frame. It was an old oak door that opened inwards. He could lock it by placing a chain around the handle and then attaching this to an old iron boot scraper that was fixed into the cement of the wall near the bottom of the door. He pulled tightly on the chain to ensure it was secure and to be certain there was no way the door could be opened. Paul then moved around to the front of the house, crawling underneath the window he previously looked through. The front door was also solid wood. It opened outwards so he was able to jam it closed by placing one of the timber pieces across. This, he wedged in place using gaps in the stone structure of the surrounding archway.

He returned to the window and checked on the situation in the living room. The scene was the same. Karl was continuing to hold court while his brothers and sisters listened. Paul went back to the front door and opened the jerrycan. He checked the letter box would open and looked inside. The living room door was closed, and the hallway was a cluttered mess of boxes and old newspapers. *Perfect*, he thought. He put the piping into the jerrycan and then placed the other end in his mouth. He sucked until he tasted petrol and then he stuck the end of the piping through the letter box. As the contents of the jerrycan emptied into the house, Paul tried spitting to rid the taste of petrol from his mouth.

Once the container was empty, he took the piece of cloth and soaked it in some residual fuel on the inside of the jerrycan, then lit it and dropped it through the letter box. The fire erupted inside instantly and within seconds, the hallway was engulfed in flames. He could feel the heat through the small opening in the door. It didn't take long for the occupants to sense what was happening and panic ensued. Paul crouched down next to the wall in front of the house. He couldn't make out exactly what was happening but there was a great deal of screaming coming from inside. He watched and had the gun trained on the window, expecting there to be an attempt at escape. It appeared that the curtains and the fixtures around the window were burning, making this route less possible. From what he could see, the old building had gone up like a bonfire.

Paul circled the house and checked the other windows. He could see Bob trying to break the frame in one of the bedrooms upstairs. He took a couple of shots at the window and Bob disappeared. He heard glass smashing and another scream. One of the women had jumped from the upstairs window at the front of the house and had fallen to the ground. She was motionless and the fire on her clothes spread until her torso was burning. More screams came from inside. Paul did a further couple of laps around the house, taking periodic shots. These were more to deter the occupants from trying to escape than to take anyone out. He wanted them to burn. He wanted them to suffer.

Flames emerged from all the windows and the only noises he heard were the roar of the fire and the snapping timber as floors collapsed. The flames unified as a single violent raging beast. He walked around and around until he was certain that no further living soul was present in the house. He couldn't see what happened to Karl but assumed he had perished like the rest of them, in the belly of the beast.

Paul picked up the jerrycan and took it and the gun over to the body in the middle stable. There, he wiped off both objects with his clothes and took the man's motionless hands and placed the fingers all over the two objects – paying particular attention to the handle of the jerrycan and the grip and stock of the gun. He stood up and took another look at the burning farmhouse. It really was a glorious spectacle to behold.

Paul took out his phone and texted Sarah.

WEF R HERE GET HELP NOW

He walked over to the corner of the room, careful to be fully clear of the blood, and lay down on the floor. He was exhausted and panted like he'd run a mile. Gwilym's body gently rocked from side to side, temporarily blocking the light from the bulb above. Paul watched the slowly oscillating shadow that was cast against the wall. He felt numb. All he could do was wait and listen to the sounds of crackling, snapping, and popping.

THIRTY

Paul walked into the interview room to be greeted by two police officers. Detective Evans was dressed in a grey suit. He was a large man with a receding grey hairline and a red complexion. Evans had interviewed Paul a few times over the last week. Next to him was a female officer in uniform, who appeared to be of a higher rank. Paul had not seen her before.

"Thank you, Mr Harris, for coming to see us once again," Evans said. "We just wanted to check your statement one last time before you sign it. This is Chief Inspector Selsby. She is here to witness your final statement confirmation."

"Okay," Paul said. "But I do need to be back in Llanffug by two for the funeral."

"Oh, that's fine, this won't take long."

He showed Paul a piece of paper. "In a moment, I'll be asking you to sign this document. But before I do that, I will summarise the events once again."

"Right."

"On the afternoon of Friday, June nineteenth, you, and Ms Davies were walking along the beach when you were approached by Mr Karl Murphy, who you recognised as an acquaintance from your home in Salford. Ms Davies then left, at which point Mr Murphy told you that he was a member of the terrorist group, the Witnesses of the External Force, and that they had abducted Ms Davies' father, Mr Gwilym Davies."

"That's correct."

"He told you that they would hurt – implying murder – him unless you burnt down the Llanffug Community House by dawn of the next day."

"Yes."

"You challenged Mr Murphy but he tasered you, leaving you incapacitated on the ground."

Paul nodded.

"As soon as you recovered, you ran back to the Golygfa Môr guest house where you told Ms Davies what had happened, and you both discussed what to do. You decided not to call the authorities at this stage because of the imminent threat to Mr Davies' life."

"We thought we were doing the right thing." Paul dropped his head.

"Based on previous experience and from what Mr Murphy told you, you both agreed that the best option was to visit Mr Robert Parry's farm two miles outside of the Llanffug village, to ask him whether he had any knowledge of the group's activities in the area."

Detective Evans paused and Paul stared at him.

"Ms Davies dropped you off and when you arrived at the farm, it was evident that something was going on. From a hiding spot near the entrance, you saw Mr Murphy and another gentleman, Mr James Faith, coming out of the central building in a row of old stables. Mr Faith was carrying an assault rifle and they both argued about something. You said it was apparent that Mr Murphy was particularly angry with Mr Faith. They stood in the courtyard yelling at each other. Then, Mr Murphy went into the house, followed by Mr Faith."

"Yep."

"You decided to see what had happened in the stable where they had emerged from. Upon entering the stable, you found Mr Davies' lifeless body hanging from a noose attached to the rafters. In shock and fear for your life you planned to escape before calling for help. However, it was at that point you saw Mr Faith emerging from the house. He appeared agitated and aggressive. From your position in the central stable building, you watched as Mr Faith took some materials from the end building and proceeded to barricade both the front and back doors of the house in order to prevent any occupants from leaving."

"I couldn't see him at the back entrance from my position, but it's what I assumed he was doing."

"Right," the detective said. "After that, he siphoned petrol from a fuel container in through the front door using a short pipe. He then tore a piece of cloth from his trouser leg, soaked it in fuel and dropped the burning material in through the front door."

"That's right." Paul nodded. Under the table he rubbed his palms on his thighs.

"As the fire took hold of the building, he then started periodically shooting the rifle into the house, presumably to deter anyone from trying to escape. One of the occupants – a young woman – did manage to make it out but she was badly burnt and died outside from her injuries. When it was evident that there were no more survivors inside, Mr Faith lowered his rifle."

"And he headed back towards the stables."

"Yes, and then he headed back towards the stable buildings. You panicked and reached for the nearest means of defending yourself, which was an axe. When he walked in, you swung at him and inflicted a fatal injury. At that stage you contacted Ms Davies, asking for immediate help. Emergency services were on-site within thirty minutes. Is that everything, Mr Harris?"

"Yes, that is correct."

"Quite an ordeal for you, Mr Harris," the detective said before leaning back in his chair. He looked at Paul and tilted his head to the side. Paul bit his lip.

He sat back up. "Anyway, if we could just ask you to sign here and here. Date here. And you can be on your way."

He handed the paper to Paul and pointed to a couple of spots on the document. Paul took it, scanned over it, and signed the document.

The detective then turned to his colleague. "Thank you, ma'am. That's everything."

She smiled at him and got up from the chair. "Mr Harris," she said before nodding and walking out, closing the door behind her.

"Am I okay to go now?" Paul asked.

"Just one thing, Mr Harris. I need to inform you the Cheshire Constabulary are very keen to speak with you so please be expecting a call in the next few days."

"What about?"

"I can't get into details right now, but they will arrange that discussion with you. They'll probably send someone down and the interview will happen here."

"Right. Okay." Paul sighed and rubbed his jaw. "Cheshire police – that's odd."

The detective pushed his chair away from the table and stood up.

"We have all we need. Thank you. Let me show you out."

They both walked from the interview room, down a corridor and then out through the reception area. Neither spoke a word. The detective opened the main doors for Paul to exit the building, and to his surprise he followed Paul. Evans took out a pack of cigarettes and put one in his mouth before lighting it.

Paul reached into his pocket for his phone and texted Jerry to say he was ready for pick-up.

"You know, you did a decent job of that," the detective said, "on the whole."

"What? What are you talking about?"

"Getting away with wiping out a whole terrorist cell."

"What? You know what happened."

"Yes, I do." Evans smiled. "But don't worry, this story works better for everyone."

Paul looked at his phone and pretended he was checking his messages. "What do you mean?"

"There was evidence." Evans looked around as if to ensure no one was listening. "Petrol on your coat. Your fingerprints on what was left of the plank used to barricade the front door. Even DNA from your hair on the chain."

Paul looked up into the eyes of the taller man. "If that was the case, then why not charge me?"

"It was considered. But compare these two scenarios. In the first, there is an argument within the terrorist group about the violent behaviour of one member towards a person they have captive. This overflows and results in that member killing the rest in a fit of rage. The cell implodes."

"Okay."

"In the second scenario, a resourceful member of the public discovers that an ideological group has committed a murder in the name of their cause and brutally kills all members in retaliation for their act. See the issue? They become martyrs. They inspire others to pick up arms and kill for the same cause."

"Quite a story," Paul said.

"Don't worry, Mr Harris. Paul. This version of events has been signed off by individuals who are high up the food chain. It works best for everyone and to be honest, you did us a favour. I just hope you don't get a taste for this kind of thing."

"I won't." Paul looked down at his phone again and then glanced up at the police officer. "And what about the other matter? The thing with Cheshire police?"

The detective took a long drag on his cigarette.

"I shouldn't tell you this but as you did us a favour, let me do you one. They want to talk to you about a murder in Delamere Forest."

"What?"

"A woman's body was found bludgeoned in the woods near a remote cottage. Until now it was assumed the husband did it, but he's missing. They had a young girl – three years old – and she was found at a farmhouse three miles away."

"What's it got to do with me?"

"Your DNA matched with something that was found at the cottage. A bloody towel in the bathroom, I think." Evans looked at Paul and raised his eyebrows.

"What about the husband?"

"At present he's still the primary suspect but the problem is the government is putting more and more pressure on the police to solve all the crimes that happened after the Revelation. And as time goes on, and the husband still fails to show, then it starts to look increasingly bad for anyone else involved."

Paul looked to the entrance of the car park and saw Jerry in his Range Rover turn in. He stroked the scar on his left arm.

"Okay, thanks. I better get going."

"We'll be in touch."

"Great."

He opened the passenger door of Jerry's car and stepped in.

"All sorted?" Jerry asked.

"For now." Paul exhaled heavily.

"You'll never be free." Paul looked in the side mirror and saw Eve sat behind him. He rubbed his hands together. They felt cold and clammy.

"You okay, bud?" Jerry asked.

Paul nodded and squeezed his eyes shut.

"How was Sarah doing this morning?"

"I didn't speak to her. Had to drop something off at the Community House, ahead of the funeral. To be honest, we haven't spoken much since the day of the attack."

They both briefly sat in silence.

"She doesn't blame you for what happened, you know."

"Yeah."

"But whatever you experienced at that farm, you need to try and put it behind you and be there for her. She's suffering, man."

"I know. I'll try."

The rest of the journey back to the village was quiet. Jerry dropped Paul off at the guest house before returning to his own home to get ready for the funeral.

Paul came downstairs wearing a black suit he'd borrowed from Dave. It was evidently designed for a different shaped man – someone with shorter arms, longer legs, and narrower hips. But for Paul it was still the best option at this stage. Sarah was stood by the window stroking Gwilym's armchair. She wore a dark floral dress that hugged her body and defined her curvy figure against the blue sky beyond the glass. Paul felt a strange, unfamiliar feeling – it was desire. But then guilt soon followed; it was her father's funeral. The wall came back up.

He walked over to her, placed his hand on hers. Her red eyes and his connected and they hugged. He felt her arms squeeze tight on his back. As he held her, he looked out of the window and saw that the hearse had arrived.

"It's time to go," he said.

Together, they walked behind the hearse as it made its way along the familiar route to the Community House. It would be Gwilym's final journey.

They entered the old building to see all seats were occupied – apart from two in the front row that were reserved for them. They walked down the aisle past numerous familiar faces. There were many there as well who Paul did not recognise. When they sat down, he reached over for Sarah's hand and held it tight.

The doors opened and a few of the village men carried in the coffin. They brought it down the aisle and placed it at the front on a short-legged table. The coffin itself had the appearance of a large picnic basket. It was made of a woven seagrass. Sarah thought the sustainable style suited her father's progressive mindset.

The funeral ceremony would be conducted by a celebrant who was an old colleague of Gwilym at the university. Sarah had met with her earlier in the week to arrange proceedings. She stood near the front, watching everything and holding a handful of papers. She was not dressed completely in black, which Paul thought a little unexpected. A suited young man sat with a cello in the corner; he watched the audience and kept an eye on the celebrant. As soon as Paul and Sarah sat down, the celebrant nodded to the young cellist and he started playing.

The instrument sounded glorious against the ancient walls. Paul closed his eyes and tried to focus on the music. But the darkness only attracted striking visions. The familiar image of the beach that had stayed with him most of his adult life came first. But this time, the Eve who lay with her head on his lap was not the young, innocent soul who he had fallen in love with, but the older, sick Eve – the one who was dying and ravaged by cancer. His mind's postcard image had become corrupted. He tried to think of something else. He was outside the pub in Belfast watching gunmen threaten his army friends. The lead gunman walked around them shouting. Then he stopped and looked out through the window. Lifting his ski mask, Paul saw Karl's smirking face. Paul shook his head again, like it was a snow globe with an image that was reset each time he did that. He was now walking through dark woods carrying a child. But the child was heavier than he remembered. He looked down and saw that he was carrying Kat. He stared at her in disbelief before looking away. Now he was in the stables of Bob's farm looking at Gwilym's body. Gwilym's eyes opened, and he gazed at Paul, silently. Paul wanted to reach up and help him, but he couldn't.

He opened his eyes and two thin threads of tears escaped and streamed down his cheeks. He wiped them with his hands. Ahead of him, a photo of Gwilym was beamed onto the white walls. As the music ended, the celebrant stood up and walked to the front of the room.

"Welcome here today to celebrate Professor Gwilym Davies' life – husband, father, academic and passionate advocate for enlightenment. The music we just heard was Bach, 'Suite Number One in G Major' – a favourite of Gwilym's. Today's ceremony has been planned with many of Gwilym's preferences in mind. Throughout his life he was a passionate advocate for history, philosophy, theology, literature, and music, as I'm sure many of you here will know. And of course, where better to celebrate than in this building in which he – albeit briefly – brought the illumination of knowledge and wisdom to many in a time of darkness and uncertainty."

The celebrant walked over to the laptop near the front and pressed a key, changing the image on the wall. It now showed a photo Paul had not seen before – Gwilym as a younger man stood in front of a room full of students.

"I worked with Gwilym for a good twenty years at the university in Bangor. One of the strange things about playing the role of celebrant at his funeral is that death and the human view of mortality was one of Gwilym's greatest passions. If there was someone who could talk about the subject matter in a reasoned, thoughtful, and entertaining manner, it would have been him."

She picked up a bound old book that Paul had seen sat on the bookshelf at the guest house and showed it to the congregation.

"Not many here will know that the title of the doctoral thesis Gwilym wrote over fifty years ago was *Fear No More the Heat o' the Sun*. It was a reference to a poem from the Shakespeare play, *Cymbeline*, which talks about why we should not fear death – it being an integral part of life that impacts us all. Jane, a friend of Gwilym for many years and colleague from the local council will now come up and read the whole poem."

Jane walked over from her seat holding a piece of paper. When she reached the front, she looked to the celebrant and nodded then looked to Sarah and half smiled.

She lifted the paper and started to read.

"*Fear no more the heat o' the sun, nor the furious winter's rages. Thou thy worldly task hast done, home art gone, and ta'en thy wages. Golden lads and girls all must, as chimney-sweepers, come to dust.*"

After the poem reading had finished, Sarah let go of his hand and she picked up a folder from the floor.

"I will now ask Sarah, Gwilym's only child, to read the eulogy."

Sarah stepped up to the front. She held the open folder tight in her hands. She did not appear as comfortable in front of an audience as her father had, who had stood in the very same spot only two weeks earlier.

She looked at everyone and forced a slight smile.

"I'm not the entertainer my father was."

There was a sympathetic titter from the congregation.

"So please, do not expect his theatrics.

"First, please let me thank everyone for coming today to celebrate his life. The last week has been a strange and difficult time. But the strength and support I have received from so many people around me – particularly those here in the village – has made it more bearable. It's fair to say my father was a man who was very comfortable with an audience. But not even he could have predicted his death would have received the attention it has."

She paused to turn the page.

"My father was a passionate man. For most of his life, he held strongly on to his faith. He believed in education and taking studies seriously. He used to say that wisdom and knowledge were the two most important tools you needed in life. He liked nothing more than a glass of wine and a deep discussion on what the ancient thinkers had to say about the various facets of life.

"Dad and I didn't always see eye to eye. When I was eight, to try and get out of going to Sunday school I told him I did not believe in God. What did he do? He marched me down the High Street to Bethania Chapel and told old Mr Jenkins that he needed to do a better job as a teacher.

"On my fourteenth birthday – quite a sensitive age for a young woman – he dressed in a toga and tried to entertain the guests at my party with a quiz about Greek philosophers, which he acted out before reading excerpts of *Hamlet* for about an hour. I was horrified."

There was louder laughter this time from the congregation.

She continued. "When I was older, he challenged my choice in university studies, my choice in career, and my choice in men. Evidently, he may well have been right about the last one."

Paul heard some whispering behind him.

"Sadly, this led to a lot of disagreement and during my time in Manchester we weren't always as close as we should have been. What I learnt, however, with time, was that he didn't challenge me out of a need for control, he genuinely challenged me to do better and find things in life that would make me happy. He had been lucky in many ways. He loved his career and was passionate about his studies. He loved my mother and could never see a better person for him than her. He wanted the same for me, but I didn't always see it like that."

She wiped a tear from her eye. Paul looked away – up at the walls and then down at the ground.

"Things changed drastically over the course of a few months around five years ago. My marriage was falling apart and then we found out Mam was ill. It was a difficult time, but it did give me a second chance to come back here and get to know my father again.

"When Mam finally died, a piece of Dad was lost as well. Not long afterwards, he found new purpose with a role in the community council. There, he could focus on improving the lives of people here in the village."

Sarah took out a handkerchief and then dabbed her eye.

"The Revelation was an event that turned the world on its head, and when it happened, I thought we'd lost Dad as well. He did disappear somewhere, for a time at least. But he returned with a new-found vigour and helped inject this little village with desperately needed energy to put it on the map. He arrived with his tools of wisdom and knowledge and put them to good use, as best he could. Sadly, at this stage, his leadership and pursuit of the greater good was his undoing. Something had changed the world in an instant, but there were a cruel few who were not ready to face a new future so quickly."

She sighed heavily and fought back the tears. Paul crossed his arms and pulled tight on his chest.

"Dad, I know you won't hear me, but I'll say these words anyway. I love you and I miss you. And I wish you weren't taken from us. Thank you for everything, Dad. *Diolch am bopeth*. Goodnight, Dad. *Nos da.*"

As she ended her reading, she broke down in tears. Paul rushed over, put his arm around her and brought her back to her seat.

*

At the end of the service, the coffin was taken outside by the pall-bearers. The rest of the congregation followed. Gwilym would be buried in a corner plot near the sea, in the same grave as his wife. Arm in arm, Paul and Sarah carefully treaded around and between the other graves. There were only whispers amongst the congregation as they gathered around the hole. The celebrant brought everyone together for her final words.

"Now we return our brother Gwilym to the earth."

As she spoke, the coffin was lowered into the hole.

"There, his body will break down and become the soil and the plants and the air around. His flesh and the surroundings will become one. His molecules return to the universe from whence they came and in the same way we all will one day. His memory lives on in our hearts and our minds but his physical being remains here for ever."

She grabbed a handful of soil, as the coffin reached the bottom of the grave.

"Now for those who wish to, please help us to return Gwilym to the earth." She dropped the soil into the hole.

"Let us help your physical being return to nature – its home and its origin."

Sarah did the same, as did Paul before walking away. Then a few others. The two stood by the wall of the graveyard gazing out at the sea. The summer air was warm and dry, and Paul could feel the heat of the sun. The wind had died down and the surface of the sea appeared calm. But there were darker clouds out near the horizon.

"There's a storm coming," Sarah said.

"I thought it'd passed already," Paul said.

"It's always coming. As soon as one has passed, then it's time to expect the next one."

Paul leant on the wall and sighed. "It doesn't end, does it?"

THIRTY-ONE

Paul and Sarah walked into the Pilgrim Inn, hand in hand. Sarah made a beeline for the bar.

"I'm off to get a wine," she said. "Do you want a Coke?"

"Sure."

Paul looked around. The pub was full, and the majority were dressed in black. Even Dave, stood serving behind the bar, was still in his suit having come straight from the funeral. There was a buffet in the function room where those peckish could fill their bellies, but thirst was the key concern of most at this stage.

Sarah came over and handed Paul a large fizzy drink with ice. They both tapped their glasses and made a delicate clinking sound. Sarah glanced over Paul's shoulder and raised her glass to someone stood behind him. Jerry came over and stretched his big frame around Sarah to give her a hug. "Sarah, baby. How are you holding up?"

"I'm okay – this helps." She nodded to the glass of wine.

"Patrick and I were just saying what a nice service it was." His partner stood near the fireplace talking to a few of the other funeral attendees.

"Excuse me for a second," Paul said. "The drink's taking effect already."

Paul left the two chatting and went to the toilet. As he returned, he walked past the fireplace, and the flickering of the flames caught his gaze. He stopped and stared into the heart of the fire. The sound of the jukebox and the chattering of those around began to fade, as though the volume dial was being turned down until all he heard were the whispers of the flames. He saw the Witnesses in the fire; their faces twisted by suffering. Karl was in their midst and his mouth moved. His voice was gentle, and he spoke in the language of the flames. "We are with you now, Paul. Forever connected, we are with you."

"Paul," someone yelled behind him, and his connection to the fire was broken. He felt light-headed and rushed out onto the decking outside at the back of the pub. He leaned over the barrier and looked out over the beach towards the sea. The pub was at the opposite side of the bay to the headland. In the distance, he could just about make out the shape of the Community House. An old man sat on a bench at the far end of the decking staring at his phone and smoking a cigarette. Paul was otherwise alone until Sarah came out carrying their drinks.

"Didn't you hear me calling you?" she asked.

"Sorry, just needed some air."

He bit his lip and thought about his next words.

"A lot has happened, hasn't it?"

"Yes," Sarah said. "You could say that."

"How are you doing? Are you okay?"

Sarah turned to look at the sea. "What do you mean by okay? Are you asking if I'm coping? Well yes, I'm just about holding it all together right now. But I feel like a house of cards that could topple at any second. On the inside, I feel broken. I feel like I've been torn to pieces. I haven't even begun to process the horrors my father experienced before his death, let alone consider that he's gone."

Paul put his arm around her.

"I'm sorry I haven't been there for you these last few days."

"It can't have been easy for you either. You had a front-row seat."

"Yes, but I think I may have been avoiding you. It's what I do when things get hard. I try and get away. Escape and evade at all costs. But I should've been there for you. I want to be there for you, Sarah. I want to stop running from stuff. I need to stop reacting to the world around me and start taking control. I need to stop blaming the universe for the bad things that happen and start taking responsibility for my own actions."

Sarah didn't respond. She turned to face Paul and looked into his eyes. Those beautiful dark brown eyes carried so much sadness. Paul grabbed her and pulled her close, tensing his arms as he wrapped them around her like a vice. She began to shudder deep heavy sobs that sounded like they originated somewhere deep within.

"It's okay," he said.

When she stopped, she stepped away from Paul and exhaled heavily before carefully dabbing her eyes.

"You alright?" he asked.

"It helps. Although I probably look like a mess."

"You look fine."

"Come on, enough of this. Let's go inside, I want to go get drunk."

"I think I might join you," Paul replied. Sarah's eyes widened then she nodded and shrugged her shoulders. She took Paul by the hand and the two returned to the main bar. Paul ordered a large glass of wine for Sarah, and a pint followed by a large whiskey chaser for himself.

*

A few hours passed, and for those left in the pub, the party was in full swing. Jerry brought out his guitar and sat in the corner playing a few acoustic numbers. He'd been instructed by Dave to keep it upbeat. A few of the others who attended the funeral were now also sat around him playing percussion instruments. Sarah was amongst them tapping along with a tambourine.

Paul smiled at her from where he stood – slightly swaying – near the fireplace. He'd lost track of the number of drinks he'd had over the course of the afternoon. He had picked at the buffet in-between pints and shots to lessen the impact of the alcohol. But he hadn't drunk anything in months, not even when tempted by Gwilym during their nightly discussions.

He was part of a conversation with three other attendees from the funeral, Lucy the butcher's wife, Rhodri, an old school friend of Gwilym's, and Jane. Sat near them – in close proximity to the fire, as always – was Bedwyr. He listened in to their discussion but was rarely distracted from his duties of tending to the flames.

"I don't think we'll ever know what caused it," Lucy said. As often happened in recent months, the discussion had moved on to the Revelation.

"With all the research and resources going into finding out what happened, it's strange that we still know nothing," Jane said.

"Or they're telling us nothing," Rhodri said.

"Of course, they know what happened." Dave interjected from behind the bar as he gathered used glasses onto a tray. "They've bloody well known about aliens on this planet for decades – all that Area 51 and Roswell stuff."

"How do you know it's aliens?" Lucy asked giving Dave a curious look.

"What else could it be? No one here on this world has that kind of power."

"But why mess with us like that and then not show themselves?"

"Why would they need to?" Dave reached across the bar to pick up an empty glass. "For all we know, humanity might just be a side project for them."

"A side project?" Jane raised her eyebrows.

Dave stopped. "Yeah. What if this planet is just a big garden or a farm? The Revelation might just have been the gardener adding some insecticide to kill off something they didn't like."

"Dave, you're wasted in this pub." Lucy smiled at the rest of the group.

"To be fair, he might be right," Rhodri said. "Or at least the reality may be stranger than we can imagine."

Paul watched Sarah sing in the corner of the room. Every so often their eyes would connect like young lovers who had just got together. But then a thought came to him and he decided to chime into the discussion.

"What happens if we don't find out? That's possible, isn't it? What if we never know what the Revelation was?"

No one had an answer.

"Daysex macarena," a voice said from behind them. It was Bedwyr.

"What was that, Bedwyr?" Jane asked.

"Daysex macarena," he repeated, and they all turned around. "It's something Gwilym said. You know how he used to go on about all that ancient Latin stuff. He said that in their plays they would often end stories by having one of their gods turn up to explain any bits that needed sorting. The actors dressed as these gods were lowered down onto the stage using ropes and pulleys, and the whole thing was called daysex macarena."

Jane started nodding. "Ah, you mean *deus ex machina*."

"That's what I said."

The others in the group looked between the two.

"God from the machine," Jane said. "It's a term that describes something unexpected or sudden that's introduced to provide a final resolution in a story."

"That's right," Bedwyr said. "Gwilym used to joke that that's what we needed for the Revelation. For God to turn up and explain what happened. Like the daysex macarena thing. But the problem was the Revelation had killed our gods so there could be no explanation."

"And no resolution as to what happened." Jane half-smiled and started shaking her head. "Oh Gwilym."

"To Gwilym," Rhodri said, raising his glass. All the others raised their glasses and repeated his name.

As they finished their toast, Paul saw that Sarah was walking over.

"Is the show over?" Paul asked.

"I need a break," Sarah replied. "I might go for a walk on the beach to get some fresh air. Do you want to come?"

"Sure." Paul thought a break from the booze might be good for him. He went to get his coat and they met by the doorway. Sarah opened her jacket and showed a bottle of whiskey she had stashed in her inside pocket.

"Dave let me have a carry-out."

"Okay, so much for the break."

"Huh?"

"Nothing. Let's go."

The air felt thick and warm outside. The sun was low in the sky as they reached the beach, and the dark skies over the seas were close. In the distance, they could hear the faint rumble of thunder.

"Where do you want to go?" Paul asked.

"Anywhere. I just wanted to get outside for a bit and breathe some fresh air."

"I thought you were enjoying the music?"

"Oh, I was. But it's been a tiring day. And the wine was making me sleepy."

"Sleepy, right." Paul grinned.

They walked along the beach from one end near the harbour, down past the stone pier towards the water. The tide was out to its furthest point and the beach appeared huge.

"I think your dad would have been pleased with today."

"Yes, perhaps." She spoke with a flat tone.

"Everyone spoke so fondly of him. He'll be greatly missed here."

"I know."

"I'm just saying this because it might give you some comfort."

"I know, Paul. It's just hard to make sense of it all. Why did he have to suffer in that way? Why does stuff like that have to happen?"

"I asked your dad that same question. He said that life is random and driven by chaos. But people need to find meaning wherever they can. They like to think they're part of a story or some grand plan. Particularly when there's suffering. The idea that terrible things happen for no reason at all is difficult for people to accept."

She looked down and smiled. "I can hear his voice now."

Sarah turned her head like she was searching for something else to focus on.

"Hey, have you been to the Saint's Cave?"

"No, I don't think so."

"It's further up the beach, below the headland. You can only really get to it when the tide is out. Come on, let's go now."

Sarah took Paul by the hand and they walked at pace towards the other end of the beach. When they reached the eastern edge, where the headland cliffs overlooked them, they scrambled over a rocky outcrop that typically defined the separation of land and sea. This was not an area normally accessible when the tide was in, and Paul had rarely ventured this far. After clambering over a large barnacle-covered rock, they reached a smaller patch of sand. A secret beach.

"Here," Sarah said.

Walking along the sand, Paul could see the entrance to a small cave. They both stood at the opening and looked inside to see interesting rock formations and the darkness beyond.

"Saint's Cave."

"Why have you never shown me this place before?"

"It's not really accessible most of the time. Also, Ben doesn't like climbing over the rocks, so I don't tend to come here much anymore."

Sarah walked into the cave and sat on a boulder. She opened the whiskey, took a long sip, and then made a face as she swallowed.

"We used to have parties here when we were teenagers. It's where I had my first kiss."

"Who was that with?"

"Gwyn the butcher."

"Right, I see." Paul's eyes widened. "Before he married Lucy, I hope?"

"Oh, well before Lucy."

Paul went and sat next to her. She offered him the bottle and he took a deep swallow.

"Can I ask you something?" Sarah said.

"Of course."

"How are you okay after what you saw on Bob's farm?"

He sighed and thought about his words. "I'm not sure if I am." Paul drank from the bottle again as he considered how best to explain it all.

"It's like I'm still there. When I close my eyes, I can hear the fire; I can feel that young man's blood under my feet like a puddle; I can see your father's body right in front of me and if I reach out, I think I can touch it." He turned to look at Sarah.

"Bad things like that stay with you. You've got to find a way of living with them. And you do eventually, but they're always there, lurking in the shadows. Jumping out on you when you least expect it. It's how it's been before and what

I am used to." Paul stretched his neck back and pinched the skin of his throat.

"Do you remember our conversation at the beach, before Bob's farm?" Sarah asked.

"What about it?"

"About getting help. I still think you should. Might be the only way you can move forward with things."

Paul breathed out slowly. "Shit, you're right. I should do. I've been living with ghosts for so long that it's become normal for me. That's not right, is it?"

She half smiled and shook her head.

Paul's head dropped. "I could get in touch with that doctor at the hospital. She could probably advise me on what to do." He took a drink from the whiskey bottle, aware of Sarah's eyes watching him. "I don't think it would be easy. Some of these things have been with me for a long time." He turned to face Sarah. "There're probably things I should tell you as well. Things about my past. They may not be pretty. But they're who I am, or who I was at least."

"I want to know." She reached over and hugged Paul.

Paul then put his arms around her. He felt her breath on his neck and sensed her head lift slightly to align with his. He then turned his head and he looked into her eyes for a moment before they kissed. Paul's heart began racing, and something stirred inside him. Sarah stopped and moved her body away from his as though she was expecting an interruption. He looked around and it was just the two of them in the cave.

"It's okay," he said before pulling her back towards him. They kissed again, this time with less restraint. They held each other like it was the first time. Or the last. Paul felt

Sarah's hand move down towards his thigh and then beyond, into the space between. At the same time, his fingertips moved from her back down to her hip and then up to her chest. Her right hand reached to open the button above his fly. Something stopped Paul. He felt very aware and exposed. He wasn't ready yet. Not in this place, anyway.

"Wait," Paul said. "Not here, not like this."

Paul got up and took Sarah by the hand. Together they walked silently out of the cave and back the way they came across the rocks at the base of the cliff to the main beach and then on along the familiar route towards the guest house. Paul felt the longing, and every few steps they glanced at each other before carrying on with determination. She walked faster and he saw her from behind and examined the curves of her body. He felt himself become hard as he anticipated what would come next.

Sarah opened the front door quietly. Julie had been tasked with keeping an eye on things while they were out for the day, so she was around somewhere. A guest was in the living room watching television and raucous laughter came from the dining area. They tiptoed through without making eye contact nor saying a word to anyone. Up the stairs they walked together, hand in hand. She guided Paul to her bedroom and there they fell into each other as soon as the door was closed. They stood by her bed kissing and they held each other like they'd been waiting for this moment for an age. She brought her hand around and reached down into his trousers, grabbing his hard penis, pulling and pushing as best she could inside the tight-fitting trousers. He squeezed her buttocks before reaching below and lifting her skirt. His hand moved inwards – to between the thighs and he pushed upwards into her panties with his fingers. He tried rubbing before feeling a spot further back where there was more give and he felt she was wet.

Sarah let go of his penis; she removed his suit jacket and unbuttoned his shirt, before running her hands over his bare chest.

"Take your trousers off," she whispered before stepping back and reaching around to unzip her dress. He struggled with the unfamiliar buttons before managing to open them and drop the trousers to the floor. At the same time, he lost his balance and fell back onto the bed. There, he looked down and seeing the black socks he had on his feet, promptly took them off. Sarah appeared out of nowhere on top of him and they continued to kiss. He turned his head to his side so he could look at her whole body; her flesh only covered by black cotton underwear. He tried to reach around and open her bra, but his clumsy attempts failed, and she intervened and did it herself. She then leant back down, and he felt her warm breasts press against his chest. His hands were all over her as he gently felt her skin while also pulling her body close to his. She then turned on her side and removed her underwear to reveal her pubic hair. She climbed on to him, now fully naked and reached underneath to pull down on his underpants. She took his penis, and he felt her guide it inside her. He almost burst at once, but he tried to hold on. He watched as she raised the top half of her body and her breasts began to bounce as she moved up and down on him. She leant down to kiss him but became upright again soon, assuming a position where she could move more freely. He had forgotten how good this felt. He had forgotten how alive it made him feel. Eve was no longer at the front of his mind.

He tried hard to hold himself back as Sarah fucked him faster and faster. She moaned and breathed heavily. In a matter of seconds or minutes – who knew – he could hold back no longer, and he climaxed. He couldn't remember it feeling like that before. Instantaneously, Sarah stopped moving and she leant forward and held him.

Afterwards, they lay on the bed facing each other. Paul couldn't stop staring into her eyes, while Sarah stroked his face. His mind – for once – was silent, and as he felt himself drifting off into sleep, they shared one last moment.

"I think I love you," she said.

"I think I love you, too."

*

Paul woke up in the darkness and sat upright. Beads of cold sweat streamed down his spine. Something was wrong. But what had he done? He reached out and felt Sarah's skin. Everything that happened after the funeral was a drunken daze. *But this should be okay*, he thought. Why would he feel panic? Why would he feel revulsion? Why would he feel like he had betrayed someone? There was a thunderstorm outside, and the window shook from the heavy droplets of rain that pelted against it.

Then he heard another sound; someone crying. The sobbing came from a familiar voice. It called to him from the shadows. He looked around the room and saw the shapes of furniture and the outline of the door and the window, but there was no one there. There were no other noises to be heard – just one lone individual weeping. Paul got out of bed, naked, and looked around the room. He struggled to place the origin of the sound. He looked under the bed and saw nothing. There was no one in the bathroom or in the wardrobe. Then, when he opened the door of the room and let in a narrow sliver of light, he saw her. Crumpled on the floor with her head in her hands and tears streaming down her face was Eve.

"What is this?" Paul whispered.

Her young, red eyes and soaking face looked up at him.

"You betrayed me."

"But you're not really here."

"You wish I wasn't, but I am. You use this woman to try and forget about me. You try to erase me."

"I don't. I'm trying to move on. I loved you, Eve, but you're gone."

"You betrayed our life and my love by killing me off. If you want to erase me then let me help you."

Eve stood up and ran downstairs. Paul went to follow but realised he was naked. He dashed back into the bedroom and searched the floor for his clothes.

"Who were you talking to?" Sarah asked as she turned over in the dark.

"I've got to go."

He found his shirt and put it on quickly. Sarah sat up in bed.

"It was her, wasn't it? Eve?"

"Can't talk now." Paul pulled hard on his trousers to get them onto his legs.

"Paul, love, she's not here. She's in your head."

He had to reach under the bed to find his shoes.

"Paul, don't go. Don't give in to her. Don't give in to your dark parts."

He put on his shoes and then hurried out of the room. Paul ran down the stairs and rushed out of the building into the heavy downpour. He looked around and saw Eve's pale figure run down the hill towards the beach. He followed her but she moved too quickly and maintained her distance ahead of him. As she headed up the hill towards the headland, he realised where she was going. On he continued after her, up the incline as fast as he could, wiping rainwater from his eyes. There were no stars, and the night would have been the darkest he had seen in a while were it not for the lightning. Flashes lit up the landscape like a monochrome photograph.

Paul reached the gate to the Community House gardens. Eve was not in sight. He went through and looked around outside the building. He thought she may have disappeared again, but there she was on the other side of the garden walls, at the cliff's edge looking out at the water. As he moved towards her, lightning hit the sea ahead and he saw her green floral dress appear iridescent in the night. He was within a few steps from her when she turned and faced him.

"I know you want to forget about me," she said. "And I'm going to help you."

"No, come back away from the edge."

"It's okay, go with your lady friend. See where it takes you. Tell her all the bad things you've done. Tell her about the real you. See how happy you are once things have settled. Once the excitement has passed."

"Eve, just come here to me."

"You do what you need to do," she said. "You know where I am."

Eve stepped back over the edge and fell, swallowed up by the turbulent waves of the Irish sea. Paul rushed forward and leapt over the wall, onto the grassy verge. He looked over the side to see where she had landed. He wiped the water from his face and squinted. Down below, he could just about make out her head and arms as she floated on the surface of the water.

Without much thought, he removed his shoes. He intended to follow her. But then a voice called to him from behind. He turned to see Sarah standing in the rain wearing her yellow waterproof jacket.

"Don't do it," she said, pleading with her voice and her eyes.

"If I don't, she'll always haunt me." He raised his voice so she could hear him above the sound of the storm and the seas. "I have to take control of this. I have to end it."

"She's you, Paul. She's something dark in you. She's not the woman you loved. That person doesn't exist anymore."

"I can't let her win like this, Sarah. I'll never be free."

"Paul, you are free. She's in your mind." She reached out her hands and stepped forwards. "I'm real. I exist and I love you."

Paul looked down to the open water and saw the figure below being lifted and dropped with disdain by the sea. He then turned to Sarah and tried to see her almond brown eyes in the dark.

A lightning flash behind him lit up her face, like one last gift from the heavens.

"I love you," he whispered before turning and leaping off the side of the cliff. He thought he heard a howl behind him. As he fell, he instantly regretted jumping. He landed in the cold sea water and the shock squeezed his chest and emptied his lungs and mind. He was submerged in a cold dark silence before he kicked and fought his way back to the chaos of the surface. There, he struggled with his orientation. There was no sign of Eve and the only company were the waves. They were his masters and they tossed him between them like a toy. Paul struggled to breathe and control his thoughts. Eve slipped from his mind, and then he saw Sarah's face again – why did he leap? Why didn't he stay with her? Panic overcame him. He felt desperate to survive and return to his real love. He tried to swim but the waves continued to play with him. To manhandle him. He was thrown closer to the base of the cliff. Paul fought with all his strength to swim away, but the unforgiving sea tossed him up and against the rocks, delivering him into darkness. And from darkness to a familiar place.

THIRTY-TWO

Paul stepped into the Sailor's Return and walked to the bar. He looked around. Not many regulars but some familiar faces. The barman, for one.

"Father Michaels?"

"Phil, please. I haven't used that title for a while. How are you, Paul?"

"Not bad, I suppose. It's been an odd kind of day."

"Funerals can be such strange events. Everyone expects doom and gloom. But they can be rather exhilarating. The catharsis brings something out in people. I saw it many times in my job. Anyway, what can I get you?"

"Pint of lager, please."

Michaels walked over to the beer taps on the other side of the bar and filled the glass. Paul looked around at the room. The place looked good.

"Geoff been refurbishing?" he asked.

"A while ago. When was the last time you were here?"

"Can't remember. Before the Revelation, I think."

"Ah yes, many things changed after that day."

Michaels brought over the drink, and Paul took a sip. He was blown away.

"That's the best pint I've ever had."

Michaels nodded in response. "Yes, most people who try it say that. It's from a brewery in North Wales. All the water comes from a clifftop well near a church."

Paul took another sip of the beer. "Look, I'm sorry about the thing with the fire. But you know it wasn't me who…"

"Yes, I know."

"I should've thanked you for how you helped me after Eve died."

"Well, you're here now."

"Yes, I am." Paul took another sip of the glorious cold beer. "I never knew your first name was Phillip. I guess it's a more appropriate name for someone who works in a pub."

The barman cocked his head.

"Phil," Paul said. "Phil the barman fills my glass."

Michaels smiled and Paul raised his pint and turned away from the bar. He looked around for somewhere to sit. The pub was very different to how he remembered it. The tables and stools were new. The bar looked polished and the mirrors behind it were clear and clean. The walls had recently been decorated. There was now even a pool table. But then when he thought about it, when was he here last? He struggled to remember, and the past was very foggy.

Paul felt something against his shins, and he looked down. It was a stool. He'd walked into the seating area. Without much consideration, he sat down and then looked across the small round table at the man sat opposite him. It was Jimmy – his old mate from the army.

"You made it then?" Jimmy asked.

"Seems I did, eventually."

There were other people sat nearby but most stared at the widescreen television that hung on the wall. A daytime soap opera was playing.

"What are you watching?" Paul asked.

"It's called *The Good Fight*. Everyone's into it at the minute. You should give it a go – I think you'd like it."

On the screen, a man read passages from an old black, leather-bound Bible to his young son. The child didn't appear interested.

"What happened to you?" Paul asked. "They found the other two in a field. Why weren't you there?"

"Oh, they took me elsewhere to be interrogated. Tortured, actually. I was shot and my body weighed down in a bog." He looked at his watch. "They'll find my remains in three or so years. What about you?" Jimmy asked. "Are you still following your dead wife around?"

"Not exactly."

Jimmy leaned over. "I'm glad, mate. We all thought she was nuts."

"But this was a man in love," said a gentle voice behind Paul. He turned to see Agnes sit down next to him. She was holding a glass of a clear, sparkling drink and still wearing her straw hat.

"Your dedication to her was exceptional," she said.

"You didn't stay long in the village after finding the well," Paul said. "Where did you go?"

"There was nowhere else for me to go. After drinking Morwell's water, I knew the truth of it all and I was content."

"I understand," Paul said. "That water made me see things very differently."

"Quiet, man," Jimmy said. "This is really dramatic."

Paul joined everyone else in the bar and looked up at the television. In the soap opera, a man was packing his bags and yelling at his wife. He told her they were on different paths and that he had important work to do elsewhere; to stay with her – and their son – would hinder his mission.

"So, the father is leaving the mother and son to go and live his own life?" Agnes asked.

"Yeah. I really feel for the wife," Jimmy said. "But that kid's going to be messed up forever."

"It's just a television programme," Paul said.

The father rushed around the house gathering his things together. The wife followed, begging him not to leave. The little boy just watched from the corner. The camera frequently showed the argument from his point of view. He looked on without saying a word. The man was ready to go, and his wife was on the floor howling and crying. He approached the little boy and handed him the same Bible that he had been reading to him earlier.

'I want you to have this.' The man raised his voice so that he could be heard over the sobs of the wife. 'There is power in this book. It's why I'm leaving. One day it will help you to understand.'

He stroked the side of the boy's face and then picked up his bag and strode out of the room. There was the sound of the front door closing and then the mother screamed. The little boy walked over to her. He tried to show her the book he'd been given. Through her tears she spat her words at him. 'This is your fault. He left because of you. God will never forgive you for this.'

The boy was silent as his mother repeated these words and bent her body and pulled her legs into a foetal position. The scene faded to black and then opened to show him sometime later, lying on his parents' bed leafing through the book. The thick blocks of text failed to engage him. He closed it and examined its cover and spine, running his fingertips across the leather. He shrugged his shoulders and placed the book on the bedside table before leaving the room. Then the end credits rolled.

"That was something," Agnes said.

"There's another one on in a minute," Jimmy said.

"I'm going to the bar for another drink," Paul said. "Do either of you want anything?"

They both declined.

Paul stood at the bar waiting to be served by Phil, who was at the opposite end tending to another customer. In his periphery, he became aware of someone approaching. He turned and saw Kat's face smiling at him.

"Have I missed anything?" she asked.

"It's okay, we can fill you in. Do you want a drink?"

"Large vodka, please."

"Really?"

"Of course not," Kat said. "Lemonade is fine. I don't want to start any fires." She winked at Paul.

Paul tried to get the attention of Michaels.

"Yes, same again for me. And a lemonade."

"So, what happened to you after…?" Paul struggled with the words.

"After I jumped from the bridge? Not much really. I was briefly conscious in the water, but the fall broke my neck, so I didn't last long."

"Right," Paul said. "I hope you didn't suffer."

Kat shrugged her shoulders.

Paul handed a note to Michaels and then received the change.

"It's strange to see you here," he said.

She turned her head and surveyed the room.

"Your mother told me about your condition," Paul said.

"I thought she would."

"Why didn't you tell me? I might've been able to help."

"It's too late for regrets."

"I guess so. I just didn't expect to see you. What are you doing here?"

"Paul, this is all your show. I'm just an extra."

Paul handed Kat the lemonade.

"Humour me, though," Paul said. "What's it like beyond?"

"What would you like to know? Has the suffering and pain gone? Sure. As has all the good stuff. You don't get to keep any of it. Shall we go and sit down?"

Paul returned to his seat with the others and Kat joined them. Jimmy and Agnes both raised their glasses to her.

"Such a shame what happened to you," Agnes said. "You must have been in such pain."

"I was but it wasn't just about that. My condition made me believe things that weren't real."

"Sounds familiar," Paul said. "You know, I didn't warm to your mother."

"She's a complex woman," Kat said. "And she had shock and grief to deal with."

"Hush, everyone," Jimmy said, signalling to the television. "The show's coming back on."

As everyone's attention moved back to the screen, Paul

heard raised voices and excitement behind him. He turned and saw a wild-looking bearded man wearing tattered robes playing pool against another of his lost army mates.

"Morwell is hammering Boyce," Jimmy said. "Who'd have thought a third-century saint would be such a whizz at pool."

"He wasn't really a saint," Agnes said.

Paul turned to see the next instalment of the programme starting.

"That theme tune is familiar," he said.

"It's that eighties band, Wheel Deal," Kat said. "Song's called 'Keep Each Other Shining', I think."

"It's not a hymn but it's very upbeat," Agnes said.

"Yeah, rather contrasts with the tone of the show," Jimmy said. "As much as I love it, it's pretty dark."

"What's happening now?" Paul asked. "Why's this guy moping around in bed?"

"He's just been kicked out of the army," Jimmy said.

"Depressed, is he?" Agnes asked, turning to Jimmy.

"Think it might be PTSD. He experienced something in action, and he's come back a different person. He won't speak to his wife about it. Spends each evening in the pub getting hammered."

"I saw the last episode," Kat said. "They showed him having flashbacks to when he and his wife got together. That scene on the beach nearly broke my heart."

"It's just television," Paul said. The others turned and stared at him. None of them said a word.

"Look now." Agnes pointed to the screen. "Many years have passed by and the man is with his wife at the doctor, who's telling her she is dying."

"So, they skipped over three decades of his life?" Kat asked.

"Guess they fast-forwarded through the unimportant years," Jimmy said.

"Is this his opportunity for redemption?" Agnes asked. "To make it up to her after all the debauchery and bad behaviour?"

"You'd think that, but the heavy drinking continues," Jimmy said. "You'll see her on her deathbed in a minute and then it switches to him sat alone in the pub on a weekday afternoon, pissed as a fart."

"That's tragic," Kat said.

"Yeah, he only starts the healing after she's gone," Jimmy said.

"What the hell kind of soap is this?" Paul got up. "I'm off to the toilet."

He didn't really need to go, but the intense storyline was getting to him. He walked over to the other side of the bar to add some space between him and the group.

Around the corner, he saw the shadow of someone skulking alone. He craned his neck and looked to see who it was, and then came the familiar voice.

"Alright, dickhead."

"Karl, what the hell are you doing in here?"

"Having a drink, like the rest of ya. Enjoying the entertainment."

"But how did you get served? Have you seen who's behind the bar?"

"It's all kosher, mate. I killed him, you killed me. Swings and roundabouts. Come and sit down for a minute."

Paul stepped up onto the bar stool next to his old friend.

"All getting too intense for you over there, is it?" Karl asked.

"There's quite a bit of scrutiny underway."

"Ah, what the fuck would they know? They weren't there. Besides, you may have been a shitty husband, but we did have some laughs, didn't we?"

Paul laughed. "That we did."

He clasped his hands and turned to face Karl. "But did it ever occur to you that it wasn't about chasing a good time, but about running away from the bad times? Running away from reality?"

"Reality is overrated," Karl said. "Everyone tries to escape it one way or another. Some through good old-fashioned drink, drugs and fucking. Others like to escape from everything they know and fuck off to another part of the world. Then there are the cults or communities or whatever you're calling each other nowadays. Seems to me you're still the same dickheads standing around in circles singing 'Kumbaya' and quoting shit said by bearded fuckers who lived two thousand years ago. Now you talk about what? Humanity? Fucking science? Philosophy?" He shook his head and sipped his drink. "You're all frightened little children – afraid of dying and even more afraid of living."

Paul nodded then stepped off the stool.

"That's what I thought. You know, Karl, I pity you. I know I've made mistakes. But at least I reached a point of realisation. I know that life can be good, if not great. I know what love can be. I may not be able to live the way I want to, but I know that life is not something to run away from. It's something to embrace and hold on to. The only thing I wish is that I'd realised it all earlier. Before I became so damaged. But at least I saw all this – the reality of what it all means –

before my time came. Before, my friend, I became like you – a twisted, bitter ghost."

As he stepped away, he heard Karl call after him. "Embrace life? Bollocks. You can't handle this madness any more than the next dickhead. I know how that noggin works – you deserve to spend your days chasing after that fricking banshee…"

Paul strode away and Karl's rant faded behind him. He walked back towards his group with his head down, feeling a strange mixture of relief and sadness. Before he got to the table, he encountered another unexpected face. This one had a wide, welcoming smile. Gwilym. He reached over and hugged the old man tightly, like a son reunited with his father.

"I'm glad I didn't miss you," Gwilym said. "Can I get you a drink?"

"Yes, please. Pint of that lager." Gwilym ordered a large glass of red wine for himself. As the drinks arrived both men leant on the bar.

"It was a nice service today," Gwilym said.

"Oh, you saw it?"

"You know I don't like to miss these things."

"Of course. I'm not sure if you're aware, but things went south afterwards. Eve will never leave me alone it seems."

Gwilym tilted his head and looked at Paul with an expression of surprise.

"You don't really think that's Eve who's been haunting you, do you?"

"It looks and sounds like her. Albeit a bit younger than how I remember her. But if it's not her then who is it?"

"My dear boy, you know as well as I do. She's all the rage, darkness, and deep sorrow that you've carried around all your life; your father abandoning you; your mother's hateful words; the violence you witnessed in Belfast and the burden you felt from survival; your substance abuse; your wife's cancer; the Revelation and all the things you witnessed along the way."

"But why her?" Paul asked. "Why does it look like her?"

"Because perhaps the guilt is the overarching face of this malevolence? And who better than the greatest victim of your story to play that role?"

Paul looked at his own reflection in the mirror behind the bar. He understood. Gwilym put his hand on Paul's shoulder.

"Your parents did quite a number on you. Especially your mother. It left you haunted from an early age, blaming yourself and believing the universe had it in for you. You hoped joining the army would help you to escape but as we all know that did not end well. For decades you tried to destroy yourself through various vices. Eve stuck with you the whole time. But eventually you lost her as well, and by the time you'd realised how lucky you were to have her in your life, it was too late. After that, of course, came your foray into the church. But it seems that not even the cosmic forces can cut you a break. The Revelation happens and then you can't even dwell and hope for salvation in the afterlife. You were left with the here and now."

"So, what do I do next?" Paul asked.

"You choose."

"Choose what?"

"To be or not to be," Gwilym said. "To exist or not to exist." He put his arm around Paul's shoulders and pulled him close. "Here's the thing. Life is hard. And I don't mean in terms of money problems or worries about work or your love life. Fundamentally, just living with the knowledge that one day you will be dead is very difficult for a lot of people to accept. What really is the point of it all? Why is there suffering? Disease, war, natural disasters – it's all chaos and chance. There is no God's will guiding your fate according to his mysterious ways. Humans are mortal animals living on a rock floating in a dark emptiness."

"So, what is the point of it all?"

"The point is, my young friend, we have each other. Our strength comes from the connections we have with ourselves and with others. From supporting one another and from enjoying the good things together; the things that make us different from all the other mortal creatures we share this planet with. Life is full of possibilities and endless opportunities for experience. And all of it is so much richer when we share those moments together."

"So, I choose to live or to die?"

"You choose the pain, the euphoria, the joy, the sorrow, the glorious chaos of life. Or you choose the painless non-existence, the return to nothingness."

"When do I have to choose?"

"You must choose now," Gwilym said. "It's time for you to make your decision. You've been in this place too long already. If you wait much longer then the sea will take the choice away from you. It's time you finally took control of your own destiny. Pick one of the doors to leave and your decision will stand."

"I wish I could choose it all," Paul said.

"I know but that's not how life works. You have to make your own decisions about how you want to live."

"And then…?"

"And then you live with your decisions. You and only you are responsible for your own choices – not God, not the External Force, not your mother. You."

Paul turned around. The television had been switched off and everyone in the pub now gazed at him. The place was silent. He nodded to Gwilym, and the old man grabbed his arm and squeezed it gently. Paul then looked over to the table where his other companions sat and raised his hand to wave. Agnes and Kat smiled back, and Jimmy gave Paul a thumbs up. He walked into the centre of the room and examined the two exits. Morwell – stood by the pool table – lifted his fists over his head to show his encouragement.

Paul stared at the two doors. He knew which one was which, and where each would take him. He took a moment to consider the options, and there it was, the decision was made. He turned back to look at Gwilym, and tears started streaming down his face.

"It's okay, my boy," the old man said. "There's nothing to fear now."

Paul nodded and walked to the far corner of the room, past the seating area, and stopped briefly. He glanced at the clock on the wall; he was right on time. He turned around, took one last look at everyone then pushed the door open.

There, stood Eve. Her smile sparkled from the darkness like a lost constellation. Paul stepped through the portal and the door closed behind him. He reached his arms around her and pulled her close. Her head rested against his chest and he felt her soft hair against his neck. She looked up and he turned his head down to meet her gaze. She gently smiled.

"You're ready to join me?" she asked.

Paul stroked the side of her face with his fingers. He started shaking his head. "So much of me wants to but I can't, I'm sorry. Not yet."

Her expression slacked and her eyes dulled. "Why would you want to stay? This is a life that has given you nothing."

"It's given me many things. It gave me you. I am the one who failed to make it work and for that I am sorry. Truly, desperately sorry. I can never make it up to you but it's crucial – at the very least – that I take responsibility for my actions. My mistakes are my own."

"Everything has been against you. There are so many reasons you've struggled. How will you overcome these hindrances?"

"I cannot change the past or the choices I've made but I need to learn to live with them and accept them."

"And what about the future and the suffering that you must face?"

"I don't expect it to be easy but so long as there's fire in me then I will continue to fight on."

He felt her hands drop from his back and she stepped away. He tried to hold her a little longer, but she pulled further from him.

"Besides, I have…" His words were cut off as a blinding white light filled his vision and he recoiled and shut his eyes tight. Before they opened again, he began to shiver, and he choked as his mouth filled with salty water. He felt his body being repeatedly twisted by external forces until it stopped, and he was motionless. His hands plunged into cold wet sand and he pushed himself onto his back.

*

Paul lay in the surf and opened his eyes. His body ached like he'd been beaten. Nearby he heard the whirring blades of a helicopter. He turned to see its large spotlight as it moved away along the coastline. The back of his head hurt, and he saw blood on his fingers when he reached up to touch the spot. He lifted his head and realised he was sat on the beach near the bottom of the cliffs of the headland. The rain and thunder had passed but the sky remained cloudy.

He cleared his throat. "What was I saying?" He sat up and saw the village lights at the other end of the beach. In-between, stretching across the bay from where he sat in the breaking waves over to the stone pier, was a light blue glowing strip. It glistened more brightly each time the crashing waves struck the sand.

"The burning of the sea." He chortled and coughed. "Nature's showing me the way home."

The helicopter disappeared around the other side of the headland and the sound of the waves and the luminescence of the water became more prominent. He looked around – as though expecting to have company. "What I was saying was, I have a home now. I have friends – a family – and a person who I love. That is what will help me to fight and overcome the suffering. Everything I've been given here and all that I've become part of is a gift. Do you understand?"

No answer came.

He raised his voice. "Do you understand?"

He looked around but no one responded.

"Stop messing with me. I'm tired of your games. I want to be free of you."

He was alone, it seemed.

He breathed in and yelled, "Do you hear me?"

"I hear you," spoke an emotional, trembling voice from behind. He turned his head to see a dancing torchlight approaching. He squinted to see who was carrying it. Out of breath, Sarah fell to the floor and sat in the sand next to Paul. As she turned to face him, her jaw dropped, and her red eyes were wide open. "What…?" She struggled with the words. "Why…?"

Paul reached over, grabbed her, and kissed her head.

Sarah looked up at him. "Eve?"

"She's gone now," he said.

"And you?"

"I'm okay." He nodded.

"You can't do that, Paul. Ever."

"I know." He pulled her face close and kissed her.

She pulled away. "I thought I'd lost you, as well."

"I'm sorry. I could never be free until I was rid of her."

"Is she really gone?" Sarah looked concerned.

"Yes, I think she is."

Sarah had a look of disbelief about her. "What happened to you?"

Paul stared down at the sand. "The sea took me, and I found myself in a familiar place with familiar faces."

"Huh?"

"I'm not sure if I understand it myself. But I know that it helped me realise what I wanted most of all was to be back here with you." He exhaled heavily. "I feel so lucky to be close to you. I always thought I'd squandered the one good thing that'd happened to me and I deserved no goodness, but life isn't like that, is it?"

"Life is what you make of it, Paul." A tear rolled down her cheek and Paul reached over and wiped it with his thumb and then lay his hand on her face.

"I realise that now and it's up to me to find the sense and the meaning in all of this. For the first time – in a really long time – I really want to." He looked into Sarah's eyes. "I choose it all – the joy, the pain, the sorrow, the glorious chaos that life brings."

"You sound like my dad."

"Ha, he spoke some sense, didn't he?"

Sarah blinked back her tears and grinned. She grabbed his hand tightly in hers, kissed it and then splashed it in the sea. They both watched as the phosphorescent light shimmered and made a luminous outline around his hand in the water.

"Magical, isn't it?" she said.

This book is printed on paper from sustainable sources managed under the Forest Stewardship Council (FSC) scheme.

It has been printed in the UK to reduce transportation miles and their impact upon the environment.

For every new title that Matador publishes, we plant a tree to offset CO_2, partnering with the More Trees scheme.

MORE TREES
LET'S PLANT A BILLION TREES

For more about how Matador offsets its environmental impact, see www.troubador.co.uk/about/